Yowliday Inn

Susan C. Daffron

An Alpine Grove Romantic Comedy

Book 14

 Published by Magic Fur Press
An imprint of Logical Expressions, Inc.
P.O. Box 383
Ponderay, ID 83852

This is a work of fiction. All names, characters, places, and events are either the product of the author's imagination or are used fictitiously. Any resemblance to actual persons, living or dead, business organizations, events, or locales is purely coincidental.

Yowliday Inn

ISBN: 978-1-61038-073-7 (paperback)
        978-1-61038-074-4 (EPUB)

Like all of my books, *Yowliday Inn* is dedicated to
my husband James Byrd,
my best friend and biggest supporter.
Thanks for everything!

<u>Books by Susan C. Daffron</u>
The Alpine Grove Romantic Comedies

Chez Stinky

Fuzzy Logic

The Art of Wag

Snow Furries

Bark to the Future

Howl at the Loon

The Good, the Bad, and the Pugly

The Treasure of the Hairy Cadre

The Luck of the Paw

Daydream Retriever

The Hound of Music

The Last Train to Barksville

Who's Afraid of Virginia's Woof?

Yowliday Inn

The Jennings & O'Shea Mysteries

Sensing Trouble

Sensing Secrets

Sensing Truth

Chapter 1

Dancing Cedars

The old saying that "you can't go home again" doesn't stop people from trying. Crammed into seat 25E waiting for passengers to exit a geriatric 737 aircraft, Erin Quinn had visual proof that a lot of people were going over the river and across the country to get to grandma's house for Thanksgiving 1997.

The skinny man in seat 25D wrapped his serpentine fingers around the armrest, jerked it upward, and leaned back into Erin's space. It was a clear breach of airline passenger etiquette, and Erin slapped her hand on the armrest, shoving it back down. After hours next to this guy, she'd had quite enough of Mr. Twitchy. He'd spent the entire flight rearranging the magazines in the seat pocket in front of him, smoothing his slacks, and organizing his carry-on items. In between these activities, he pulled a small notebook from his shirt pocket, looked at it, and put it back.

He squirmed in his seat, twisted, and put the armrest back up. Widening his eyes at Erin's irritated expression, he whined, "People are hitting me with their suitcases."

Erin pressed her lips together, repressing the snide comment related to her desire to whack him over the head with a Samsonite. No matter how satisfying, that would *definitely* be a breach of airline passenger etiquette. The long flight was over and the plane was on the ground, so she could take comfort in the fact that in a few minutes he'd disappear into the crowd, never to be seen again. Her therapist would be proud of this moment of rationality. Christie always said that just because you think a thought doesn't mean you should act on it. Erin could imagine her smooth, calm voice advising not to "believe everything you think."

If Erin had acted on her thoughts about this trip, she'd be headed in the opposite direction, not visiting her hometown of Alpine Grove. She'd managed to avoid returning to the small mountain town for decades and hadn't even seen her parents for more than two years. But Mom and Dad had waged a phone campaign, even recruiting a few family friends to encourage her to visit for the holiday. Because Erin never answered the phone, her answering machine took the calls. Her "extended family" was more than a little unusual, and some of them were downright nuts. The messages reminded her why she'd left Alpine Grove in the first place. After so many calls, she finally relented. Between the family pressure and the plane ticket her mother had sent, she ran out of excuses. Mom was extra determined this year.

Erin closed her eyes and counted backward from ten, trying to center herself. Instead of being calming, it allowed her to focus on her environment, reminding her that Mr. Salami was sitting on the other side of her in the window seat. His slobbery consumption of a gigantic deli sandwich had left unpleasant olfactory remnants. Yuck.

She opened her eyes and found Mr. Twitchy crouching like an anxious house cat, poised to leap into the aisle. He finally made his move and Erin waited for others to step into the walkway behind him, so she could avoid being in close proximity to him again. Once he was safely away, she removed her luggage from the overhead bin and followed the shuffling masses off the plane.

As the crowd meandered up the jetway, Erin visualized her parents' faces. Even though she had talked to them recently on the phone, the fact that she hadn't seen them in person for so long made her anxious. Agitated butterflies swirled erratically in her stomach. When she emerged into the crowded airport, she blinked a few times at the bright light, and looked around for the signs to baggage claim.

She got on an escalator heading down, reveling in the anonymity of being in a huge airport. It was the antithesis of Alpine Grove, where everyone knew who you were, whether you liked it or not.

Erin often thought Alpine Grove was like an exaggerated, larger version of the bar in the old TV show, *Cheers*. Not only did everyone know your name, they knew all your relatives, where you lived, which schools you attended, who your friends were, and probably your grade-point average. Part of the reason she'd been so desperate to leave the area was to could escape being labeled as the gangly, serious oddball. When she was young, her family had moved into town, and she'd felt like an outsider, always trying to fit in. All she'd wanted was to be normal for a change.

Erin stood in front of the shiny metal carousel, waiting for both her suitcase and her parents to show up. Murphy's Law dictated that her suitcase would be the last one unloaded from the plane. And her parents were always late, except to their own events. They showed up on time for speaking engagements without fail. Anything else was dicey.

The crowd began to thin as one by one, people snatched their precious cargo from the spinning metal machine.

Mr. Twitchy and Mr. Salami disappeared. Luggage started emerging more slowly and an older woman snatched a lone suitcase that spewed off the conveyor belt after everything else. The pink hard-sided suitcase was unwieldy, and she was assisted by a man passing by. As the empty carousel spun in anticipation of more luggage, a sinking feeling settled in Erin's gut. Deep down, she'd known checking a suitcase was a bad idea. When the carousel came to a stop, she repressed a filthy expletive. As if this trip weren't bad enough, apparently her clothes would be spending the holiday somewhere else.

She leaped at a tap on her shoulder and whirled around. An extremely tall man with a ponytail of long wavy brown hair, a close-cropped beard, and brilliant blue eyes blinked at her, startled at her reaction. He looked like he'd just come down off a rugged mountain hiking trail somewhere. Erin said, "I don't suppose you know where my luggage is, do you?"

He shook his head. "Nope. Sorry. I'm here to pick you up."

Erin scanned his face, examining him more closely. He was a lot older and taller than the last time she'd seen him, but she recognized the mischievous sparkle in those stunning baby blues. "Ziggy?"

His face lit up in a boyish grin. "Hey, Stardust. It's been a long time, huh?"

~

Erin wasn't sure how to handle a social situation with someone she hadn't seen in twenty years. Did you hug? Shake hands? Lacking any inspiration, she simply stood and stared up at him. "What are you doing here, Ziggy?"

"Most people call me Dylan now. And I told you. I'm picking you up from the airport."

To be fair, no one called her Stardust either, but it was difficult to think of him as anything other than Ziggy. "Please call me Erin. How did you get stuck with airport duty?"

"It's my day off." He gestured toward the empty luggage carousel. "I guess you need to deal with your missing suitcase first, huh?"

He wasn't wrong about that, and now that the awkward do-we-or-don't-we hug moment had passed, Erin bent to pick up her shoulder bag. In a voice more confident than she felt, she said, "That looks like the office over there."

He stood quietly while Erin filled out the pile of forms that theoretically would help restore her suitcase to her someday. He was so tall, it was like she was standing next to a mighty oak tree. When had Ziggy gotten so tall? The last time she'd seen him they were about the same height, but now he had to be six eight or nine. When she was done, she put down the pen and looked up at his face. "I appreciate you coming all the way here to get me, but where are my parents?"

"Tokyo, I think. Their flight was delayed for a day or so."

How typical. Erin's parents always prioritized work, so why should she be surprised? She cleared her throat and cast through her mind for some small-talk ideas, but didn't come up with much. She was out of practice. "Do you still live in Alpine Grove or are you visiting too?"

"I work at my parents' Christmas tree farm." He picked up her shoulder bag. "The parking lot is this way."

She hustled to keep up as he strode toward the exit. The automatic doors slid open, and she was greeted by blazing

Southern California sunlight. They walked in silence through the maze of parking areas. Erin wasn't sure what to say. She didn't know about the Christmas tree farm or anything else.

Way back when, her parents and Ziggy's—or Dylan's—parents had fallen out of contact because of some sort of feud or disagreement. Erin had no idea what happened, but the net result was that Ziggy was the last person she would have expected to end up stuck with the task of picking her up at the airport.

He pointed at an old maroon pickup truck that was so filthy it had an overall grayish-brown patina. "That's our ride."

An enormous black canine head popped up in the window and Erin stepped backward with an involuntary yelp. The dog's gigantic pink tongue lolled from his mouth and he was wagging his long serpentine tail.

"That's Moose." Ziggy said. "Don't worry. He's friendly."

Erin thought a few additional adjectives like huge and drooly were also appropriate to describe the aptly named Moose, but she kept that commentary to herself.

Ziggy tucked her canvas carry-on bag behind the driver's seat and gestured toward the truck. "It's not locked."

Not a surprise. Even in the big crime-laden city, having an oversized dog in your truck probably discouraged theft. She got in and tried to politely shove the wide expanse of dog butt across the bench seat toward Ziggy. She wrinkled her nose. "I don't mean to be critical, but did something die in here?"

"Moose might have eaten something that disagreed with him. Sometimes he finds things out in the woods."

Erin rolled down her window. "Like dead things?"

"Yeah. Eating them tends to make him fart."

"Oh." Erin pinched her nose and leaned toward the window. Sucking in smog was better than eau d'Moose.

The traffic getting out of the city was typically horrible, and Erin gazed out the window, happy to let Ziggy focus on navigating the congested freeways in silence.

He glanced at her. "I forgot to mention it, but I also have to pick up your parents' dog, Casey, at the boarding kennel. Then I can drop you and Casey at your parents' house."

Erin made a face. "I don't have a key. Do any of the motels take dogs?"

"There's one place, but it's probably full because of the holiday weekend. We've got an extra room out at the farm, and it should be cool for you to hang out. I've never met your parents' dog, but he's got a cute name. Is he okay with other animals?"

"Casey is named after 'Casey Jones.'"

"Grateful Dead?"

"Yes. Although I haven't seen Casey in a while, I remember him being short, brown, and friendly."

"As long as he doesn't cause trouble ahead and trouble behind, it should be okay." Ziggy glanced at the massive dog panting happily between them. "Moose likes everybody."

Erin looked around the dog at Ziggy, amused that he still knew his song lyrics. "I'll tell Casey to watch his speed. And unless my mom put him on a diet, we probably don't have much to worry about."

No one she'd ever met in her years on the East Coast had been a Deadhead. But they hadn't spent their early years living in a hippie commune like she and Ziggy had either.

Yet another reminder of the vast differences between her childhood and her adult life.

Although she was curious what he'd been doing for the last couple of decades, Erin didn't feel compelled to make conversation during the drive. For the last two years, she'd spent a lot of time avoiding small talk and situations where she might have to explain what she'd being doing lately. The awful, stupid, terrible event, aka TASTE, was always there, lurking like a shadow she couldn't escape. And she did *not* want to talk about that with anyone for any reason.

Fortunately, Ziggy was probably the most mellow person she'd ever met, so it didn't feel weird sitting silently next to a guy she hadn't spoken to in more than twenty years. She wasn't struggling to think of something to say because she knew he didn't mind. Ziggy had a relaxed, peaceful air about him, an internal stillness that made him easy to be around.

Maybe it was because he was the antithesis of herself. He'd always been this way. Always sure of what he liked and disliked, not concerned about what people thought of his opinions, whether it was the merits of peanut butter or the parade of ugly plaid clothing in the seventies. Unlike Erin, Ziggy had always given people the impression that he didn't care what anyone thought about him at all. He'd always behaved as if he were content to do his thing, whatever it might be. And right now, his thing was driving.

The city fell away behind them and the vegetation started to change as the road ascended to higher elevations. Because it had been so many years since she'd been to Alpine Grove, even the drive seemed foreign. Why had her parents decided to move back *there*, of all places?

Apparently exhausted from watching the traffic like a sentinel, Moose collapsed in a heap next to her and placed his large black muzzle on her thigh. With a glance at Ziggy, she shrugged and stroked the wide expanse of smooth black fur on the dog's head. It was the size of a bowling ball. And not one of the kiddie ones either. Moose's head was akin to a full-size, adult, eight-and-a-half-inch ball. What breed of dog was this beast?

Ziggy looked away from the road at her. "Your leg is probably gonna fall asleep. Sorry about that."

Erin smiled at the expression on Ziggy's face. He had round eyes that gave him an air of innocence, which she knew wasn't accurate. When they were kids, he used to get away with everything because of that guileless expression. It drove her nuts that everyone bought it. Meanwhile, she'd go into long, complicated explanations for her bad behavior, which mostly served to either annoy the adults or put them to sleep.

Ziggy slowed when they reached the outskirts of town, and Erin was assaulted by memories. Where was the cafe? What happened to the Frederickson's building? Since when did Alpine Grove have an advertising agency? And why? Bea Haven Gifts? That must be the store Bea was starting up around when Erin's family moved away. Why on earth had her parents wanted to return here?

Ziggy stopped at the single stoplight in town. "Welcome home." As he pulled forward, he waved at a man in a brown suit who was standing outside an office.

"It looks different. But the same." Erin's stomach tightened. She should ask Ziggy about what had happened over the years. Part of her felt left out, but the other part didn't want to know. "Where is this dog kennel?"

"It's out in the trees a little south of Dancing Cedars. The owner inherited Abigail Goodman's old log house."

"Abigail died?" Everyone in Alpine Grove had known Abigail. Erin couldn't imagine the town surviving without her. Although Abigail hadn't been a member of the Dancing Cedars commune, she'd helped many members over the years with countless problems.

"It's been a couple years ago now. I went to the funeral. Half the town was there."

Erin gazed out the window as they turned down the road that led out to the forests where Abigail had lived. How could she be gone? She wasn't that old, was she? Not really.

Ziggy tapped her forearm. "Hey, I'm sorry. I thought you knew."

Erin shook her head. "My parents haven't told me anything about what's going on in Alpine Grove or why they were so insistent that I visit this year. This is going to be weird, isn't it?"

"Probably."

~

Ziggy turned off the road and drove the old truck up a remarkably long tree-lined driveway. The massive cedars had undoubtedly grown in the last twenty years, but they'd been huge before, so the overall impression to Erin was the same. The driveway itself was in vastly better shape than the muddy tire tracks Erin remembered. Someone must have spent a lot of money on road gravel.

Ziggy parked in front of the kennel building. The old log house was farther up the driveway behind a gate. When Erin got out of the truck, she was greeted by the sound of many canines barking. The kennel buildings were obviously new, but the log house looked different too.

Ziggy pushed a button on the wall of the kennel and Erin walked around the car to stand next to him. "Putting a covered entryway on the house was a good idea."

"Kat said that the steps up to the house were covered with blue carpet and falling apart."

"You said Kat is Abigail's niece, right?"

Ziggy nodded and they both turned at the sound of a door slamming. A petite woman with a long dark braid descended the steps and started down the driveway. She was wearing an oversized green coat and hiking boots. Her hands were stuffed in the pockets and the braid swayed back and forth as she walked.

Erin squinted. "She looks like a younger version of Abigail."

"It kinda freaked me out the first time I met her." Ziggy shrugged. "Kat's a lot shorter though."

Kat walked up and glanced at the truck. "Hi Dylan. I don't have Moose on the schedule. I hope you don't need to board him because we're completely out of space. In fact, we're a little overbooked."

"I'm here to pick up Casey. The Quinns are still in Tokyo. They were supposed to call and let you know. This is Paul and Jennifer's daughter, Erin."

Erin put out her hand. "Zig…I mean Dylan…picked me up at the airport. My parents didn't call me either."

"Maybe they left a message." Kat gestured toward the kennel. "I'm sure Casey will be thrilled to see you. It's a little noisy in there. I'll get him for you."

"A little noisy" wasn't an accurate description of the hysterical cacophony of barking and howling, and Erin was perfectly happy to remain outside in the relative quiet, gazing up at the trees. It was beautiful here. When she was a kid, Ziggy's parents sometimes dropped them off here on their way to town so she and Ziggy could play with Abigail's critters. There always were dogs and cats around, and sometimes Abigail took care of other animals like sheep and goats.

Back then, owners who couldn't care for their animals tended to drop them off here. The animals stayed with Abigail until she found them new homes. Erin and Ziggy used to have fun running through the forest with the various dogs and petting any cats who would permit it. Sometimes Abigail would let the kids dig weeds with her in her garden. Technically it was work, but she'd made it seem like a scavenger hunt or a contest to see who could find the most weeds. To Erin, those carefree days felt like a lifetime ago.

Kat returned with Casey, who barreled over to Erin wagging his tail so hard his wide brown body wiggled along with it.

Erin crouched down to pet the dog. He was significantly heavier than the last time she'd seen him and his dark muzzle had more gray, but it was sweet that he seemed to remember who she was. Casey's heritage was anyone's guess. He had short legs like a corgi, brown fur tinged with black like a German shepherd, and the floppy ears and short fur of a retriever. But the soulful dark brown eyes were all his own.

She took the leash from Kat, who was holding a piece of paper in her other hand that looked suspiciously like a bill. Erin did some mental math, reflecting on her dwindling bank balance. How much did dog boarding cost anyway?

She cleared her throat. "Um, my purse is in the truck. I'll be right back." She hustled back to the cab and pulled out her checkbook. Uh oh.

She walked back to the group, and Kat handed her the piece of paper. Erin tried not to gasp. Her parents had been gone for three weeks?

Ziggy leaned over to take a look. "Stardust, are you cool with this?"

"I might be a little short." More like *a lot* short. "Is there any way you can wait a couple days until my parents return?"

Kat made a face. "We really…."

Ziggy pulled a beat-up leather wallet from the back pocket of his jeans. He riffled through some bills and handed them to Kat. "Thanks for taking good care of Casey. You can keep the change. Have a great Thanksgiving."

Kat held out one of the twenties. "Thank you, but are you sure?"

"Buy an extra turkey. It's the holiday season, right?"

"Well, I'm a vegetarian, but I'm sure I'll think of something. Thanks." Kat stuffed the bills into her coat pocket. "Please wish the Quinns a happy Thanksgiving for me."

Erin and Ziggy said their good-byes and watched as Kat started walking back up to the house. Ziggy clapped his hands together. "Okay, the next trick is trying to squish Moose into the extended cab. He hates sitting back there."

Casey stood next to Erin, and they watched as Ziggy moved tools and other junk around behind the bench seat to make room for the huge dog. He then cajoled and maneuvered Moose around the seat and into the narrow extended cab area. Once Moose was crammed in place, Ziggy waved. "Okay, load up Casey."

Erin lifted Casey onto the bench seat, and Moose craned his neck over the seat back so the two dogs could sniff. Casey was unfazed by the large animal. Maybe after weeks at the kennel, he'd seen it all.

Ziggy started the truck, and they slowly made their way down the driveway. At the road, he stopped and Erin read the sign. "The Wag On Inn. That's a cute name."

"You know it must be the holiday season because there's no room at the inn."

Erin laughed involuntarily. The sound was so rare it was startling, and she whacked his arm. "How long have you been waiting to say that?"

"A while. The name was on the invoice too. I can't believe you didn't notice. At least you finally read the sign."

Erin smiled. They'd shared so many dopey jokes like that when they were kids, running around playing at the commune. They'd been inseparable. Her mother used to say that half the time no one else knew what they were talking about because it was like they had their own language.

She said, "You haven't changed much, have you?"

"Nope. But you have. What happened?"

"Nothing." Nothing and everything. But there was no way she was getting into it with Ziggy. She gave him a potent subject-changing school-marmish finger shake so he'd stop looking at her with those wide eyes. "How come you're carrying around so much cash?"

"I prefer cash. I grabbed some before I left."

"I sure wouldn't wander around a big airport with that much money stuffed in my pocket. What if someone stole it?"

"But they didn't."

"But they *could*. There are muggers and pickpockets everywhere. What would you have done?"

"Told Kat I got ripped off and I'd pay her tomorrow."

Erin put her palms over her face. "Even after all this time, your logic still drives me nuts."

"You going to tell me what's wrong?"

She looked up. "No."

"Okay."

~

Kat walked inside the house and was greeted by loud barking from the dogs hanging out in the downstairs hallway. "Hi guys. It's me. I still live here."

The five dogs standing at the gate at the bottom of the stairs gave up the brave-defender-of-the-homestead routine and milled around for a moment before settling into their favorite sleeping locations.

She opened the refrigerator and peered inside, seeking inspiration for dinner. Nothing looked particularly interesting. She tried the freezer. Also uninteresting. She wasn't in the mood to make anything hard. Moments like these were exactly why people ordered delivery pizza or take-out Chinese food. But when you lived miles from anywhere, amenities like food delivery and garbage pickup weren't an option. Cooking and trips to the local dump were mandatory.

Kat's husband, Joel, walked through the front door and the canine welcoming committee resumed their barking until he pointed out that shutting up would be a good idea. Joel had been out at his cabin, affectionately known as The Shack, which he'd rented out after he moved in with Kat.

He strolled into the kitchen and gave Kat a hug. "Did the long-term boarder finally leave?"

"Yes, Casey is gone." She held up a bag of potatoes. "How do you feel about spuds for dinner?"

"What kind of spuds?"

"Mashed?"

"With what else?"

"I don't know." Kat set the bag on the counter with a thud. "Everything sounds hard. I don't feel like cooking."

"It's your turn." He pulled several potatoes out of the bag. "I'll peel these if you think of something to go with them."

"We have celery." Kat threw the bag on the counter. "And carrots."

"That sounds like soup."

"I guess." She carried the carrots to the sink and began washing them. "That's not so bad I suppose. It's getting cold out there. I saw more feline paw prints in the dirt on my car. I hope they're from Butch or Sundance cavorting on the hood and not some poor lost refugee kitty seeking shelter."

"Me too." He set a peeled potato on the cutting board. "I have some kind of bad news."

"Are Jack and Becca okay?" Kat turned to face him. "Nothing's wrong, is it? No one is sick or dying or anything, are they?"

"No." He raised an eyebrow. "Where are you getting that?"

"Sorry. The worrywart disaster mechanism kicked in." She set a carrot on the cutting board next to the potato and faced him. "What's up?"

"They gave me their notice on renting the Shack."

Kat was surprised. Becca and Jack had been living in Joel's small cabin for almost two years. The couple had met after being stranded there during the massive Thanksgiving weekend blizzard of 1995. Becca loved the place because she said it saved her life. As a forester, Jack loved the huge trees that surrounded the cabin.

Kat looked up at Joel. "If they move out of the Shack, where are they going to live?"

"Becca found a house that's larger and closer to town. It has enough trees to keep Jack happy, and she put an offer on it. Unless something goes wrong with the closing, they'll be moving out at the end of December."

"I guess we need to find someone else to rent the Shack." Kat put another carrot on the cutting board. "We'll never find tenants as great as they were though. They love that place."

"Actually, I'm thinking of selling it."

"You can't sell the Shack!" Kat pointed a carrot at him. "You built it. You *can't* just sell it."

"Of course I can. And I probably should." He shrugged. "It's just a bunch of wood, nails, and screws."

"You spent years building it though. I can't imagine you not owning it anymore. That makes me sad."

"Hold off on the sadness. We don't have to decide now." He put his arm around her shoulder, pulled her close, and kissed her temple. "In fact, you should be in a great mood. Boarding Casey for weeks must have netted some big bucks."

Kat looked up at him. "It did. And get this, he paid in cash. I was fondling the bills in my pocket all the way back up to the house. Riffling through all that money made me feel like a multimillionaire."

"You're a dog boarding mogul now. But since when do the Quinns pay in cash? I thought they always wrote checks because they're passing off dog boarding as a business expense."

"Their daughter picked up Casey this time. Except she didn't pay. Her friend did. Some guy named Dylan. He has a big dog named Moose and you've probably seen him around town. His eyes are this amazing blue color."

He wiggled his eyebrows. "You seem impressed. Should I be worried about this guy?"

"No, but I'm not kidding when I say he's got amazing eyes. Remember when we were hiking in Hawaii and we looked down from the trail at those brilliant blue sections of ocean?"

"Yeah, you called it Caribbean blue, even though we weren't even close to being in the Caribbean."

"Yeah, I know. Details, details. My point is that his eyes are almost exactly that color. They're so gorgeous that you end up staring at them, which is sort of embarrassing."

"If you start humming "Caribbean Blue" by Enya, I'm going to have to kill you."

Kat flashed an evil grin. "I would never do that."

"I had that song stuck in my head for our entire honeymoon. You're lucky I didn't divorce you."

"That's just because there's only two or three words you can understand and it melted your analytical mind. It's a beautiful song, like a waltz that goes twirling on and on." Kat started humming, "Blah, blah, blah Caribbean Bluuuuue."

He put his hands over his ears. "You need to cut that out or I'm not helping you with dinner."

Kat pulled his arms down and tickled his ribs, causing him to double over. She leaned close to his ear and crooned, "Blah, blah, blah Caribbean Bluuuuue."

He grabbed her around the waist, hoisted her to the living room and plopped her on the sofa. Settling in next to her, he leaned in close and said, "Do you remember how we got that song out of my head?"

"Oh yeah." She grinned. "We had to distract your brain from trying to figure out all those missing lyrics. Getting you to stop thinking about it was fun."

When he kissed her, the tune vaporized and Kat forgot the two words of the lyrics that she knew. Dinner could wait for a while.

Chapter 2

The Jingle Bear

Much to Erin's relief, Ziggy concluded his brief interrogation, and they settled in for the return drive south to Alpine Grove. Erin watched the trees zoom by, trying not to think about the fact that because she had no car or even a driver's license, she had no control over where she could go, unless she wanted to walk extremely long distances. In such a rural area, public transportation simply didn't exist.

Then there was the matter of seeing Ziggy's parents again. It was likely to be odd at best. He mentioned that they probably would prefer that she call them Greg and Melody rather than Zappa and Moonshadow. One time at the commune, Erin had asked if Melody's nickname was Moonshadow because she was such a space cadet. Everyone laughed and told her she was hilarious, but Erin had been completely serious.

The old truck rolled by the shops in town again, and south of Alpine Grove they turned off the highway. The road crossed expansive golden pastures that had been harvested, and several turns later they returned to the forest.

Ziggy turned at a sign for The Bryant Tree Ranch and drove past rows and rows of perfectly trimmed evergreens. Although Erin didn't know what types of trees they were, the ranch obviously had a wide variety of conifers you could select for your Christmas tree.

Erin looked up at the vast expanse of Christmas trees that seemed to march up the hillside in the distance. The house was a long, single-story ranch with white siding that sat behind a wooden fence. Out front were piles of lumber, evergreen boughs, machinery, and various decorations that looked as if they were being readied for holiday visitors.

Erin pointed at a wooden shed with a sign that said it was Santa's Hot Cocoa Station. "That's cute."

"It was Mom's idea. Kids looking for the perfect Christmas tree often get cold. When they start to whine, it kills the holiday mood." Ziggy parked the truck and pulled the keys out of the ignition. He patted Casey's head. "Ready to roll, Casey?"

They unloaded the dogs from the car, and Moose leaped around the yard ahead of them, clearly thrilled to be out of the truck. Casey waddled sedately next to Erin, unconcerned by the acrobatics and antics of the large black dog.

Ziggy opened the front door and Moose barreled inside. A woman's voice said, "Oh, Moosie, calm down. You made me spill the sprinkles."

Ziggy indicated that Erin should follow him to the kitchen. They entered the room, which had cookie-making paraphernalia and ingredients covering every available surface. A woman with a reddish pixie haircut wearing a long kitchen apron stood behind a gigantic bowl on the kitchen island holding her hands up away from Moose's inquisitive nose.

"Hi Mom." Ziggy set Erin's canvas bag on the floor. "You remember Erin Quinn, right? Bea asked me to pick her up at the airport."

The woman looked confused for a moment and set the spoon she was holding on the counter. "Erin?"

"It's Stardust, Mom." Ziggy raised his eyebrows at Erin, who took the hint and said, "It's nice to see you again, Mrs. Bryant."

"Please call me Melody. Everybody does."

Ziggy walked around the island, leaned over to peer at the cookbook lying on the counter, and surveyed the ingredients littering the countertops. "Mom, where's the sugar?"

"Sugar?"

"One-and-a-half cups." He licked the tip of his index finger and took a dab of the white substance from the bowl. "This is a little salty."

Melody examined the cookbook and pointed at the page. "It says salt, right there."

"One-and-a-half teaspoons," Ziggy replied.

Melody put on a pair of reading glasses. "Hmm. Well, okay."

He bent to give her a one-armed hug. "Stardust doesn't have a key to her parents' house, so I told her it's okay if she and Casey crash here."

Melody looked confused for a moment, then scowled. "Saffron and Arrow never were considerate. For heaven's sake, who would lock their child out of their home?"

Ziggy glanced at Erin, who responded with a slight raise of her eyebrows and an "I have no idea" shrug. It wasn't a stretch to think that her parents had been inconsiderate back when people had called them Saffron and Arrow, but she had no clue what they'd done to inspire Melody's ire.

Melody turned, maneuvered around Ziggy, and grabbed a bag of sugar from a cabinet and set it down. Ziggy got a funnel from a drawer and poured the salt out of the bowl into the salt container. Melody grabbed a measuring spoon and dipped it into the bag of sugar.

Ziggy took the spoon from her hand and handed her a one-cup measure. "One-and-a-half cups of sugar."

"Hmm."

Erin got the impression this wasn't the first time Ziggy had helped his mother remain focused. Their movements were almost choreographed, each of his actions a reaction to hers. Considering how large he was and how small the kitchen was, it was a remarkably graceful performance.

"I'm going to show Erin where she's staying." He pointed at the bag of flour. "Three cups of flour, right?"

"Of course. I've made cookies before, you know."

Ziggy turned away from her, rolled his eyes melodramatically at Erin, and grabbed her bag on his way toward the door. "The guest room is back here."

She followed him down a hallway, craning her head to get a few peeks at the other bedrooms. The master bedroom was large with its own bathroom. A second bedroom had clothes and papers strewn across the bed. Moose charged past her and leaped up on the bed, causing a paper snowstorm. Ziggy glanced behind him and mumbled something uncomplimentary about the dog's lack of coordination.

Casey looked like he wanted to join Moose in the fun, but Erin tugged on the leash to encourage him to stay with her. She followed Ziggy into the last bedroom and stopped short. The room was painted a deep green with bright red trim. The walls were lined with shelves filled with every Christmas ornament imaginable. Hundreds of Santas, elves, reindeer, trees, wreaths, and sleighs were stacked everywhere. Ziggy flipped a switch and Christmas lights twinkled from strings that had been draped over almost every available surface.

Erin turned her head to scan the room. "Wow. Merry Christmas."

"I know it's like Kris Kringle barfed in here, but you get used to it after a while."

"I guess."

Ziggy dropped the bag, sat on the end of the bed, and patted the red and green quilt. The fabric sported little dancing snowmen and twirling candy canes. "Take a load off. You look exhausted."

Erin picked up Casey, stepped over Ziggy's long legs, and sat down next to him, settling the dog in her lap. "Thank you for letting me and Casey stay here."

"Sorry Mom griped about your parents. I don't know what that was about."

"She had a point. My parents tend to focus on their business to the exclusion of everything else."

He slapped his palms on the bed and pushed himself up off the Christmas quilt. "Welp, I guess I should let you get settled in. The bathroom's across the hall, and clean towels are in the linen closet in there. I need to check to make sure Mom hasn't added anything else to those cookies before things get nasty."

Erin smiled. "Good luck."

He left and closed the door quietly behind him. Erin flopped back on the bed, stretching her arms wide. Casey marched off her lap and curled up beside her.

Erin stroked the soft fur as she watched the Christmas lights blink overhead. Why on earth had she let her parents talk her into this trip?

~

Erin started awake at a knock on the door. Casey was still snoring next to her, and Ziggy's voice came from the other side of the door. "Hey Stardust, are you alive in there? Erin? It's almost time to eat."

Erin reassured him she was still among the living, got up, and hurriedly changed her clothes. After a quick trip to the bathroom to wash her face and remove the remaining scents of airline travel, she felt significantly better. Fortunately, she'd put her toiletries in her carry-on bag since her suitcase could be anywhere at this point. Maybe the ugly Samsonite was having a swell time in Tahiti or some other exotic locale.

Feeling more human again, she ventured down the hall to the kitchen. Ziggy was rolling out cookie dough, and his father had joined him in the baking extravaganza, using cookie cutters to shape cookies into trees, bells, stars, and Santas.

The man Erin formerly knew as Zappa had a lot less hair than he had in the seventies, but other than that, Greg Bryant looked almost the same as she remembered. The thin wiry man looked up from his task and gave her a wide grin. "Stardust! Look at you. Wow. The last time I saw you I think you were ten or eleven years old."

"I was twelve and a half when we left the commune and fourteen when we left town."

Greg put down his cookie cutter and walked around the counter. "You probably remember, but I'm a hugger. Come here."

Erin let him wrap her in a big bear hug, which felt odd because it had been so long since anyone had embraced her. She slowly put her arms around him, feeling awkward and out of practice.

After what felt like hours to Erin, but was probably only a couple seconds, he released her, gave her a final pat on the back, and returned to his cookies. "I heard you became a lawyer."

"I went to law school and passed the bar." Erin clasped her hands tightly in front of her, hoping they wouldn't ask about what happened after that.

"That's great." He glanced at a tray of gingerbread men his wife was decorating. He picked off a few red and silver nonpareils that had been placed in strategic locations.

Erin scanned the cookies and realized that the decorations were anatomically correct. Almost pornographically so. Melody was creative in her use of sprinkles and sugar toppings, and she'd done some interesting things with pieces of crushed peppermint and M&Ms as well. Hmm.

Greg passed his tray of cookies to Melody. "Okay, last one."

Ziggy pulled a ladle out of a pot that was simmering on the stovetop. "I'm glad you're finishing up. The soup's done, and I'm starving."

"Didn't you eat anything on your trip, Zig?" Melody asked.

Erin smiled to herself. If Mom still called him Ziggy, she wasn't going to feel bad. He just didn't look like a Dylan to her. Pointing at the dog near her feet, Erin said, "We had to pick up Casey before the kennel closed."

Ziggy said, "Moose must have eaten something disgusting, so we had to stop twenty-nine times on the way down the hill. I thought I would be late for the flight."

"I'm sorry," Erin said.

Ziggy waved the spoon at her. "It's not your fault that dog is gross. You had to put up with his stink all the way back up the hill. He's not on my list of favorite creatures right now. Even the goats are looking better."

Melody said, "The goats are adorable, and you know it."

"I suppose," he grumbled as he pulled soup bowls from the top shelf of a cabinet.

Erin helped Ziggy carry the bowls into the dining room while his parents tossed the cookie-mixing bowls into the sink. Everyone settled into four of the chairs at one end of the wooden farm table.

The soup was delicious. Erin hadn't realized how hungry she was after traveling all day. She knew she probably should say something instead of just gobbling down the soup. It tends not to be socially acceptable to crash at someone's house and then not speak.

Of course, it wasn't kosher to hole-up in your house sleeping on the couch in ten-year-old elastic-waist sweatpants for weeks on end either, but she had been doing that for more than two years. She'd needed to venture out into the world from time to time to earn money, even though she desperately would have preferred to lead the life of a shut-in. Work had the unfortunate effect of throwing her into social settings routinely, but she had gotten surprisingly good at avoiding meaningless small talk.

She put down her spoon reluctantly, because the glacial silence was getting increasingly uncomfortable. "This soup is delicious. Do you have the recipe?"

Ziggy shook his head. "I made it up. Leftover surprise, which isn't terribly surprising, since we ate it yesterday. Today, I opened the plastic containers, threw it in a pot, and added water. Now it's soup."

Ziggy's approach to repurposing dinners was similar to her own. Erin stirred the soup in her bowl slowly, trying to think of a follow-up comment. "It came out well." Okay, it was an utterly lame statement, but she was running out of steam. She turned to Greg, "It looks like you're getting set up to sell Christmas trees. When do you open for the season?"

Greg looked up from his soup and gave Ziggy a meaningful stare. "The day after Thanksgiving. We're almost out of time, and there's still a lot of work to do."

Melody added, "I'll be doing more baking tomorrow. I can't believe Christmas is just around the corner again. I'm feeling a little stressed about all the shopping and preparations I have to do. It's a busy time."

"Mom, I told you. I'll take you to the store tomorrow." Ziggy stood up and pointed at Erin's bowl. "Want a refill?"

"Yes, please." Erin handed it to him with a grateful smile.

When he returned, Erin ate her soup and listened as he and his parents discussed all the things that had to happen before the big opening. Ziggy was going to be working hard. Apparently, Melody didn't like to drive, so either Greg or Ziggy took her on major grocery-shopping expeditions.

After all the cookie baking, no one seemed interested in dessert. Erin offered to help clean up, and Greg and Melody left her and Ziggy to the task of hosing down the kitchen.

Erin suggested that she wash the dishes because she didn't know where anything was stored. She put the dishes in the dishwasher, then filled up the sink so she could scrub the pots and pans. Ziggy dried and put everything away.

When they were done, Ziggy tossed the dish towel over his shoulder and leaned back against the counter. "Thanks for offering to do dishes. Normally that's my job."

She took a position next to him leaning on the sink. "You seem to have a lot of jobs."

"This is what happens when you live at home." He flashed a wicked grin. "On a positive note, no rent."

Erin glanced at the doorway, then back at him. "Is your mom, um, okay?"

"She's the same as she's always been." He shrugged. "Mom has lots of ideas, but not the greatest follow-through. She loses focus sometimes because she self-medicates, if you know what I mean. If she doesn't get her morning Mary Jane, she's a swirling ball of anxiety."

"I guess she was always a little high-strung."

"Kinda different than being around a bunch of smarty-pants lawyers, huh? Where do you work? Do you go to court a lot?"

Erin turned away from him. "Actually I don't work as a lawyer."

"You said you passed the bar. That's hard, isn't it?"

"It is, but…" Erin waved her hands, desperately wishing she could avoid talking about this with him. "I work as a temp."

"Like a temporary lawyer? I've never heard of that."

"I don't work as a lawyer. I'm a temp as in a temporary employee." At his blank stare, she continued. "Suppose you have an office and your receptionist goes on vacation. You need someone to fill in, so you call a temporary agency. The agency sends me out to answer the phones. When the regular receptionist comes back, I'm done, so they can send me out on a different job whenever one comes in."

"Okay. So how often do jobs come in?"

"Not often enough, unfortunately. I've downsized and I have savings, but..."

He set a dish in the drainer and turned to look at her. "You're the smartest person I've ever met. Why would you answer phones instead of doing what you went to school to do? That doesn't make sense. What are you *not* telling me?"

Erin bowed her head and put her hands over her face. Even when they were kids, she never could lie to Ziggy. He had this way of seeing through her. "Something bad happened. TASTE."

"What do you mean 'taste?'"

"T-A-S-T-E." She dropped her hands and felt the tears slide down her cheeks. "It's an acronym. TASTE is the awful, stupid, terrible event. The one that killed my fiancé. When he died, everything spiraled out of control. I hate talking about it. I hate even thinking about it. That's why I turned it into an acronym. It doesn't help much though."

"I'm sorry." Ziggy reached for her hand and gave it a squeeze. "I know I haven't seen you in forever, but at Dancing Cedars we were best friends. I'm so sorry about your fiancé. I had no idea."

"It's not like TASTE happened yesterday." She looked up to meet his wide blue eyes. "It's been more than two years.

I'm supposed to be over it by now. But I can't seem to get past what happened. Every time I think I'm pulling myself together, another wave crashes, and I sink back down to the bottom of the ocean."

"I can't imagine."

"Don't try. I have no idea why I'm telling you this. It's old news. Over and done." She let go of his hand and wiped the fifty-thousandth tear from her cheek with the base of her palm. "But the reason I'm not practicing law is that nothing in my life has made sense. We were engaged for years—supposed to get married last year. We waited because I wanted a June wedding. It was going to be perfect. But then he died. So mostly all I want to do is to sleep and pretend TASTE never happened. But all that sleeping makes it hard to hold down a job."

"I don't know what to say." He put his arm around her shoulder and pulled her close. "Just that I'm so sorry that TASTE happened, Stardust. I really am."

"Yeah, me too."

~

The next morning, Erin opened her eyes and was greeted by a pair of black canine nostrils inches from her face. Where was she? She lifted her head and sat up to look around. Oh yeah, she was in the Land of Christmas room. This must be what it would be like to live inside a Christmas-themed snow globe. All she needed was some plastic snow swirling around the room.

She flopped onto the bed again and rolled onto her back. The night before, she'd taken a sleeping pill, aka Erin's Little Friend, aka ELF, which was more than a little ironic, given all the tiny men in red suits littering the room. Although the yellow pills made her feel groggy and sluggish in the morning, it was better than insomnia. She'd dug out an "emergency" pill from a tiny side pocket in her purse, but the prescription bottle was in her suitcase. Somewhere.

Casey stood up, stretched deeply, and yawned, exposing an impressive set of white teeth. The voices coming from the rest of the house indicated that everyone else was awake and moving about. ELF's ability to induce coma-like sleep was apparently unaffected by the change in Erin's location. She stumbled out of the bedroom and crossed the hall to the bathroom to deal with her morning routine. From the sounds of it, a Bryant family argument was in process and she was reluctant to see what her hosts were up to in the kitchen. She was also embarrassed that she'd completely fallen apart in front of Ziggy.

Finally, she ran out of teeth to brush and faces to wash, so she ventured into the fray. Melody was stirring something in a pot on the stove while Greg supervised. His arms were folded across his chest and he was glaring at Ziggy.

Ziggy waved his arms at his parents. "I'm sorry, but this is a bad idea. I'm not doing it."

Melody waved the spoon, and gray goo glopped onto the floor. "But the kids will love it."

Greg grabbed a paper towel, crouched down to clean up the mess, and stood up. He threw the gooey towel in the garbage and put his fists on his hips. "Listen to your mother. You know she comes up with great ideas."

"Not this time." Ziggy pulled a bowl from a cabinet. "I am absolutely not dressing up as a jingle bear. I don't even know what that is supposed to be."

Melody said, "We can call you Beary Belafonte!"

"No," Ziggy said, punctuating it by thumping the bowl onto the counter.

Greg said, "Beary Manilow?"

Ziggy turned and gave him an incredulous look. "Are you kidding me? A thousand times no."

"Chuck Beary? Beary Mason?" Melody said.

"We tried this with Santa, and it didn't work." Ziggy waved his arms in exasperation. "The kids didn't buy it. They all recognized me. And you know I hate dressing up."

"But this would be different," his mother protested. "With a bear suit they can't see your eyes. It solves the whole problem."

Erin didn't want to say anything, but it wasn't only Ziggy's eyes that kids would recognize. How many seven-foot-tall Christmas bears were there? Children might think he was Bigfoot out for a holiday stroll and run screaming for the hills.

Greg grabbed a bowl from the cabinet. "Kids love teddy bears. It would be cute."

"No. Way." Ziggy took his bowl to the stove and slopped some oatmeal into it.

Without thinking, Erin said, "You could hire someone else to dress up as a bear. Maybe you can find a teenager who's looking for some extra work."

Ziggy stopped, set his bowl on the table, and turned to give her an incredulous gaze. "You're a genius."

"I'm not paying some kid to do it," Greg said. "This is a family business."

"I'll pay him or her," Ziggy said. "No matter what it costs, it would be worth it for me not to dress up in a bear suit."

Melody furrowed her brows. "I don't know. I'm not sure I'd feel comfortable with someone else being the jingle bear."

Erin ate her bowl of oatmeal quietly, listening to the back and forth and regretting that she'd said anything. Way to splash into the deep end of the pool and drown in a family argument.

The phone rang, interrupting the discussion. Greg answered it and chatted for a moment, then said, "Sure, I'll tell him." He hung up and said, "That was Bea. She said Erin's parents will be returning this afternoon, so she can go home."

"Thank you for letting Casey and me stay here," Erin said quickly. "I appreciate it."

"I'll take you over to their house later," Ziggy said. "In the meantime, you can help me finish the cocoa hut."

"It's called Santa's Hot Cocoa Station," Melody interjected.

Ignoring the comment, Ziggy focused his attention on Erin. "So how are you at wielding a paintbrush?"

"I'm happy to help," Erin said. She couldn't remember the last time she'd painted anything, but it would be a great excuse to get away from the elder Bryants, who probably hated her for giving their favorite jingle bear outlandish outsourcing ideas.

Ziggy lent her some old paint-covered overalls and an ancient work jacket and gloves. Even though she ended up looking disturbingly like a poorly dressed scarecrow, Ziggy didn't seem to notice. He gathered up the supplies, and they went outside. He stopped in front of the small building and handed her a four-inch paintbrush. "This may come as a shock, but the plan is for the cocoa hut to be red with green trim."

"You must be a little tired of red and green."

"You have no idea." He jammed a fuzzy cover onto a paint roller attached to a long wooden pole. "They start pulling out the red and green paint chips whenever I walk into Lowell's Hardware. It's sad."

"I'm sorry that I've ended up in the way during such a busy time for your family." She crouched and used a metal paint-can opener to pry the lid off the green paint. "You obviously have a lot to do."

"The preparations are almost done." Ziggy stirred the red paint. "The work on the trees is over, and once I finish painting this, the setup is done. Then the day after Thanksgiving, it's Christmas tree shoppers all day, every day."

She looked up from her task. "From the tone of your voice, I get the impression you're not looking forward to it."

"You know how I am. If I had my way, I'd go off for a hike in the forest and wouldn't come back until after the new year."

Erin smiled. "That does sound more like how I remember you."

"I haven't changed." He sat down cross-legged on the ground next to her. "What you said about hiring someone. I think that may be the best idea I've ever heard. You're brilliant."

"Oh brother. Give me a break."

"I'm serious. I haven't had a Christmas off in, well, I don't even want to think about how long. I would love to have some holiday in my holiday season for a change. After so many years of working, I'd like to experience all that 'joy of Christmas' stuff everyone talks about."

"Well don't ask me about it." Erin pressed her palm to her heart. "My parents refer to me as the Grinch because I've avoided visiting them over the holidays for the last two years. I've holed up in my apartment by myself."

"I admit that doesn't sound very festive."

"Everyone says you're supposed to be happy around the holidays. I wasn't. Trying to force myself to not be sad made it worse."

"How does forcing yourself to not be sad even work?"

"It doesn't. Willpower doesn't work on feelings. It's like you've been thrown off a building and you're flailing at air but continuing to fall. You're powerless to do anything, which makes you panicky so you feel even worse."

Ziggy rolled the fuzzy roller back and forth against his palm. "Worse than just feeling sad?"

"Instead of only being sad, you're also mad at yourself for being sad. Frustrated and ashamed because you can't get over what happened and be happy like normal people. The whole world is a giant Christmas-themed Norman Rockwell painting that you're looking at while you're hating yourself for being a rotten person who avoids her family."

"You're not avoiding your family now."

"I would if I could. I know they're going to give me lots of worried looks and be careful what they say to me. They treat me like I'm some fragile piece of porcelain, but at the same time, they also think I should be done grieving by now." Erin paused. What was wrong with her? Why was she dumping all this on Ziggy? He had enough on his mind.

Ziggy watched the roller as he continued to move it back and forth on his hand, then looked at her. "So why are you here?"

"Mom sent me a nonrefundable plane ticket and made me feel so guilty for avoiding them that I couldn't refuse. She says there's something she wants to talk to me about in person."

Ziggy stopped rolling. "That sounds ominous."

"I know. I finally agree to a holiday visit so I can get some horrible news." She waved her paintbrush in exasperation. "Thanks Mom. Like that's going to cheer me up. As if I weren't already convinced the world is full of random bad things waiting to happen to good people."

Ziggy looked thoughtful for a moment, then leaned forward, widening his vivid blue eyes at her. "Here's an idea for you. Sometimes when I'm wandering around among the trees, I think about all the bad things that don't happen to me."

"What do you mean?"

"Like yesterday, I cut down a tree, and it fell in the other direction, so I didn't get killed."

"That's nice, although I imagine you have quite a bit of practice felling trees."

"I do, but I could screw up."

"But you didn't."

"And that's great, isn't it? Maybe you can ease into the holiday spirit by celebrating all the stuff that didn't happen to you."

Erin raised her eyebrows. "Like not getting squished by a grand fir?"

"Exactly." He waved his roller at her. "Did you *not* get whacked in the face by a paint roller today? Woo-hoo! Let's have a party."

"Well not yet anyway. Be careful with that thing."

"Did you *not* get attacked by a rabid squirrel today? Or bitten by spiders from Mars? Nope. You also weren't thrown in jail for beating up an elf. And you even avoided meeting Sasquatch. Let's celebrate that!"

"I forgot what a weirdo you are." Erin smiled in spite of herself. "You didn't have to dress up as a bear either."

"Yes!" He laughed and raised the paint roller in a mock toast. "Cheers to another big win!"

~

Painting the cocoa-hut trim was mindless work. While Casey napped, Erin and Ziggy chatted amiably about what had happened with their families over the last twenty years.

Erin was so surprised when Ziggy told her that his brother Harrison had joined the Navy, she accidentally splashed some green paint on a window. "Little Harry joined the military? Your mother must have completely freaked out. She spent years protesting the Vietnam War."

"Dad wasn't too pleased either. Mom tells people that Harry is overseas on a boat. What she doesn't say is that the boat happens to be an aircraft carrier."

"Where is the ship now? Is he coming home for Christmas?"

"Someplace classified and we're not sure." Ziggy dipped the roller in the tray of green paint. "He was only here a couple of days last year and wisely avoided the time leading up to the big day. People who get their Christmas trees on

Christmas Eve are often stressed-out procrastinators, so it's a day worth missing."

"I can imagine."

Ziggy was still excited about the idea of finding someone to fill in for him for the holidays. He said he planned to ask around. Erin wasn't sure who he might ask, but it wasn't her problem to solve. She was still fretting about whatever her mother wanted to say to her.

They were in the process of cleaning up when Melody came outside to let them know that Bea had called to say that the Quinns were back home in Alpine Grove.

Once Melody was out of earshot, Erin said, "Does Bea mind being the intermediary between our parents because they won't speak to each other?"

Ziggy took off his gloves and rubbed his hands together. "Nope. She's convinced it's temporary, and they'll come around."

"Twenty or so years doesn't seem very temporary to me. Do you know why they hate each other?"

"Nope. Mom and Dad refuse to talk about it. Something happened at Dancing Cedars. I've always thought it might be related to why everyone left."

Erin shook her head. "I've never understood why we had to leave. The worst thing about moving to town was having to go to public school. I hated it."

"Me too."

"How would you know? You weren't there. People all thought I was a freak. You disappeared so I had no friends."

"They thought I was a freak too. I didn't need that, so I avoided the whole thing by getting myself expelled."

"Hold on. I knew you left, but are you saying you got expelled on *purpose*? Nobody told me that."

"Remember the 'smoking dragon' that the grownups used to pass around at Dancing Cedars?"

"Of course. Puff, the Magic Dragon."

"After we moved to town, I hated going to school, so I didn't very often. My parents noticed when I got in trouble for ditching."

"I noticed too."

"It wasn't a sustainable plan. Then one day I found Puff in a box in the living room, and I had an idea. I figured that if you bring a huge bong shaped like a dragon to school, you're likely to get expelled." He grinned. "It turns out I was right."

"What did your parents do? There's only one junior high school in Alpine Grove."

"They had to drive me to Western Junior High in Gleasonville every day. Dad was furious, and he told me that the next step would be to ship me off to some school for 'problem kids' in Colorado. Western wasn't so bad because no one knew who I was. Being the new kid isn't great, but at least there I wasn't the funny-looking kid from the commune."

"I think part of why my parents moved away from Alpine Grove was because I was so miserable in school."

After they cleaned up, Erin packed up her things and went to load Casey into Ziggy's truck. The process was complicated by a small orange cat that shot across the yard like a bullet in front of the cocoa hut. Casey lost his furry mind barking hysterically at the feline interloper. Erin finally managed to convince him that he needed to be inside the truck and not chasing the cat through ten thousand Christmas trees.

Once Casey was safely in the cab, Ziggy got into the truck. "The weather has been odd this year. Two years ago, we had a blizzard over Thanksgiving weekend. But this year the weather has been mild, and we seem to have a lot of stray cats around. I didn't want to mention it, but I think whatever Moose ate was the leftovers from a cat's bird-hunting expedition."

"Eww. That's disgusting."

"Yeah, the partially digested slimy feathers he horked up were pretty nasty."

Erin's parents owned what they told her was a cute cottage downtown that they'd purchased when they decided to cut back on work. Her father referred to the move as their semi-retirement, but nothing much seemed to have changed as far as Erin could tell. The couple still traveled all over the world giving self-improvement seminars. The only difference was that now they lived a lot farther from a major airport.

The Bryant Christmas Tree Farm was about fifteen minutes from town. Ziggy told Erin that her parents' new home probably was near the old Whitaker place on Spruce Street.

"When I was a kid, I thought it was a castle because of the tower." Erin rested her palm on Casey's back. "I wished I could live there so I could be a princess. Wasn't it supposedly a boarding house in the twenties?"

"I heard the woman who owned it was part of the Temperance Guild, but she had a parrot that liked to recite dirty limericks. I always wondered how he learned all those bad words if she was such a goody two-shoes."

"Everyone used to say the woman's ghost wandered around in the turret. Maybe she was chasing after her naughty bird."

Ziggy turned onto Spruce Street and slowed down. He scanned the numbers on the houses, and suddenly pulled over to park at the end of the block. "Number 604 *is* the Whitaker house. You didn't tell me your parents were the ones who restored it."

"I didn't know."

"That's cool they bought a place with its own ghost."

"If you believed the rumors, every old building in Alpine Grove is haunted." Erin looked up at the large edifice, which sported huge porches on two sides. The two-and-a-half-story house sat on a corner lot. A tower on the corner of the house extended up beyond the roofline with swooping curved eves that looked almost like a hat. Topped with a finial to emphasize the peak, the tower had windows on both the first and second floors that were set into the five exterior sides, providing a view out to the meticulously landscaped yard below.

Ziggy put his hand on Erin's forearm. "Aren't you going to get out?"

"I'm working on it." She gestured toward the house. "Restoring this house must have cost a fortune. The last time I saw it, this place was falling apart. The wood was gray, the paint was peeling, and the whole thing was decomposing."

"I've been watching the work progress over the past year or so. They did an amazing job, although I'm not sure I would have opted to paint it green. But that's probably just me. What is it that your parents do?"

"They teach seminars. Self-help stuff about nurturing better relationships."

"That must a lot more lucrative than selling trees."

"I think you're right."

Erin got out of the truck and lifted Casey to the ground. She pulled her carry-on bag from the back seat and set it next to the dog.

Ziggy walked around the truck and stood next to her. "I doubt your parents want to see me, so I guess this is good-bye. It's been nice to see you again, Stardust."

He had a look like he might want to give her a good-bye hug, so Erin leaned down and grabbed the carry-on strap, yanking it up over her shoulder. "It's been nice seeing you too. Thank you for everything."

Ziggy took a step back away from her. "No problem. Have a good visit. I'll see you around."

Erin gave him a quick smile as one of their lame jokes flashed from her memory. "Not if I see you first."

Chapter 3

Secret Agent Man

Erin walked up the sidewalk, up the steps, and across the porch to the door. She knocked and then waved at Ziggy as he drove off. When the door opened, she turned to face her mother. "Hi Mom. Welcome home."

"I could say the same to you." Jennifer Quinn grabbed her daughter in a fierce hug and dragged her into the entryway. Her long oval face was devoid of makeup and her thick straight gray hair was loosely gathered into a low ponytail. She was wearing a red t-shirt under an unzipped black sweater, black cotton pants, and fuzzy slippers.

Pulling Erin into the living room, she dropped the book she'd been holding onto an end table, took a seat on the sofa, and called Casey over to her.

Erin smiled as her mother ruffled the dog's ears and told him he was a very, very good boy. Erin let her bag slide down off her shoulder to the floor and settled onto the couch next to her mother, recognizing the scent of Mom's favorite patchouli soap.

Jennifer pulled Casey onto her lap and stroked his ears as she scanned Erin's face. "I can't believe I'm finally looking at you. It's been so long. I'm sorry we weren't able to pick you up at the airport."

"It's okay, although I'm not sure where my suitcase is."

"Bea called, and the airline says they're looking for it. From what she said, it might arrive here in the next few days." She gestured toward the windows. "But who knows with the holiday? You can borrow some of my clothes if you need to. Or we can go shopping if you like."

Erin didn't have any money for new clothes. "If you don't mind, I'm sure I can find something in your closet."

"That was kind of Ziggy to pick you up. He was such a funny kid. I can't imagine him as an adult. What's he like now?"

"A lot taller."

Jennifer laughed. "I would hope so. One thing I remember about Ziggy is that he was an amazing reader. You two were always nagging to go the library. Then you spent all your time talking about books."

When they were kids, many of the adventures Ziggy had thought up had related to the books they were reading. Saying anything could incriminate them in some bad behavior Mom probably didn't know about. Time for a change of subject. "You never told me you bought the Whitaker house. I can't believe you didn't say anything."

Jennifer put her hand on Erin's arm. "You haven't wanted to talk, honey, and I didn't want to push you."

"The house looks beautiful."

Jennifer clapped her hands together. "Isn't it amazing? It was built in 1906 and is considered a good example of the popular American Colonial Revival style with Queen Anne features. I'm trying to get historical status for it because it's one of only a small group of houses here that can be considered a Queen Anne. The style had become less popular by the time most of Alpine Grove was built. That's why you see more bungalow-style houses in town. And as you probably remember, this house is the only house in town with a tower."

"I used to draw pictures of this house when I was little."

"That's one reason I wanted to buy it. You're staying in the upstairs bedroom in the tower. It's wonderful. I know you'll love it." She put Casey on the floor and grabbed Erin's hand. "Let me show you."

Erin followed her mother to the stairs. "Where's Dad?"

"Oh, he'll be back soon, I think. He walked over to the bookstore to see if he could find the latest mystery by that local author."

"What local author?"

"Oh, I can't remember his name. But he's Margaret's son-in-law."

"Margaret Connelly still owns the bookstore?"

"I don't think she'll ever give it up." Jennifer spread her arms, inviting Erin into the bedroom. "Here it is. They finished painting the last of the trim a couple of weeks ago. I hope the paint smell is gone."

Erin ran her palm up the bright white trim on the door frame. "It's so pretty." Sunlight streamed down from the windows in the steep sloped roof and the five windows in the room's perimeter. Outside, the branches of an enormous maple tree slowly waved in the breeze.

"Finding this house was one of those capricious miracles that you can't explain." Jennifer sat down on the bed and ran her palm across the blue and green quilt. "It went on the market the same day we went to talk to a realtor. It has incredible energy and everything unfolded the way it was supposed to."

Erin tried not to sigh. Her mother tended to read a lot into signs and symbols. She couldn't even remember how many times her mother had done something because of good vibes or feelings. "Maybe you got some extra-good karma from helping all those people who attend your seminars."

"I'm sure all those positive interactions and helping to heal peoples' relationships couldn't hurt." She pulled Casey onto her lap. "By the way, we're going to Dancing Cedars for Thanksgiving. The Sullivans invited us to a potluck Thanksgiving. We've been so busy, and Bea said she'd like to see us—and you too, since you're in town."

Erin frowned. "There's no electricity out there. How are we supposed to cook?"

"The old woodstove is still there. And Bea still has some of those old propane stoves we used to use." Jennifer uttered a pretty laugh. "It will be like camping out."

"I hope we don't set the place on fire."

"Oh Erin, that type of negativity will keep you from enjoying yourself. It's a great opportunity because I've been wanting to talk to Bea about the property."

"What about it?"

"The land is just sitting there, but it could be a wonderful space to hold events." She stroked the dog's fur slowly with a dreamy look on her face. "The energy is incredible. Don't you remember?"

"I was a kid, and I don't remember feeling any particular energy." Mostly she remembered feeling tired because she spent all day chasing Ziggy around. He used to come up with ideas for complex adventures that involved climbing trees, splashing in creeks, or getting lost. Only Ziggy would think getting lost on purpose was a good idea.

"Being in a beautiful environment will enhance the possibilities for warm, accepting therapeutic relationships to develop. I'm thinking of doing women's retreats to help people identify and correct distorted thoughts."

Erin glanced out the window. Where was her father? How long did it take to get a book? "What does Dad think about that? I thought you worked with couples. Wouldn't he be a little out of place at a women's retreat?"

"To be honest, he seems more interested in retirement. But I'm not ready to do that yet."

"I'm sure you'll figure it out." Erin's parents' lives had been about fixing interpersonal relationships for so long, maybe Dad was sick of talking about cognitive restructuring and problem-solving. She couldn't blame him for wanting to do something different.

Jennifer reached over to Erin and grabbed her hand. "Please sit down. I need to share something."

Erin settled in. Uh-oh. This must be the news. She gave her mother an expectant look. "Is everything okay?"

"You're staying here, so it will be obvious, but your father and I have separated. His room is down the hall. Mine is the one next to the bathroom."

Erin struggled for a response. "I'm not sure what to say other than I'm sorry. Are you okay?"

"We're both fine, and I don't want this to affect your visit." She put her arms around Erin, but let go when Erin stiffened. "I know you're still working through your own issues, but I'm so happy you're finally here. I've missed you."

"Are you and Dad getting a divorce?"

"We're taking some time to explore our individuality. The web of life is complex and we've been intertwined for so long, we've agreed to take some space for ourselves."

Erin wasn't sure what that meant exactly. She didn't want to get into intimate details, but there was an obvious business problem. "How does this affect your seminars? They're about relationships, and if you and Dad are separated doesn't that ruin your credibility?"

"Tokyo was the last trip for a while. We're still exploring options. I'm hoping seeing Dancing Cedars again will help you heal." Jennifer put both hands to her chest. "I would love it if you would stay here for a while. That's why I sent you an open ticket. What if you helped me with the retreats? Mother and daughter."

"I don't know…this is a lot to take in, Mom."

"I'm just putting it out there. Giving it voice, so you can consider it. Sometimes the secrets of the universe manifest when you least expect and shape your choices."

"Maybe we should see how Thanksgiving goes before I make any big decisions."

Jennifer hugged her again. "Good idea."

Erin was sitting at the table in the kitchen with her mother when her father, Paul Quinn, returned. He was one of those men who seemed to get better looking as he got older. At the commune, he'd had a messy beard and long, scraggly hair like everyone else, so for years Erin had had no idea what the bottom half of her father's face looked like. It turned out that when clean-shaven, Paul had a square jaw and chiseled features somewhat like Sean Connery's. Now his dark brown hair was starting to go gray, which made him look like a wise professor. Erin always figured that the tweedy teacher thing he had going probably played well at the seminars.

After the initial welcome, never one to avoid conflict, Paul asked, "Did your mother tell you about our situation?"

Erin confessed that yes, she knew her parents weren't sharing a room. She added, "I don't plan to stay long, so I'll be out of your hair in a few days."

Paul folded his arms across his chest. "You aren't in our *hair*. We've been begging you to visit for more than a year."

"I know, but I need to get back."

"I hear what you're saying. This house is unfamiliar, and you've been pulled out of your safe environment. How does that make you feel?"

"Dad, I don't want to talk about my feelings." Erin stood up. Time to make a break for it. "My suitcase hasn't turned up, and I'd like to go look through mom's closet and see if I can find something to wear for tomorrow."

Erin could hear her parents murmuring in hushed, concerned voices as she ascended the stairs. Maybe she was too harsh. She knew they meant well, but going through her complicated and depressing feelings all the time was exhausting. Why did they always have to talk about everything? She was sick of talking. Why couldn't they let it rest? Her parents had spent a lot of time with Andy over the years and were well aware that he'd died before he and Erin got married. What more could there possibly be to say at this point?

Later at dinner, the conversation was a little stilted until Erin asked a few questions about the Tokyo trip. It was a safe topic, and once Mom and Dad got going telling her about all the mini-dramas and adventures they'd had during their trip, time passed fairly quickly. After painting and socializing over the course of the long day, Erin was ready to go to bed. Once she was done helping with the dishes, she bid everyone goodnight and retired to her tower room.

Being alone again was a relief, but sleep might be elusive without ELF. The little yellow pills hanging out in her long-lost Samsonite were probably having a grand tour of North America at this point. She wanted to write a "wish you were here" postcard. Insomnia was frustrating all by itself, but the side effect of worrying about having insomnia wasn't much better.

After completing her evening skin care and dental ministrations, she closed the door to her snug tower room and curled up under the covers. The room had been painted a soothing creamy yellow color with bright white trim. The only wall that wasn't full of windows had several framed photographs hanging in two neat rows. Dad liked to photograph landscapes and had a particular fondness for taking sunset shots on their travels.

She rolled onto her back, closed her eyes, and began the deep breathing exercises that were supposed to calm her. Counting backward from ten, she tried to force her muscles to relax one by one, starting at her toes and moving up. Without ELF, it could be a long restless night, but if she kept counting maybe she could keep her brain occupied, so it wouldn't tread down pathways that led to bad mental spaces.

Outside the window, the wind increased and rain started up, making splattery tip-tapping noises on the curved roof. The sound of her parents' voices came from downstairs, and from the hall, Casey's claws clattered as he toddled along the hardwood flooring on the other side of the bedroom door.

With the curtains over the five windows closed, the room was like a warm cocoon, isolated from the rest of the house as if she were in a cabin in the woods with the falling of silent snow muffling the noise of the outside world.

The gentle white flakes fluttered all around her, catching on her eyelashes and dusting the cobblestones below her feet. She moved through the whiteness and stared at a tall man with dark hair. He was wearing a long red coat, and even in the dim glow of the street light, the contrast of the crimson against the snow was striking. He reached out and gripped her hand. His touch was so familiar, and she detected the clean scent of the gelatinous, bright green shampoo Andy used to like. She could feel the cold of the snow on her skin and yet, somehow, she knew she was dreaming. But this was a dream she didn't want to end. "Andy? Is that you?"

He let go of her hand, turned away, and Erin screamed, "No, don't leave me." He turned back to look at her, and she reached out her hand to touch him again, but he vanished into the white haze. She jerked awake and rolled off the bed, crashing to the floor.

As she crawled back into bed, she tried to remember how she knew it was Andy. She couldn't see the man's face very well because of the snow. Did it even look like him? Andy had never dressed like Santa as far as she knew. Maybe the time she'd spent at the Bryant Ranch had messed with her head. She rubbed her hand where Andy had touched her. How could a dream feel so real? Normally, she didn't remember her dreams at all.

Andy had worked on Capitol Hill as a legislative assistant and later a legislative correspondent. He worked long hours and had never even gone to a Christmas party. Politicians didn't get all warm and fuzzy about the holidays. The legislative body went back to their home districts during the recess, but for the staff, it was all about the work all day, every day.

Erin hugged her pillow to her chest, mentally reviewing what she'd seen in the dream. It was snowing and hard to see, but Andy must have been standing in front of their apartment building in Georgetown. Where else were there cobblestones?

She hadn't lived there in two years. Like everything else, she'd left it behind after TASTE. Andy died right after she had passed the bar exam. He'd had to go on a business trip with the Good Senator and she hadn't gone with him because she'd had a job interview. How many times had she wished she could rewrite history and join him on that flight? If only she'd insisted on rescheduling her interview and gotten on that plane with him.

He'd talked her out of it, saying, "This trip is all about me getting coffee and Jimmy Wonderful glad-handing constituents. You'd have a horrendous time. Go slay that interview, get the job, and I promise we'll celebrate when I get back."

Except he'd never come back. Erin snuggled down under the covers and tucked the quilt under her chin. It was unfair. They'd had their whole future planned. For years, they'd worked and worked so she could become a lawyer. Andy never complained about her long hours at school and work, and he always gave her time to study.

He used to say that when she was a powerful lawyer saving the planet, she could pay him back by "supporting him in his dotage." Whatever that meant. Becoming a lawyer had seemed far-fetched when she was working as a lowly paralegal for Natural Justice, an environmental firm on the Hill. But when her boss Carson Ballantine had encouraged her to take the LSATs and apply to law school, she did it almost on a lark. Why not? And then when she actually got into Georgetown Law and received a merit-based scholarship, she and Andy had thrown one heck of a party.

Erin gripped the covers more tightly. Everything had been going so well, she should have known that it wouldn't last. If only she'd gotten on that plane. Or simply never met Andy at all.

~

The next morning, Jennifer and Paul invited Erin to go with them to the grocery store. They needed to get started on the cooking for the big Thanksgiving potluck at Dancing Cedars, and the project required a serious store run.

Wading through an incredibly crowded grocery store wasn't appealing, and Erin offered to take Casey for a walk instead. After the rainstorm the night before, everything was scrubbed clean, but the temperature was still mild. She hadn't walked around Alpine Grove for years, and she knew from zipping through with Ziggy on the way to the boarding kennel that quite a bit had changed in the last couple of decades.

She leashed up Casey, wished her parents good luck on the shopping expedition, and headed out into the pretty morning. Casey trotted along jauntily as they strolled through the quiet residential neighborhood. Most of the leaves had fallen off the deciduous trees. Only a few hangers-on wobbled on the bare branches.

Erin had also wanted to get out of the house so she could think about her dream. After she'd worked through the initial shock, she'd gone through all of her relaxation exercises and was able to go back to sleep. She'd slept soundly for the rest of the night and when she woke, she felt better than she had in ages. The tower room's cocoon factor aided sleep, which was nothing short of a miracle. She needed to remember to tell Mom how much she liked the space.

Erin and Casey walked by a few people working on fall garden cleanup who waved cheerfully. One pair of wavers seemed to be having an unusually complex negotiation related to stacking firewood.

Erin had felt out of touch with the mundane workings of daily life for so long it was odd to see people going through typical pre-winter preparations. All these people looked happy and normal, thinking about the future and excited by the upcoming holiday season.

Seeing Andy so vividly in her dream had shaken Erin more than she wanted to admit. For two years, she'd been enveloped in a gray depressive fog, moving through her life like an observer but not engaging in much of anything. She was bored and unhappy, but not sure what to do about it. She went to temp jobs, drank her coffee, answered the phones, and went back to her studio apartment, going through the motions of life without really living it. Often she felt like she was watching a rerun of an unhappy life every day. But she never seemed to be able to change the channel.

At the single traffic light on Alpine Grove's main street, a man in a brown suit was standing outside an office, watching the traffic go by. From such a distance, Erin couldn't tell if she knew him. But she did wonder why he was just standing there. Didn't he have anything to do? Back in Washington, D.C. no one stood still. All the worker bees hustled from one appointment to the next. The only people who weren't in motion were people sitting on park benches on nice days, hurriedly gobbling down lunch before their next meeting.

At the time, being among so many productive people committed to making a difference in the world had been energizing. Now the idea of so much activity made her feel cynical and tired. She'd worked at an environmental firm and had made zero impact on anything. What was the point?

Casey paused to take care of some personal needs, watering a small patch of grass alongside the sidewalk. Erin encouraged him to keep moving, and they continued strolling along checking out the various businesses. Although she lamented the loss of the cafe, some old standbys remained. The two disgusting dive bars, the 311 and the Mystic Moon Soloan, looked exactly the same as they had decades ago. Odds were good that the interiors and the beers were as skanky as they'd ever been.

Although many businesses had changed hands, physically Alpine Grove looked like she remembered it with lots of two- and three-story brick buildings lining the main street. Like the cafe, the old Garden Restaurant had disappeared along with its rustic wood and glass building. Now there was a real estate office in that spot. Maybe the restaurants had burned down. Had she read something about a fire in Alpine Grove sometime in the eighties? She couldn't remember anymore.

The big brick buildings at the south end of the street still housed the government offices. The photo store was still there along with Bea Haven gifts. The old Alpine Motel had been added onto and now was called the H12. Did the number twelve indicate it was twice as good as a Motel 6? From the looks of it, probably not. Near the H12, the old Cupboard Restaurant was now a deli.

The drugstore was now a paint store. She and Casey crossed the street, walking slowly. Erin was looking at the window displays and signs while Casey seemed to be discovering thrilling scents along the ground. Long ago, there'd been a second-hand clothing store, where Erin's mother took her shopping. Somewhere there had been a dime store that had cheap toys too, but there was no sign of it now. The only clothing store sold "quality outdoor goods and footwear." Judging by the brands of clothes in the window, Erin couldn't afford any of it.

Erin stopped to look at the glittery display at Bea Haven gifts. It had a star theme with hanging stained-glass stars, wind chimes, mobiles, and crystals reflecting the sun. Stacked silver and gold boxes contained displays of pretty ornaments, glass animals, hearts, and butterflies.

The front door opened with a jingling of bells and Ziggy said, "Hey, I didn't expect to see you here."

"I'm taking Casey for a walk. What are you doing here?"

Ignoring her comment, Ziggy turned back and yelled into the store, "Bea, come say hi to Stardust."

Before Erin could try to run off, Bea Sullivan was in front of her wrapping her in a hug. "I can't believe you're here. It's absolutely wonderful to see you."

A memory involuntarily flashed into Erin's mind of Bea hugging her when she was a little girl. Bea was one of the many "aunts" she'd had at the Dancing Cedars commune and was easily one of the nicest people Erin had ever met. When the commune had disbanded, adjusting to suddenly having only two parents had been difficult. All the "aunts" and "uncles" and other kids she'd lived with were gone, and the absence of that community had added to her loneliness and feeling like an outsider after she moved to town.

Bea released her and held her shoulders, scanning her up and down. "I know I'm going to see you on Thanksgiving, but do you have a moment to sit down on this bench with me for a minute and enjoy this beautiful day?"

Erin sat as instructed. "How are you?"

"I'm doing well. Looking forward to the holiday, seeing everyone, and eating lots of food. Tracy and her boyfriend Rob will be there."

Ziggy said, "Stardust, you probably remember Rainbow, right?"

Erin nodded, remembering the little girl with bone-straight white-blonde hair who used to sit at the bank of the creek making mud pies.

Bea looked up at Ziggy. "She gets a little twitchy if you call her Rainbow, so you might want to stick to Tracy." She focused her attention back to Erin. "I was so sorry to hear about your fiancé."

Erin didn't say anything because a woman with a huge smile on her face was approaching them. She waved at Bea as she walked by them and went into the store. Bea stood up. "I have to go, but we'll talk tomorrow. I want to hear how you're doing."

Bea went into the store and Ziggy sat on the bench next to Erin. "I've got a secret, but you have to promise not to tell."

"So now you're secret agent man?"

"'Secret Agent Man' was performed by Johnny Rivers. Later covered by Devo."

"Devo is a little out of our purview." Erin was amused that he remembered their habit of testing each other on song titles and their artists. Because the radio had been on all the time at Dancing Cedars, they both had an encyclopedic knowledge of music from the sixties and seventies. She pulled Casey into her lap. "I promise nothing. Why are you here? Aren't you supposed to be working?"

"This is work." He held up a bag. "I had to buy teddy bears. Mom is now obsessed with Christmas bears. She's making little outfits for them."

"Little jingle bears?" Erin giggled. "Do you get to hand them out while you're wearing your furry suit?"

"Shut up. And no." He waved his hand toward the street. "Somewhere out there are people willing to dress up as large mammals. But *I* am not one of them."

"No ursidae for you, huh?"

"Finally!" Ziggy grinned widely and shoved her shoulder. "You're starting to sound like you again. Only you would throw a little Latin into the conversation."

"It helps with all the legal jargon I had to learn. So what's the secret?"

Ziggy leaned back on the bench and stretched his long legs out in front of him. "Don't tell your parents, but my family is going to Dancing Cedars for Thanksgiving too."

"That can't be a good idea."

"Yeah, I know. Bea hasn't told my parents or yours that the other couple is showing up."

"That's underhanded. She was always so straightforward with everyone. It doesn't seem like her style."

He shrugged. "She's got something up her sleeve I guess. Sorry she brought up TASTE."

"Everyone seems to feel like they have to say something when they find out." Erin set Casey back on the ground and leaned forward, putting her elbows on her knees. She gazed down at Casey's gray muzzle. "I know people mean well, but it's hard for me to talk about."

Ziggy leaned forward and looked into her eyes. "What was your fiancé like?"

"He was a legislative correspondent for a senator on Capitol Hill."

"I didn't ask what he did, I asked what he was *like*."

Erin sat up quickly and fingered the leash in her hands. "Andy was, well, I don't know. I loved him."

"I know that. What was he like? As a person. You know, personality, looks, favorite color, whether he liked Brussels sprouts, whatever."

"He had brown hair and brown eyes. He wasn't a fan of Brussels sprouts." Erin paused, letting her mind wander. "Other than that…he was smart. Brilliant, really. And funny in kind of a sarcastic, cynical way. It's hard to explain."

"Interesting."

"I had a dream about him last night. It was weird because it felt so real." Erin stopped short. What was it about Ziggy that made her blab every last thing on her mind like she did when she was twelve? "I don't know why, but I've been thinking about Andy more lately."

"What happened in the dream?"

"He reached out and took my hand like he wanted me to go with him somewhere."

"Did you go?"

"No. He let go of my hand and disappeared." A tear slipped from her eye and she brushed it away. "Do you think the dream means something?"

"I have no idea." He reached down to give Casey a pat, grabbed his bag full of bears, and stood up. "Maybe we can talk about it tomorrow while our parents are yelling at each other. This could be a rip-roaring Thanksgiving, complete with fireworks."

"Only at Dancing Cedars do you get to have a little Independence Day flair with your Thanksgiving."

"You know it'll be totally far out and groovy too." He grinned. "See you around, Stardust."

"Not if I see you first."

Chapter 4

The Radiance of Santa

Erin strolled slowly through the residential neighborhoods until Casey indicated that his arthritis was acting up and he was tired of walking. The elderly dog undoubtedly didn't typically go for three-hour walks, but it was such a beautiful day, Erin enjoyed being outside exploring on foot. She apologized to him for dragging him all over town and carried him for a little while to make up for it.

When she returned to the house, her parents were putting groceries away and arguing about something related to their seminars. Erin didn't want to get involved, so she unclipped Casey's leash and let him go survey the scene. She went up to her tower room and took off her shoes.

She opened the closet door to throw her sneakers inside, but found the floor was covered with boxes. She put the shoes on top of a box and yanked off her jeans. She pulled an old pair of sweatpants off the stack of Mom's old clothes she'd laid on the nightstand the night before. After changing, she hung up her jeans and the Mom cast-offs.

One of the boxes had *Erin* written on it in big, bold letters. Curious, she bent to open it and settled cross-legged on the floor to investigate. She pulled out a framed photograph of her first boyfriend, Eric. He was holding a football and grinning like a goof. She hadn't thought about him in years. She'd had a terrible crush on him, but it was one of those crushes that was far better as a fantasy than a reality. He was a sweet guy, but such a jock that his conversational skills mostly consisted of talking about plays in the latest game. She had no idea what had ever happened to him, but she didn't miss sitting through tedious televised sporting events.

She dug down and encountered stacks of birthday cards, a ticket stub for an Elton John concert, and her freshman college ID cards. The lamination was frayed around the edges, and it was perhaps not the most attractive photo she'd ever had taken. Eeek. Way to have a seriously bad hair day.

She pulled a sky-blue macramé plant hanger that she'd made a million years ago from the box. Underneath was her favorite blue and purple elephant mandala wall tapestry that had hung above her bed at Dancing Cedars. She opened it up, and a few beads from a beaded curtain that had been in the ancient VW van rolled onto the floor. After losing beads for years, maybe the curtain had finally completely fallen apart. What had ever happened to that van anyway? Maybe it was still sitting in the field along with that old Subaru station wagon.

She reached into the bottom of the box and found a pink beaded necklace with a plastic peace-sign pendant, a blue McGovern-Shriver headband, and a tie-dyed bandana. Wow. How very seventies. Why had Mom saved all this stuff? Did she truly think Erin would still want it?

She opened up another box and dug in. This one was focused on memorabilia with a few of her debate team trophies, science fair ribbons, and a scrapbook. She opened the binder, which was filled with newspaper clippings. Mom had saved the articles about Erin's various awards and scholarships. She started reading and looked up at a tap on the door.

Her mother smiled. "Are you taking a trip down memory lane?"

Erin closed the scrapbook and set it aside. "I can't believe you saved all these things."

Jennifer bent down, reached into the box, and pulled out a photo album. "I wondered where this ended up. I was afraid we'd lost it."

Erin remembered sticking snapshots into the album. When she was little, she'd thought that how photos clung to the sticky cardboard under the plastic film was nothing short of magic.

Jennifer sat on the floor next to her, lifted the red plastic cover, and covered her mouth to suppress a giggle. "Do *not* let your father see this one. He may not adequately appreciate this jumble of phenomena."

Erin leaned over. "I don't remember this at all. Is he wearing a pumpkin plant?"

"It was a winter squash. Specifically, an acorn squash I believe, although he referred to it as cosmic nourishment."

"Good thing that leaf is so large or the employees at the photo store would have gotten a sneak peek at Dad au naturel. Squash plants are sort of prickly, aren't they? You'd think that would be scratchy on bare skin." Erin raised her eyebrows at her mother. "I'm not sure I want to know the answer, but why did Dad take off all his clothes and cloak himself in winter squash?"

"We weren't terribly good farmers." Jennifer traced the outline of a leaf. "It became a joke that your father and I were like the plant plague. Anything we tended had a habit of dying. This was proof that we could successfully get a plant to grow and thrive."

"Although I'm pleased to hear about your green thumb, that image might give me nightmares."

On the opposite page was a photo of a little girl with long, light brown hair dumping a bucket of water over a dark-haired little boy. Jennifer pointed at the photo. "Back then, we didn't have much money to get film developed, so we didn't take many pictures. But I've always been pleased that I did get a shot of one of the legendary Ziggy and Stardust creek-side skirmishes."

"Ziggy was relentless. That was the day I got him back."

"Oh, here's one of your Aunt Julie's wedding. You were so pretty."

"I looked like one of Dad's winter squash. The puffy sleeves on that dress were hideous."

"That's a subjective assessment mired in insecurity. I think you look nice."

"Yuck." Erin pointed at a photo of two women in matching crocheted ponchos. "This is a cute picture of Kristen and Lila. Have you heard from them lately?"

"According to Dean, they're still living in San Francisco, embracing their evolution."

Erin wondered what that meant exactly. Their evolution to what? They'd been a couple for probably twenty-five years. "How's Dean doing?"

"Getting older like the rest of us. We all look so young in these photos. That was such an extraordinary vortex in our personal timelines. Now we're all facing the reality of our mortality. The last time I saw Dean, he had a gray beard."

"I'm guessing he wasn't wearing short cut-offs or a t-shirt with a marijuana leaf on it either."

"Well, no. He looks a bit like Burl Ives now."

"Is that the guy who played Kris Kringle in *Miracle on 34th Street?*"

"No, that was a different actor. His name was Edmund Gwenn. I only know because I've seen the movie three hundred times. Burl Ives and Edmund Gwenn do have a similar radiance."

"The radiance of Santa Claus?"

"Yes, although Dean doesn't appreciate being compared to Santa. He says he looks nothing like jolly old Saint Nick." Jennifer smiled. "I told him if he lost some weight, people wouldn't so inclined to make the comparison. He didn't embrace my suggestion."

"I can imagine." Erin pointed at a snapshot of people wandering around a large old building. "This is how I remember us back then. A dirty ragtag group. I know everyone was into going back to the land, but the commune was filthy. *I* was filthy."

"I suppose." Jennifer traced the outline of the log structure in the snapshot. "It did take a while for me to adjust to the amount of work farming requires. And I admit that fighting off spiders in the outhouse in the dark during a snow storm wasn't a lot of fun. Or waking up in the middle of the night from the cold because Dean forgot to put more wood in the stove, so the fire went out. There were definitely hardships, but I loved the camaraderie. Sitting around debating the problems of the day with my friends while eating home-cooked meals are some of my best memories."

"Then why did you leave?"

"Oh, it's complicated. Like I said, life on a farm is hard. All that menial labor takes a toll. And over time, we lost tolerance for some things and interpersonal squabbles. But I don't ever regret the experience."

"More power to you." Erin shook her head. "I couldn't do it. Give me electricity, indoor plumbing, and a job in a nice clean office any day."

Jennifer patted Erin's knee. "Well, that's what you have now and you don't seem particularly happy."

"That has nothing to do with where I live, Mom, and you know it."

"I hear you, and I understand. But I hope you're thinking about what's next for you."

"I keep telling you, I'm *fine*."

"I've known you since the moment you were born, and you're not fine. I've seen fine, and this isn't it." Jennifer stood up and walked to the doorway. "Dinner should be ready in about an hour."

"Thanks." Erin would have loved to come up with some snappy rejoinder about the state of her life, but she had nothing. Never argue with a mom when she's right.

~

After dinner, Paul went to the closet and pulled out a box. "Who's up for doing a puzzle? I got a new one and I'm itching to get started."

Erin acquiesced reluctantly. Her father took jigsaw puzzles extremely seriously. Some might say *too* seriously. He had a special puzzle table, and no one was allowed to put any beverages near it or, heaven forbid, actually *on* it.

He opened the box, and they sat around the table picking edge pieces from the box and laying them out. Erin picked up the lid of the box. "What is this photo supposed to be, Dad?"

"It's an underwater scene."

"The image is all shades of blue."

"That makes it more challenging." Paul held a piece up to his glasses. "You work on that aquamarine section over there."

"As opposed to the aquamarine section over here?"

"That one is a lighter color." Paul moved one of Erin's pieces to a different place on the table. "See, that's a lighter one."

Jennifer held up two pieces and put one down. "These are not destined to be joined."

Erin grabbed the rejected piece and wedged it onto a section of the edge of the puzzle.

Paul gasped. "That doesn't fit." He grabbed the two pieces and wiggled them to pry them apart. "Don't damage the puzzle, honey."

Erin gently fit pieces together, making a special effort not to disturb the sacred purity of the blue cardboard. Puzzles were boring. She glanced at her father and recalled the giant acorn squash leaf. It was difficult to equate distinguished Paul Quinn, relationship coach, quietly doing a puzzle with Arrow, the naked guy with a huge squash plant covering his crotch.

When they'd left Dancing Cedars, Erin had proclaimed with the forcefulness of teen angst that having more than one name was mortifying. She'd declared that no one was allowed to call her Stardust ever again. Mom had promised to only refer to her as Erin from then on. She'd said it was okay to leave the names behind along with the commune because they'd adopted those names when they shed the trappings of conventional life. Now that they were "returning to the world," they could go back to their given names.

Most people at Dancing Cedars had been looking for a fresh start with no judgments about their past activities. Adopting the new names helped give them a sense of closure from their past and a new identity for their future. At the time, Erin had thought it sounded like a bunch of hippie claptrap, but now she could see the value starting over might have. Having no history and its associated baggage sounded pretty good.

Erin didn't share her father's love of puzzles, and after about an hour, she was tired of squinting at twenty-five shades of blue, so she excused herself and retired to her tower room.

Because she'd finished the book she brought with her on the plane, she curled up in bed with a book she'd found on the bookshelf. She hadn't read Dickens' *A Christmas Carol* for years, but the holidays were approaching, and it was better than self-help books or tomes about conflict management with titles like *Abstract Interdependence*. Erin had no idea what that meant, and she was pretty sure she didn't want to know.

She opened the old green hardcover and was distressed to realize that the opening scene was about death. Hmm. Given her dream about Andy the night before, maybe this wasn't the greatest choice for nighttime reading, after all. Even the first sentence said Marley was dead. The narrator wanted to be sure everyone was clear that old Marley was as dead as a doornail and Scrooge knew it too, so having the ghostly dude wandering around was cause for alarm.

Erin had forgotten how annoyingly perky Scrooge's nephew Bob Cratchit was. The guy went on and on about falling in love. No wonder Scrooge wanted to be left alone. He didn't have a wife, and his best friend had been dead for seven years. Why did Bob feel compelled to rub it in? Erin had a low tolerance for pushy faux cheerfulness. Get real. No one was that happy.

It was like her mom gushing about those photos of everyone at Dancing Cedars. Erin had gladly left that life behind. Why would she want to remember being desperately poor and living in a rickety, drafty dwelling with no electricity that was located precisely in the middle of absolute nowhere? Her mother had completely romanticized their time at Dancing Cedars. It was freezing in the winter and buggy and dirty in the summer. At least Ziggy had been around to keep her from going totally insane.

Erin rearranged her pillow and looked over at the boxes in the closet. She closed her eyes. So much memorabilia. So many boxes. So many photos. Was there a big door knocker at Dancing Cedars? What about the townhouse in Georgetown? Somewhere she'd lived there was a door knocker. But where?

She waved her arms as if she could push the snow aside. Andy was walking down the cobblestone street ahead of her. Emotion overwhelmed her as if it were the day they'd met. Memories flipped by like newsreel footage. She liked him. He liked her back. Then the sparks flew. The chemistry. The beating of her heart when he was nearby. Their long talks. Blushing. Smiling. And then the joy of waking up next to him. Eating breakfast. Being together every day. She shouted, "Andy!" repeatedly, but he refused to turn around.

Erin was shaking and furious, partly because he was always so stubborn and partly because she knew this was a dream. What did it mean when you knew you were dreaming *while* you were dreaming? Then the snow faded away, and she was left sitting in her studio apartment. What was going on? Ziggy sat cross-legged on the floor across from her, unpacking a box that said Erin in big black letters. He held up a teddy bear dressed in an elf suit. "Why are you unpacking here? This place is bleak."

"I know. I hate it too. But I had to move."

"And get rid of everything you own?" He pointed at the circle of boxes in the empty white room. "This is messed up. You don't even have furniture."

"I had to get out of the place we shared, so I would stop seeing reminders of Andy in every room. He was everywhere. I had to get rid of his soap, his clothes, his shoes, the furniture he sat on, the sheets, the laundry detergent. Everything. Even the neighborhood. I kept running into neighbors wishing me well, giving me pitying stares. I had to get out of there."

Ziggy threw the jingle bear at her, and Erin sat bolt upright, clutching her pillow to her chest. She sniffed it because she thought she caught a whiff of Andy's shampoo again. Flopping back down on the bed, she stared at the ceiling and rubbed her arm where it had been smacked by the flying teddy bear. Okay, no more reading Dickens at bedtime. Definitely not. That was way too weird.

Shadows danced on the ceiling almost as if they were scolding her. Speaking of scolding, what was a twelve-year-old Ziggy doing in her apartment griping about her lack of furniture? A guy who still lived at his parent's loopy Christmas-themed house didn't have a lot of room to talk about her life choices. Sheesh.

By the time Erin got going the next morning, scents were wafting up from the kitchen, indicating that cooking was already in progress. The only good news about her bizarre vivid dreams was that afterward she slept like the dead. Maybe all that dream intensity wore out her brain for anything else.

In any case, she felt remarkably well rested again. Maybe losing her luggage and ELF had been a blessing. The yellow pills had helped her sleep, but left her feeling groggy and dull. Even though the dreams were disturbing at night, sleeping like a normal person again made for better days. Life was full of trade-offs.

As Erin went down the stairs, she was assaulted by a demanding olfactory memory. Mom was making lentil loaf. Oh, no. No one liked lentil loaf in 1973, and it was unlikely it would be any tastier now. She walked into the kitchen, where her parents were busy chopping vegetables.

Paul handed her a chef's knife. "I'm glad you're up. We've got a lot to do."

Jennifer passed her a cabbage. "We're making the casserole."

Erin surveyed the counters, which were covered with a wide array of produce. It was like a farm stand had exploded in the kitchen. Although she was a vegetarian, her tastes tended to be more on the side of spiced ethnic foods. When she and Ziggy were kids, cabbage casserole used to be code for something you disliked. As in, "That bug is gross—like *cabbage casserole* gross." The way the dish smelled while it was in the oven was almost as revolting as the entrée itself.

Erin stood in front of a cutting board and began chopping. "So, um, Mom are you sure you need the casserole? Maybe someone wants turkey."

"We're making all vegetarian food." Jennifer paused, holding her knife in the air. "I can't imagine bringing meat to Dancing Cedars. Back then, being a vegetarian was a political statement—a part of the counterculture. Not eating meat showed that you cared about the world and the beings who share Mother Earth with us. It was a reflection of who you were and your choices."

Erin said, "What else are you making?"

"Eggplant puree for dipping, marinated kohlrabi, sauerkraut soup, and lentil loaf." Paul said. "Oh, and prune salad supreme too."

Jennifer said, "Yes, we can't forget that—it's a family tradition. The recipe won the Betty Crocker cooking contest in 1955."

"I thought it was 1956," Paul said.

Erin had heard about this contest for years, and she couldn't fathom how such a horrifying assemblage of incompatible ingredients could possibly have won anything. Were the judges missing taste buds? For reasons she failed to understand, a lot of recipes from the fifties seemed to involve gelatin. Mom had adapted the treasured family recipe because gelatin isn't typically vegetarian. So Mom had adjusted the recipe to swap out the lime Jell-O for agar-agar and lime juice. The substitutions didn't make the concoction taste any better though. The salad was green because it had lettuce, prunes, and olives floating around in the gelatinous mass.

Then to ensure you felt completely sick, the recipe suggested throwing a dollop of mayonnaise on top as a garnish. It was right up there with cabbage casserole at the apex of Erin's most-loathed-foods list.

"You haven't considered making some dishes that might be, um, a little more contemporary?" Erin inquired. She would need to eat before they went out to Dancing Cedars or she would starve.

"These are our traditional recipes," Jennifer said. "Creating these intricate culinary choices has infused our family culture for years."

Paul opened the pantry door. "Jen, we forgot about the carrot pudding. Did you get raisins?"

"No, I didn't think of it." She walked to his side, and they rummaged through the cabinet. "Could you run out and get some?"

Paul was already heading for the front door to remedy the raisin emergency. Erin tried not to sigh. Carrot pudding was a gooey mass of carrots, raisins, sugar, flour, and cinnamon that tasted a little bit like paste. Even dessert wasn't going to be any fun. She had zero nostalgia for commune food.

Erin chopped and listened to her mother hum a mysterious tune of her own devising.

Jennifer set her bowl of grated carrot aside, turned to lean against the counter, and cleared her throat significantly.

Erin looked up from her pile of cabbage. "Yes?"

"Have you thought about what we talked about?"

"You mean the photographs of hippies?"

"No, honey. About staying here. Working with me doing women's retreats at Dancing Cedars." Jennifer stretched her arms out wide. "I'm so excited about this idea. The land is a spiritual place, and I'd love for others to share the magic and joy of that space. It could give to others what it gave to me."

"I don't think so." Erin laid down the knife. She didn't want to hurt Mom's feelings, but this was a hard no. Dealing with Thanksgiving was one thing. Moving here? Not on a bet. And doing women's retreats was so far off her radar, it was in outer space. No way.

"Why not? I think it would be a good experience for you."

"I have to go back home, Mom. I have an apartment. All my stuff is there." Well, such as it was.

Jennifer took one of Erin's hands in both of hers. "Honey, I'm worried about you. What do you have to go home to? A temp job? I'm offering you a real job, so you can put your life back together. Maybe make some new friends and become part of the community."

"I'm sorry, but it's not something I'm interested in doing, that's all."

"Well, what *are* you interested in doing? You were a paralegal and lawyer. Couldn't you do that here? I'd feel so much better knowing you were nearby."

"I'm not interested in that type of work. Even if I were, I'd have to pass the bar again, which I'm not sure I want to do. The state of California has no reciprocity with other states. I'd have to take the exam again, and it's considered one of the hardest ones to pass. I'm not up for that." Erin took a deep breath. That was the understatement of the year.

"Your consciousness isn't in alignment with your current reality. You've always been a brilliant, articulate communicator. An overachiever who skipped two grades and received scholarships. Yet now you barely speak and work low-level temp jobs. This isn't who you are."

"Sorry I'm not achieving my potential, Mom."

"You're not happy either."

"Didn't we already have this conversation? Could you just let it go?"

Jennifer turned back to her vegetables. "We're not done talking about this."

Erin was sure they weren't done, but if she could make it through two more days, she could leave and then maybe Mom would forget about it. They chopped in silence, and when Paul returned with raisins, the rest of the food preparations proceeded without incident.

After the long day of cooking, that evening Erin lay in bed thinking about her mother's demand that she get her act together. Why couldn't people just leave her alone? The pressure to figure out her life made her want to run away all the more. Unfortunately, running away was challenging at the moment. It was a long walk to the airport, and she was too big of a chicken to hitchhike.

Too bad there weren't any trees. Back at Dancing Cedars, when Ziggy got into trouble—which was often—he'd go climb a tree. The bigger the trouble, the taller the tree. When he was in seriously deep doo-doo, he'd go for the biggest conifer he could find. Some pines were so bushy that if he went up high enough, no one could see him at all. The adults would freak out wondering where he'd gone.

At the time, she thought he was nuts risking his neck like that, but in retrospect he might have been on to something.

Prune Salad Supreme

For Erin, the night was mercifully free of dreams, possibly because she'd stowed Dickens back on the bookshelf and stuck to counting backward. Boring was better than disturbing, and when she woke up, she felt positively normal. Her mind wasn't running a mile a minute trying to digest a weird dream, and she wasn't groggy from evil ELFs either. Good thing too because there was no way Thanksgiving at Dancing Cedars was destined to be anything but strange.

When she went downstairs the next morning, her parents were packing food into coolers while Casey looked on. She picked up a plastic container from the counter and handed it to her mother. "This is even more food than I thought. We'll never be able to eat it all."

"Bea said she invited some other people," Jennifer said.

Erin had a flickering notion that maybe she should divulge the big secret that Ziggy's family would be attending the feast, but thought better of it. Her parents would find out soon enough. After so much intense time with Mom and Dad, she was looking forward to having more people around to dilute the conversation. Mom would be less likely to badger her about life choices when they were in a crowded room with lots of food.

The commune property was located north of Alpine Grove, even farther out in the hinterlands than the boarding kennel. Erin sat in the back seat listening to her parents chat and gazing out over the hills and fields that had been turned over, awaiting the inevitable blanket of snow. The drive seemed longer than she remembered. Finally, they made the last turn onto Misty Meadow Lane, the gravel rural road that dead-ended at the rusty livestock gate that blocked access to the commune land.

The hundred and sixty acres that made up the Dancing Cedars property included multiple tracts of forest, pastures, and a rustic log homestead, aka The Hodgepodge Lodge, where many of the commune residents had lived. Other residences had at various times included temporary dwellings like tents, tipis, and old school buses, along with more permanent structures like a geodesic dome and a log-and-plywood shed. According to Jennifer, years of snow had taken down both the dome and the shed, which wasn't a surprise since the people who had built them had little-if any—construction experience. Even in 1975, the makeshift chicken coop and goat shed had been rickety, and apparently, they too had returned to the land.

Someone had already opened the gate, and Paul drove the SUV up a rutted single-track path that meandered into the trees. The sunlight filtered through the pine boughs, which waved in the light fall breeze.

Erin rolled down the window and listened for the sound of water. The burbling creek that ran through the land was like the soundtrack of her childhood. She and Ziggy had spent hours playing in the small clearing alongside that creek, making up elaborate games and stories. All the commune kids had enjoyed complete freedom to wander the vast stretches of woods and fields that made up the property. She and Ziggy had built countless forts and lean-tos among the trees as part of their ongoing tales of action and adventure.

The road, or goat trail as they used to call it, was overgrown with grass, which disguised the many rocks and holes. As they slowly thumped along up the incline, Erin was glad that her parents had a four-wheel-drive vehicle. The slow traverse was claustrophobic because of the branches of large trees that loomed over the road. All the birch and aspen had lost their leaves, but the pines towered alongside the vehicle, creating a shady tunnel.

The trees fell away as they entered a clearing. The Hodgepodge Lodge was at the far end, looking much like it had in 1975. The old building had at one time been a simple rectangular log building, but over the years, a number of additions had been tacked onto it. As the story went, some long-forgotten person passing through the commune in the early days had commented the building was a hodgepodge of fine craftsmanship and incompetent workmanship. The name had stuck.

Several acres of golden weeds waved in the breeze as they proceeded across the meadow and parked in front of the building. Erin got out and leaped when her foot touched something that hissed. An angry orange cat hissed again and ran under the SUV. She stepped away from the vehicle and bent to peer underneath. "Hi little kitty. What are you doing here?" Yellow eyes glowered, and the feline growled to add a bit more emphasis to his displeasure. Maybe she'd leave him alone.

Casey was standing in the back seat, eager to get out of the vehicle, but smart enough to realize that he was too old to jump down without hurting himself. He hadn't had a positive reaction to the cat at the Bryant Ranch, so Erin picked him up and carried him away from the vehicle before she put him on the ground.

She looked up at the sound of the door opening. Moose charged toward her and Casey. She put up her hands in defense. "Moose! Sit!"

The dog didn't sit, but he didn't jump on her either. Instead, he engaged in some mutual sniffing with Casey as they reacquainted themselves with one another.

Ziggy strolled through the door and lifted his hand at Erin. "Happy Thanksgiving. Welcome back."

Paul and Jennifer came up alongside Erin, carrying food. Jennifer tilted her head, looking up. "Ziggy?"

He took the foil-covered pan from her, "Yeah, well, most people call me Dylan now."

Erin suppressed a smile, "Well, except his family. And me."

He ignored Erin and focused on Jennifer. "It's nice to see you again."

Jennifer shot Paul a look of concern and said in a polite tone, "It's nice to see you too. Erin was right. You *are* taller."

Erin waited next to Ziggy while her parents filed through the doorway.

He nudged her arm with his elbow and whispered, "This smells like a bad memory. They didn't bring the cabbage casserole, did they?

"'Fraid so."

He looked down sadly at the pan in his hands. "Do you think anyone would mind if I dropped it?"

"The other stuff is worse."

"Jeez, not the green jiggly goo. Really?"

"I'm sorry to say that the award-winning prune salad supreme has arrived."

"Oh man. That stuff is nasty."

"I ate something before we left."

He grinned at her. "You always were the smart one." He balanced the casserole on one palm like a waiter and waved his other arm in a sweeping gesture toward the door. "After you."

Erin walked inside the building and turned her head to look around. The walls were made from massive hand-hewn timbers that had been stacked lengthwise with dovetail corners. The mud-daub chinking that routinely fell out from between the logs had clearly continued to fail over the years, so daylight shone through here and there. The lodge had always been drafty, but now a tent would be better at keeping out the elements.

Fortunately, the focal point of the open downstairs living and dining area was a huge woodstove, or they never would have survived winter back in the day. Erin remembered stuffing an old pair of jeans into a gap in the wall next to her bed on the second floor. She walked over to the huge stove and Casey sat next to it. Near the door, the temperature inside wasn't much different from the great outdoors, but next to the stove, it was nice and toasty. She took off Casey's leash, and he turned around a few times before settling onto the stone hearth pad, clearly pleased that he'd found a warm spot to hang out.

The long wooden farm table was in the same place, surrounded by old ladder-back chairs. Along the far wall, the plywood workbenches that served as kitchen counters looked the same as ever. At one end, a rusty hand pump perched over a metal water tub. The cabinets that had been salvaged from a nearby house presumably still contained various pots and pans. Although all the personal items had left with their owners, it was remarkable how little the bones of the place had changed.

A kerosene lantern sat on the table where Erin's parents were talking to Bea Sullivan and her husband, William. He'd been known as Leaf back in the day, but Ziggy had mentioned to Erin that Leaf wouldn't respond to that name anymore, so she shouldn't even try.

Both Erin and Ziggy had been half afraid of Leaf/Bill when they were little. He'd been on the road a lot, and when he was at Dancing Cedars, he was often intensely working on projects in his tipi. The kids were under strict advice not to disturb him when he was working, so they gave the tipi and Leaf a wide berth.

Ziggy's parents, Greg and Melody, were sitting at the other end of the long table talking to a blonde woman and a youngish guy with glasses that Erin didn't know. Maybe that was Rainbow—or Tracy—and her boyfriend. Bea had mentioned his name, but Erin couldn't remember what it was anymore.

Erin walked over to Ziggy, who was standing at the counter peeking under aluminum foil to find out what dangers lurked within. Given the expression on his face, he seem too pleased with his discoveries.

Erin nudged him. "Did your parents bring anything normal, like stuffing or potatoes?"

"Mom had a little issue with preparation, so we had to feed what was going to be the stuffing to the chickens. The mashed potatoes came out okay, and we brought some of the cookies to compensate."

Something zipped through Erin's peripheral vision and shot up the stairs. Casey and Moose leaped up to follow. Who would have thought Casey could move so fast? He was pretty spry for an old dog.

Ziggy started for the stairs, followed by Erin. At the top of the stairs, she paused to catch her breath. Was the second floor still stable? That would have been good to consider before she was standing up here pondering the integrity of floor joists.

Ziggy yelled, "Moose! Where are you?"

Erin figured if the floor could handle Moose, it should hold her weight. She called for Casey, treading cautiously through the empty hall. There were four rooms upstairs. Erin walked to the first doorway and found Casey in the corner of the room poking at something on the floor with his paw.

Erin rushed over to the dog and bent to shove Casey's butt out of the way. A black and white kitten was being a tiny hero, hissing furiously at the dog, who took a few steps back, looking confused. The kitten sprinted for the door and disappeared. Was the whole lodge full of cats?

She picked up Casey and carried him out of the room. Ziggy had found Moose, who looked guilty. She tightened her hold on Casey. "Moose didn't eat a kitten, did he?"

"There were at least two of them." Ziggy said as he clipped a leash on the dog. "They ran off, and Moose couldn't figure out which way to go. I encouraged him to stay with me."

"You know, it doesn't smell that great up here." Erin wrinkled her nose. "I think the lodge may have become a giant litter box."

"I think we need to keep a closer eye on the dogs. These feral cats keep popping up everywhere. I know they're supposed to be afraid of people, but we invaded their space." He pointed at the doorway. "You might not want to go into the room across the hall. There's a decapitated mouse in there. And a lot of feathers."

"Eww."

They went back downstairs, where everyone was still sitting at the table deep in conversation. They clearly weren't paying attention to the crowd of cats that had gathered on the counter. The sneaky feline group was ever-so-quietly pawing at the foil and plastic wrap, but a gray tabby got a little too excited and broke the silence, thwacking a container onto the floor. All the cats immediately skittered back upstairs.

Everyone at the table turned around to look, and Melody got up to survey the damage.

Ziggy peered around his mother's shoulder, turned, and gave Erin two thumbs up. He strolled over to her and sang sotto voce, "Ding, dong, the green wiggly slime is dead."

Erin whispered, "If a cat takes out the kohlrabi, things will really be looking up."

Melody scooped the broken glass and gelatinous mass into a metal garbage can lined with a black bag. She didn't seem terribly disappointed about missing out on the award-winning food and returned to her place at the table.

Erin joined Ziggy in evaluating any potentially edible food options, but then turned her attention to the raised voices at the end of the table. Greg and Paul were, to put it kindly, having words, and Bea was attempting to keep the argument from devolving into a fistfight. Beating each other up wasn't conducive to the holiday spirit.

Nudging Ziggy, Erin said quietly, "I think I missed something."

"Sounds like there was some free love going on in 1972."

"*What?*"

"Shhh."

The gist of the argument between the two men was that Saffron and Zappa had shared a lot of quality time in his Microbus. In other words, Jennifer and Greg had a fling, and when Paul found out about the indiscretions in the Volkswagen, he reciprocated by having his own party of two with Melody in his tipi.

Erin raised her eyebrows at Ziggy. "Did you know any of that was going on?"

"Nope." He shrugged. "We were little kids. I wasn't paying attention to whatever the grownups were doing."

"Me neither. Maybe that was a good thing."

Melody yelped, "I don't know. Stop asking me!"

"Harry deserves to know," Paul said.

Bea put her hand on Paul's arm. "Harrison isn't here. Why don't you find a way to talk to him together? All four of you should speak to him. Calmly and honestly. Let him decide how he feels about the situation."

Erin gaped at Ziggy. "Hold on. Are they saying Harry might be my half brother? Holy…"

"Shhh."

"Does that make us related?" Erin leaned back against the counter. "This is bizarre. I barely even know Harry."

Ziggy whispered, "Would you shut up, Stardust? I'm trying to eavesdrop here."

Tracy and her boyfriend sidled up next to Erin. She was cradling a dachshund in her arms and held out her hand. "Hi Stardust, that's my boyfriend Rob, and this is Roxy, my spoiled dog. She was digging her claws into my leg, so we needed to get out of the fray."

Rob waved halfheartedly and Ziggy said, "Shhh!"

Erin inclined her head toward Tracy. "Hi Rainbow. You probably were too little to remember it, but there was a lot of drama at Dancing Cedars."

"I guess so." Tracy nodded so forcefully her straight blonde hair slapped her chin. "This is like a soap opera."

Ziggy said "Shhh!"

Erin rolled her eyes melodramatically at Tracy. "*Days of Our Lives* has nothing on Dancing Cedars."

~

Once Bea had defused the situation, she encouraged everyone to help heat up the food on the stoves. Melody and Jennifer each selected a propane stove and retrieved their pans from the counter. Bill and Paul sat at the end of the table talking and Greg went outside. Rob and Tracy went to help Bea with the food they'd brought.

Erin and Ziggy were still standing around holding the dogs on their leashes in case any more felines joined the holiday party. The situation was awkward, and Erin felt completely out of place. She shoved Ziggy's arm. "Should you go see if your dad is okay?"

"What am I supposed to say?"

"I don't know. Be supportive."

"Supportive of *what*? Their fight has nothing to do with me. Go talk to your parents if you're so worried."

Erin shrugged. He had a point. "Maybe later. They look busy."

"Chicken." He turned and dragged Moose toward the stairs.

Erin looked around. Everyone truly was busy, so she picked up Casey and followed Ziggy upstairs.

She peeked in the doorways, and found him sitting cross-legged on the floor in a corner of one of the rooms, with Moose lying next to him.

Settling in next to them, she put her hand on Ziggy's knee. "Are you upset?"

"Maybe. I don't know. Should I be?"

"If you're not upset, why are you sitting here in an empty room that may contain rodent and bird carcasses?"

Ziggy leaned his head back on the wall and closed his eyes. "Do you remember all the meetings around that big old wood table? Everyone had to unanimously agree on chores and responsibilities and priorities. There was so much talking all the time. Everything took forever to decide."

"We called them perpetual powwows or PPs. We used to think it was hilarious to say that the grownups were going PP."

"I usually thought up a reason to go play elsewhere when they started ranting at each other." He opened his eyes and looked at her. "That was on purpose."

Erin hadn't thought about it before, but he had come up with some of their best adventures when the adults were busy going PP. "I guess I knew that, in a way."

"When I think back on the lecture you gave them about how they needed to follow Roberts Rules of Order, I understand how you became a lawyer."

Erin had forgotten about that little diatribe. "I told you. I never *was* a lawyer, but considering I was nine, I think I made a persuasive argument."

"Too bad it didn't work. The thing is, I'm not like you. I hate quarreling, shouting, and debates. If you get more than two people together, inevitably there's a fight. Everyone has a grudge or feelings get hurt. There's always so much emotion and strife. Why do they have to *talk* about everything all the time?"

Erin patted his knee again. "You're a big softie."

"I'm not good with groups or arguments. They wear me out." He rubbed his eyes with the base of his palms. "And sometimes you hear stuff you wish you hadn't."

Before Erin could say anything, Bea called from downstairs. Dinner was ready.

Erin and Casey followed Ziggy and Moose down the steps. The long table was laid out with food, and everyone was cheerfully loading up their plates. Whatever Bea had done to settle everyone down had worked because both Erin's and Ziggy's parents looked significantly more relaxed. They still weren't sitting anywhere near each other, but it was a start. Good thing the old wooden farm table was so large.

Erin sat next to her mother. Jennifer wrapped her arm around her shoulders and gave her a big hug. "Where did you run off to?"

"I was talking to Ziggy."

"Just like old times." Jennifer squeezed her shoulders, let go, and passed her the potatoes. "I'm so disappointed about the prune salad supreme. Do you see the cabbage casserole anywhere?"

"I think it's way down at the other end. I'll go retrieve it for you."

Erin returned with the noxious-smelling casserole and demurred when her mother offered a huge scoop of it. "I ate too many cookies earlier."

One of the cabinet doors slammed and some metal pots crashed together. Erin got up. Maybe it was another feral cat looking for some more prunes.

Tracy leaped from her seat and ran to the cabinets. "Roxy! That had better not be you in there. Come out of there *now*. You know you don't like it when I extract you from kitchenware."

A few more rustling and crashing noises arose, along with a little yip that was definitely not feline.

"Get out of there." Tracy slapped her palm on the cabinet door. "You are in *such* big trouble."

At another yipping sound, Tracy opened the cabinet door, and Roxy bolted out with a louder irritated yelp, taking a few old pots and pans along with her. Considering the dachshund had only three legs, she was remarkably agile. Tracy picked up a saucepan and put it back in the cabinet. "Sorry everyone. Roxy thinks hiding in cabinets is hilarious. Unfortunately, no one else ever thinks it's funny."

Erin went back to the table, relieved that it wasn't a cat, Moose, or Casey causing trouble for a change. She'd be so glad when this meal was over. With the holiday behind her, she could go back to the peaceful, quiet sanity of her apartment and regular life back in DC.

Bea stood up and held up her glass. "Today is a day of gratitude, and I want to say thank you for sharing this special meal in this special place."

Everyone smiled and toasted, and Bea took a sip of her drink, but didn't sit down. She clearly had more to impart. "I know we've had our differences and haven't all been in touch with one another lately, but there's something I need to talk to you about while we're all gathered together today."

Jennifer said, "That's a great idea. I'd like to share something too."

Bea said, "As most of you know, a lot has changed since we started the Dancing Cedars experiment, including land prices. Since we all went our separate ways, any time we've talked about a fair way to split up the property, the discussion hasn't gone well."

Paul said, "That's for sure. Listening to people rant about how much more they contributed than anyone else…"

Bea waved her hands, "Yes, I remember. Let's not dredge all that up again."

Paul continued, "And then of course Kevin, the math whiz, and his definition of equitable and what constitutes a contribution…"

"I don't want to split the land, Paul." Bea said. "But I see a lot of people at the store, and over the last few years, developers have been sniffing around. There aren't many large parcels like this anymore, and the trees and the land have value."

"Developers? No!" Melody exclaimed. "We can't let them turn Dancing Cedars into a strip mall or a big ugly chain store."

Erin wanted to roll her eyes at the comment. Given the remote location, this wasn't exactly prime commercial property. But Bea was probably right about the timber. An enterprising developer could clear-cut the trees, split the land into tiny parcels, sell them off, and net a tidy fortune.

Bea took another sip of water. "I've talked to some people and have an idea how we can save this land for future generations to enjoy. We could do a conservation easement with a local land trust."

Melody said, "I don't know what that is."

"A conservation easement would be an agreement between us as landowners and a land trust that would protect Dancing Cedars from development. The easement transfers the development rights to the land trust. With a conservation easement, we'd continue to own the land, but it couldn't be developed. A conservation easement is perpetual and must be adhered to by future owners. So the land would stay the same, even after we die."

Jennifer said, "Everyone has to agree though. And I'm not sure I like this idea."

Bea said, "I haven't talked to the other owners yet, but yes, we'd all need to sign off on it. I did pay for a survey and forest management plan. It looks like we could do a selective thinning of the trees to improve the health of the forest. It might net all of us a little money in the short term. There also are some tax benefits."

Greg said, "I definitely need more information before I could make a decision."

"I was hoping that I could buy Dancing Cedars," Jennifer said emphatically. "It's not doing anything, and no one has been here for years."

Melody glared at her. "You want to turn it into a strip mall too?"

"No, of course not," Jennifer shot back. "I want to do retreats. I'd use the land for private, elite training for women who want to embrace their power."

"I'm all for powerful women, but I don't want to give up my rights to this land," Bea said. "I want my grandchildren to be able to come out here whenever they like."

Tracy said, "Uh, Mom, let's not get ahead of ourselves here."

"I agree," Rob said.

There was a thump at the door and Ziggy got up. "Sorry to interrupt. I think Moose wants in."

The huge dog barreled into the lodge, dragging a revolting smell in with him. The noxious skunk cloud caused everyone at the table to gasp and shy away from the large, stinky dog.

Greg bellowed, "Get him out of here!"

Ziggy grabbed Moose's collar and dragged him back toward the door, "I can't take you anywhere, can I?"

~

The speed at which people pack up food after a big meal increases substantially when the room smells like skunk. Erin wasn't sorry that the meal had ended abruptly. She was exhausted and secretly hoping that she'd have another chance to see Andy in her dreams. Sure, it was ridiculous to want to see him in a dream, but even though it wasn't real, she couldn't help wishing for another chance to hold his hand.

When she woke up the next morning, she remembered nothing about her dreams, although she'd slept well. Maybe the two vivid dreams with Andy had been a fluke because she was so stressed about coming to Alpine Grove. The idea that she might not dream of him ever again made her desperately sad. It was confusing. For so long, she'd done everything she could to avoid thinking about Andy because it hurt too much. Now she was actively seeking dreams with him in them.

By the time she meandered down to forage for breakfast, her mother was in her study talking on the phone. Most people took the day after Thanksgiving off, but not her parents. Since they'd been on the speaking circuit doing seminars, work had become their life.

Although Mom had brushed off the effect her separation from Dad might have on their business, a separation was easy to conceal. The escalation of Mom and Dad's feud with the Bryants couldn't be helping their marriage much. If they ended up getting divorced, it could have some public relations fallout.

Erin made herself some toast and reflected on Thanksgiving. What a surreal experience. Visiting Dancing Cedars had been like being transported back to 1975. Time had stood still, mostly because much of what was there had always been there. The hills, the trees, the creek, and even the lodge were largely unchanged. She could understand why Bea was suggesting the conservation easement. She'd heard the "origin story" about the founding of the commune many times over the years. In 1967, her parents, along with a number of friends, had put a down payment on the 160-

acre homestead on the hilltop in the forests north of Alpine Grove. The payment was split among the group, with the idea that the like-minded friends would create a safe space away from big cities and the protests and conflict surrounding the Vietnam War.

The Dancing Cedars commune became a way station for artists, hippies, friends, anti-war activists, runaways, and other people who were looking for a different way of life or had reasons to leave the conventional world behind. The only financial expense was the mortgage, and people who stayed were asked to chip in whatever they could. Some people paid money, but most people paid by working in the garden or building or repairing the buildings. The financing of the land hadn't involved a bank. Every month, Paul drove to town and paid the mortgage directly to the elderly couple who had sold their family farm to the group of hippies.

The mortgage had been paid off years ago, so now the main expense was the property taxes, which were shared by the people whose names were on the deed. Six of them were at Thanksgiving: Paul, Jennifer, Greg, Melody, Bea, and William. But there were six more people who jointly owned the land. Over the years, Erin had heard third-hand complaints about how difficult it was for Bea to wrangle everyone to pay the taxes every year. Often she and Bill had to cover other peoples' shares. Sometimes her parents had chipped in extra too.

So far, all the former commune members were still alive, but what would happen when they were dealing with heirs who had no interest in the land at all? It was a complicated mess waiting to happen. And having gone to law school, Erin knew that legal entanglements could be protracted and expensive. The extremely personal interpersonal issues wouldn't help either. Clearly, a trove of old resentments and grievances still simmered among the former residents of Dancing Cedars.

Erin wasn't sure where her father had gone and Mom was busy chatting up sponsors, so after she finished her toast and cleaned up the kitchen, she leashed up Casey for another walk.

With the holiday behind her, what she wanted to do was get on a plane and leave. The bad news was that her suitcase was still MIA. Presumably, it would turn up eventually, and she could finally take it back home.

Outside, the weather was cloudy and breezy, but still not bitterly cold. While Casey took care of some personal needs, Erin gazed up at the gray sky. It wasn't cold enough to snow yet, but it felt like the warm snap might be ending. Fortunately, Mom's nice warm coat had gloves in the pockets.

She strolled through the neighborhood out to the main street through town, retracing the route she'd taken the other day. The revelations from Thanksgiving swirled through her mind. Harrison was likely to get a big surprise the next time he talked to his parents. It was odd that a week ago she was alone and unconcerned about anything to do with Alpine Grove. Now everyone else's actions from years ago were dominating her thoughts.

For one thing, she might be related to the Bryants. Or at least Harrison. How weird was that? Would the two families reconcile their differences now that it was all out in the open? Or would dredging up all the old affairs drive them further apart? Ziggy probably had the right attitude. It wasn't her problem and at this point, having an adult brother out there somewhere wouldn't have much of an impact on her life.

Near the H12 Motel, Erin stared into space while Casey seriously snuffled a shrub. The dog appeared to be pretty convinced that other dogs had visited recently, and he wanted to know all about it. Erin wasn't in a big rush and Casey was tired, so she didn't particularly care if he took some extra time to inhale deeply.

At a tap on her shoulder, she leaped forward and almost stomped on Casey. "Hey!"

Ziggy smiled, "Sorry, Stardust. I didn't mean to startle you. I thought you saw me over there."

She collected herself and crouched down next to Casey to make sure he was okay. The dog's stern glare indicated he was annoyed, but unharmed.

She stood up and pointed at the motel. "What are you doing at the H12?"

"Walking by, same as you."

"I thought the day after Thanksgiving was a big Christmas tree day. Don't you have to work?"

"Nope. I took your advice and hired someone."

"I didn't *advise* that. It was just an idea. And your mother thinks it's a terrible one."

"Well I didn't. I found a kid who needs money. His mom works at Bea's store, and she told me that he applied early decision to college. If he gets in, he'll need all the cash he can get."

"Why are you wandering around Alpine Grove?"

"I'm killing time while Moose is getting cleaned up." He held up a cloth bag. "I went to the library and got some books. My truck seriously reeks, so I was going to find a place to hang out and read."

"Why didn't you read at the library?"

"It was story time and there were a bunch of obnoxious kids, so I went and hung out in the deli for a little while, but then it got busy, so I felt guilty hogging a table."

"So are you headed home?"

"No way. My parents…uh, well, I'm glad I hired someone because they have to be polite to each other while Barry is around."

"Wait. You've got to be kidding. The jingle bear kid is named Barry?"

"Short for Bartholomew. He says Barry is better than Bart."

Erin could easily imagine the situation. Her parents weren't having "constructive conversations" either. "So you're wandering around town to avoid your parents?"

"Aren't you?" He threw his cloth bag of books onto his shoulder, reached out and grabbed her gloved hand, and started marching down the street. "Let's walk together."

Too surprised to yank her hand away, she relented. "Okay."

They walked down the street past the Italian restaurant and stopped to look at the photographs in the window of a real estate office.

Erin was shocked at the prices. "No wonder people are starting to ask about Dancing Cedars."

"Times change. What once was a useless, empty tract of land with a dilapidated farmhouse now is called pristine acreage."

"Pristine acreage is expensive." She pointed at a house in one of the photographs. "That place is a dump on less than an acre. Who would pay that?"

"You live in the nation's capital, which has some of the highest real estate prices in the country, and you're asking *me?*"

She looked up at him. "So how much do you think Dancing Cedars is worth?"

"I don't know, but my parents gripe about the taxes every year."

"Mine too."

"I like Bea's idea for the land. It would kill me to see it logged to crap." He took her hand again, and they resumed strolling. "And it's not just because I spend so much time wandering around Christmas trees. There's always been something special about those hills and the creek."

"I know what you mean. Going back there, I was expecting to be annoyed by the cold, drafty Hodgepodge Lodge with its rusty pump and beat-up farm table. But I wasn't expecting how seeing the land again would make me feel. This will sound silly, but I feel like its beauty is timeless. The sound of the creek and the sense of peace there isn't like anywhere else I've ever been."

"It's not silly." He stopped and tugged her hand to face her. "I don't think anyone who didn't live there gets that at all."

Erin smiled at his wide-eyed, incredulous look. "Let's face it. We have a shared weird experience."

"We really do." He squeezed her hand. "Bea wants me to ask you if you'd be willing to look over the paperwork. She got surveys and a management plan, but doing the conservation easement requires a bunch of legalese. There are contracts and a whole bunch of legal junk to deal with, I guess."

"I can't. I'm going home soon."

"When are you leaving? Could you stay longer? It would really help her out because you're a lawyer."

"Technically, yes, but I can't practice here. Someone else can deal with the contracts. There has to be at least one lawyer in Alpine Grove."

"No one else would understand like you do. Can't you just read over the paperwork? Then you're not practicing law. You're reading."

Erin shook her head. "I'm not…"

"Come on. Say you'll think about it." He widened his eyes again, giving her that innocent, imploring stare that always got him out of everything. *"Please."*

"Fine. I'll think about it." Sheesh. She was such a sucker.

"Yes." Ziggy threw his arms around her in a giant bear hug. Erin stiffened in surprise, but being hugged by a seven-foot bear wasn't so bad, so she relented and hugged him back.

He released her and grinned. "Let's save the land!"

She returned his grin in spite of herself. "Yeah, well, we'll see how it goes."

Chapter 6

Literary Fantasy

Ziggy wanted to keep walking, but Erin could tell poor little Casey was running out of steam, so she turned toward her parents' house. They walked by Bea Haven gifts and waved to Bea through the window.

Erin said, "I know everyone gets older, but in my head Bea is still blonde. It's odd seeing her with gray hair."

"Well gray hair is better than no hair like my dad."

"Mom told me Dean looks like Santa Claus now. We were looking at old photographs, and there are some funny ones like when I dumped water all over you."

"Funny to *you* maybe."

"There's another one where my dad is wearing a squash plant."

Ziggy laughed. "I think I remember when that was taken."

"I suppose you were doing the stealthy spy thing."

"Or hiding from my dad because I was in trouble."

"So, do you think Harry is my half brother?" Erin glanced at him to check his reaction. "I know at this point in our lives it shouldn't be a big deal, but I keep thinking about it."

"He could be." Ziggy moved his shoulders slightly in a half-shrug. "To be honest, I've never been sure if Dad is actually my father, biologically speaking."

"You don't look much like him." Erin had always thought Ziggy looked a little like Melody, but neither of his parents were extremely tall or had his unusual eye color.

"My parents weren't married until after I was born. My birth certificate didn't have a father listed. Dad legally adopted me after they got married."

"I know Harry was born at Dancing Cedars. When did they get married?"

"Before they bought into the commune. They tied the knot at a courthouse somewhere, I guess. From what Dad said, it was mostly for legal and financial reasons. They wanted to make sure I was taken care of if anything happened to them."

"After the commune broke up and we moved to town, my father got a teaching job and Mom hung out with me." Erin stopped in front of her parents' house and gestured toward the pretty restored home. "They made big money doing seminars, but I found out not too long ago that they were living on inherited money while we were at Dancing Cedars."

"That's interesting. After Dancing Cedars, my mom worked at Bea's store part-time for a while because she could take little Harry with her and price merchandise in the back." Ziggy sat on the bumper of Paul's SUV that was parked in the driveway. "Dad worked construction and did a bunch of odd jobs. He even worked at the Hadley ranch for a while. Although he's not a big fan of cattle, there weren't a lot of alternatives. Then he got a part-time job at the tree farm, and the rest is history."

Erin sat next to him, and Casey curled up at her feet. "So he bought the tree farm?"

"Yeah, the former owner, John, had a dream of becoming a Christmas tree millionaire, and he planted a bunch of seedlings. But the dream didn't pan out. My dad had worked there a couple years and then John had a stroke. Since John couldn't do much work anymore, they struck a deal. Dad moved us into the house and did a lease-to-own thing. Mom and Dad took care of John and made payments. When he died, we took it over."

"Your experience here was so different from mine."

"You left."

"I know. From the way they describe it, after college, my parents bought into the commune almost on a lark because they wanted to 'tune in and drop out.' I'm not sure they ever truly believed it would be some permanent utopia. But then there were people like Gardenia, who was a single mom with a tiny baby. She was desperate for a safe place to live. And people like your parents, who were somewhere in between."

"My parents put all their money into the Dancing Cedars down payment. They thought they'd live there forever, so when it fell apart, they had nothing. They assumed that with a place to live and lots of help, everything else would work out."

"Except it didn't."

"Yeah."

"I don't think I've ever talked to anyone about any of this before."

"Me neither."

Erin rubbed her hands together. The temperature was dropping. "Are you cold? Do you want to come inside?"

"Nah, I should go. I doubt after yesterday your parents want to see me again."

"Or your dog."

He laughed. "I'm not sure *I* want to see my dog either. But I should walk back to my stinky truck, hold my nose, and go retrieve him."

"You said Moose is getting cleaned up. What sane person would agree to do that? Where is he?"

"The boarding kennel has a groomer, and I begged her to take him. She said she has a de-skunking recipe. I sure hope it works. I'm not sure what to do about my truck. Maybe drive it off a cliff."

Erin stood up and tugged at the leash to rouse Casey. "Maybe the groomer will share her recipe."

"I should roll." Ziggy wrapped her in another big bear hug and then locked his gaze with hers. "Don't forget. You promised to look at the Dancing Cedars paperwork. Don't leave town without telling me."

"I wouldn't do that." She smiled weakly. Yes she would. He knew her way too well.

"Do you promise?"

"Yes, I promise."

"Okay. See ya, Stardust."

"Not if I see you first."

Erin took Casey inside the house and pulled off her gloves. Her parents were in the kitchen shouting at each other. Erin hung the coat on the hook, picked up the dog, and scampered up to her tower bedroom. Yikes. From downstairs her mother's voice said, "Our interdependence is stifling. I won't let you suppress my spirit any longer. Even a symbolic representation of positivity isn't possible anymore."

A door slammed and a heavy cloak of silence settled over the house. Erin sat on the bed with Casey on her lap, stroking the fur between his ears. The little guy seemed upset. "How long have they been fighting like this, Case?"

Casey didn't seem to have any answers, and it seemed like the combatants had retreated to their corners for the moment, so Erin took the little dog back downstairs. Her parents' marriage was in far worse shape than she'd thought. Being trapped in the middle of a relationship that was falling apart was the last thing she needed. Maybe the airline had delivered her suitcase and she could get out of here.

Erin found her mother sitting at her large desk in the study. She was facing the window, and when Erin tapped on the door, Jennifer turned around. She set aside a folder and smiled, "How was your walk?"

"I think Casey is tired, but it was nice. I ended up meeting Ziggy, and we talked for a while."

"It's so strange to see him as an adult. I'm sorry I didn't get a chance to talk to him yesterday."

That was because she'd been busy fighting with his parents. Erin sat in the visitor chair and folded her hands on the wide mahogany desk. "Mom, what's going on with you and Dad?"

"We're just going through a difficult time." Jennifer glanced out the window. "Seeing the Bryants didn't help. I can't believe that Bea sprang that on us that way. I would never have attended if I'd known they would be there."

"I think the idea was that you'd put the past behind you and discuss what to do about the Dancing Cedars property."

Jennifer raised her eyebrows in surprise. "You aren't seriously lecturing me about living in the past, are you?"

Okay, Mom had a point. "I think the conservation easement is worth looking into. It seems like a fair way to make sure everyone can enjoy the land and ensure it doesn't get turned into a strip mall someday."

"Now you sound like Melody." Jennifer picked up the folder and slapped it open. "It's much simpler if I buy the land. Everyone gets their money, and I get to create an exclusive retreat. Then it's over and done and we all move on. No strip mall."

"How do you know? After you turn it into the retreat, the land still increases in value. You die, then it gets sold off, subdivided, logged over, and turned into condos." Erin put her hand to her chest. "Maybe you don't believe me, but I can't stand the idea of that land ever being destroyed. It's special, and I want it to stay the way it is forever. I know it seems impossible to imagine little Alpine Grove growing and expanding out that far, but having spent the last ten years in DC, I can tell you that open spaces are disappearing at an alarming rate everywhere. It will happen here too. It's only a matter of time."

Jennifer leaned forward. "I think that's the largest collection of words you've put together in my presence in more than two years. You're serious, aren't you?"

Erin sat up straight. "I guess I am."

~

Erin's suitcase still had not appeared by the time she went to bed that night. What was the airline doing? She vowed to call the customer support line the next morning to see where, literally, on the great blue planet her suitcase might have ended up. Because her parents were arguing or sitting in steely angry silence, being in the house was increasingly uncomfortable. She was beyond ready to go home.

She prepared for bed and was joined by Casey in the tower room. One thing she would miss was spending time with the mellow old dog. He gamely trudged along on her walks without complaint and loved sitting in her lap. Maybe she should think about visiting an animal shelter and adopting a dog when she got back to DC. There were probably lots of older dogs like Casey who needed a loving home.

She curled up on the bed with an ancient copy of *Pride and Prejudice* she'd pulled off the shelf. After the disturbing *Christmas Carol* dream, she needed to stick to books that didn't involve ghosts. In Jane Austen's novels, all the polite conversation was among the living, so she hoped it would be less likely to mess with her psyche.

She opened the book and Elizabeth Bennett was thrilled at an invitation to the lake country. "What delight!"

That was an interesting choice of words. Erin couldn't remember the last time she'd been delighted about anything. Elizabeth was pretty fired up: "You give me fresh life and vigor. Adieu to disappointment and spleen. What are men to rocks and mountains?"

Erin set the book aside and closed her eyes. Maybe she should go back out to Dancing Cedars before she left. She wanted to see it without the distraction of twenty-year-old commune angst, so she could simply experience the land itself. Maybe she'd ask Ziggy to go too. It was fitting that she'd met him on his way from the library. When they'd lived at Dancing Cedars, they'd spent hours there. No matter how chaotic things were out at Dancing Cedars, the library had always given them a sense of quiet stability.

It was winter, and flakes of snow danced around her face. She was standing near the old cafe in town and in front of her a man in a brown coat with a hood was carrying a bag of library books. She yelled, "Hey Ziggy, wait up."

When he turned around, she gasped in surprise. "Andy, how can you be in Alpine Grove?"

"You tell me. How can it be 1975?" He gave her the half-grin that never failed to melt her heart. "We have to get going and start on Christmas dinner."

"What? Go where?"

"Come on." He waved the book bag as an invitation. "Don't over-think it. Have some fun."

Erin knew she was dreaming, but she followed Andy through the snow to, well, she had no idea. As they walked, images flashed of the years of holidays she'd spent with him. Drinking wine and laughing with his parents in front of a fire crackling in the hearth. Watching Andy carve a turkey poorly and teasing him about his pathetic knife-wielding skills. Baking dozens of batches of cookies. Decorating the sad little Christmas tree they'd gotten at a lot late on the first Christmas Eve they were together. Andy had been funny and brilliant. Sometimes his quick wit had infuriated her, but he made her laugh and he made her think.

Her mind flashed to the incredibly ugly cinder-block dorm where they'd met as undergrads. The walls were painted blue and gold, which she'd always thought was a particularly hideous color combination. He'd been a political science major, and she was into botany.

She felt as much as heard his laugh next to her as they walked. He used to say she was his favorite tree hugger. Miss Save the Planet. When they graduated, she followed him to DC. They moved in together, and she worked for the environmental firm as a paralegal. Andy hadn't been perfect, but during the years they'd been together, he'd pushed her to be her best, working to help put her through law school and giving her time to study.

The snow was getting deeper, turning into a blizzard, and she was struggling to keep up with Andy. "Slow down! Where are we going?"

A massive evergreen tree crashed in front of her, and she fell backward away from it, landing with a thud. She reached out her hand, crying out, "Andy! Where are you? Come back to me."

She brushed away something wet in her ear and opened her eyes. Casey's paws were on the edge of the mattress, and he was poking her face with his black wet nose. She sat up and lifted the dog onto the bed with her. "Sorry to wake you up."

She stroked the dog's head and tried not to cry. If she had to say good-bye to Andy every night, she might lose her mind. Where was her suitcase? If it ever showed up, she would gleefully pop ELF pills again so she didn't go completely nuts. The dreams also reminded her why, no matter how much she might like the idea, she shouldn't adopt a dog, much less ever have a serious relationship again. Saying good-bye was too hard. Never again.

Casey stood up and spun in a circle before curling up beside her. Erin wrapped her arm around his warm body, closed her eyes, and started counting back from ten, hoping for some mercifully dreamless sleep.

When she woke up the next morning, although the rest of the night hadn't been dreamless, at least the dreams hadn't been disturbing. Instead of losing Andy again, she'd had multiple mini-dreams about hanging out at the Alpine Grove library as she so often had when she was a kid.

In one dream, ten-year-old Ziggy was in one of the big, puffy, cozy reading chairs with his leg flopped over the arm, reading a magazine with a jingle bear on the cover. She'd been sitting in the chair next to him, but whatever she'd been reading was lost to the ether of the dream. In another snippet, she and Ziggy had been sitting at one of the tables creating a secret code based on something they'd read in *Harriet the Spy*. The dreams had a misty quality, almost like a silent movie with swirling gossamer threads of memories. The dreams left her with an overriding sense of calm, which was a nice change of pace.

She went downstairs and fed Casey breakfast. Her parents were at the kitchen table reading the newspaper in silence. At least they weren't arguing.

Erin sat down with a bowl of cereal. "So, do you have any plans for the holiday weekend?"

Paul said, "I'm going to see if I can dig up the Christmas lights and untangle them. If that goes well, I might figure out how they could work on this house."

"After working all day yesterday, I plan to relax." Jennifer flipped down the newspaper and peered over it at Erin. "I was hoping you could go through those boxes in your closet and donate or throw away anything you don't want."

"All right. This morning, I was thinking I might go to the library." Okay, maybe she was being superstitious, but after all her weird dreams, she felt like she had to go see the place for real.

Erin took Casey for a short walk around the block and then explained that he was off the hook for the longer excursion. If she didn't know better, she'd think the old guy actually looked kind of relieved. He probably wasn't used to all these long walks.

As her parents had planned, Mom was lounging on the sofa watching TV, and Dad was immersed in untangling wires. They seemed content, so Erin turned around and went back outside, headed for the library.

It was cold but still sunny. There was talk of a storm moving in, but it hadn't arrived yet. Walking every day had helped Erin clear her mind of the confusing dreams, commune-related drama, and parental disputes. She took a deep breath, enjoying the crisp fall air.

Erin walked up the concrete steps of the Alpine Grove library. Built in the 1920s, the stately two-story brick building had cast-concrete decorations around the arched doorways and huge wooden doors that led into the lobby and reading-room area.

Even though the chairs in the reading area had undoubtedly been swapped out for new ones some time over the last couple of decades, they looked similar to the ones she remembered. And when she walked in, Erin found Ziggy draped over a comfy-looking chair reading a novel, much as he had been in her dream. The view was different because he was a whole lot larger and his legs were sprawled out in front of him. But the fact that his nose was in a book like it had been twenty years ago made her smile. This was *such* a small town. Practically every time she went outside, she ran across Ziggy.

She sat in the chair next to him, and raised her eyebrows when he glanced away from his book at her. She whispered, "Skipping out on Christmas trees again, huh?"

"Hey, Stardust. What are you doing here?"

"Just seeing what's changed at the library."

"Not much." He squinted at her and gestured at the stacks. "Still lots of books. What's the real reason?"

Was she really such a bad liar? "I was thinking about all the time we spent here, and I dreamed about it last night. So I wanted to stop by."

"You dreamed about the library? That takes literary fantasy to a new and dull place."

"You were sitting in this chair."

"Me?" He sat up, set the book aside, and gave her a big grin. "You dreamed about *me*? That's more interesting."

"You were ten."

"And we're back to dull. I thought you said you were dreaming about your fiancé …what's his name? Andy."

"I keep having vivid dreams about him. Maybe the house really is haunted. After I read *A Christmas Carol*…um, never mind. But the dream I had about the library was more like different memories about both of us being at the library when we were kids. Well, except for a couple random jingle bears thrown in here and there."

"We did spend a lot of time at the library."

"It was better than the dream I had where we're in my apartment and you were griping about my lack of furniture."

"I've never seen your apartment."

"Hey, it was a dream. You were helping me unpack but being a jerk about it. Then you threw a jingle bear at me."

He placed his palm on his chest and gave her the wide-eyed innocent look. "I would *never* be a jerk."

"Oh please."

"Okay, I would. And I'd definitely throw a jingle bear."

Erin shoved his shoulder. "Even in my dreams, the adult you isn't that different from the ten-year-old you."

"Except when I was ten, we were playing with our Snoopy erasers, having them mountain-climb through the stacks. Joe Cool was the best."

"Sorry, my heroic Flying Ace battling the Red Baron was way cooler, despite Joe's egotistical moniker."

"I think you should stay in Alpine Grove for a while. You're getting your snark back."

"Excuse me, but I'm not snarky. And if I were, that seems like all the more reason to leave."

"I mean it in a good way. Being snarky is part of who you are." He picked up his book. "I need to go check on Moose and make sure he hasn't done something nasty in my truck."

"Why isn't he at home?"

"I'm paying that kid to dress up as a bear, and he seems to love it, which is remarkable to me. But the bad thing is that I can't leave Moose at the house. My parents are busy, and that guy can't be expected to embrace the holiday spirit in a bear suit *and* watch my dopey dog."

Erin shook her head in mock horror. "Heavens no. That would be unreasonable."

"Hey, the kid has enough to do, and Moose isn't good at listening to people who aren't me."

"If you're going to read all day, why don't you do it at home?"

Ziggy stuffed his book into a bag and stood up. "Are your parents getting along?"

"No."

"I rest my case, counselor. I should go."

Erin grabbed his arm before he could get away. "Are you busy?"

"Depends on whether Moose trashed my truck."

"Would you be willing to drive me out to Dancing Cedars? The weather is supposed to turn, and I want to see it again before I leave Alpine Grove."

"You're not leaving until you look at papers, remember?"

"I know, but I can do that when it's raining and reading that stuff isn't going to take long."

"I'll drive you out there, but only if we stop by the gift store and get the papers from Bea first. You promised."

"All right."

"And if Moose did something to my truck, you have to help me fix it or clean it up."

"You drive a hard bargain." Erin gestured toward the door. "After you."

They walked outside to the old truck, which was parked across the street. Moose panted happily from within, fogging up the windows.

Ziggy said, "It's not locked."

Erin shoved Moose aside and examined the bench seat, which seemed to be free of anything revolting. She slid in and immediately rolled down the window. "The magic skunk recipe needs some refinement."

"Hey, I tried. I need to dip the whole truck in it, which isn't as easy as it sounds." He turned the key, and music blasted from the stereo, startling everybody in the cab. Quickly turning the knob to stifle the sound, he said. "Sorry. Sometimes you have to take it to the limit."

"It's okay, I like the Eagles, and I've taken it to the limit way more than one time."

He turned the volume up to a reasonable level and they crooned their way over to the gift store. Although the truck was a rusty old clunker, it had a swanky high-quality sound system. He parked, told Moose to behave himself, and they went inside.

Bea was behind the counter and beamed when she saw them. "You two look happy."

"Aren't you the one who used to say that singing is good for the soul?" Ziggy said. "I brought Erin here to pick up the papers."

Bea clapped her hands together. "That's wonderful. I'll be right back."

Erin glared at Ziggy. "You didn't make it sound like I'm going to do something heroic here, did you?"

He didn't say anything, and Bea returned with an accordion file. "Here's everything we have."

Erin took the brown folder and tucked it to her chest. "I'm not sure how much help I can be."

"But she's going to read everything," Ziggy added. "We both think the conservation easement is a good idea."

Bea set her palms on the counter. "I'm not sure how to get everyone on board with it. There are so many of us and so many personalities. Not to mention everyone is spread out now."

"Bring everyone together," Ziggy said. "You managed to get our families together for Thanksgiving. It's a start."

Erin said, "Well, I'm not sure how great of a start it was."

"I know it could have gone better." Bea crossed her arms. "But it opened a dialogue. These conflicts have been festering for too long. Dylan is right. We need to bring everyone together and talk about the future."

Erin wanted to roll her eyes. This is what they always did with the perpetual powwows. A PP of this magnitude couldn't possibly go well. "How would you bring everyone together?"

"It's almost Christmas," Ziggy said.

Bea's eyes lit up. "Even more important, it's the thirty-year anniversary of the founding of Dancing Cedars. Not everyone celebrates Christmas, but we always made a big deal about the solstice. I might be able to convince everyone to come out to Dancing Cedars to celebrate the anniversary and solstice. People could stay over and we could talk."

"Wait a minute," Erin said. "We were just there. Dancing Cedars is overrun with feral cats, skunks, and who knows what else. No one wants to go there."

"You do," Ziggy said. "Didn't you just ask me to drive you?"

She turned to glare at him. "That's different."

He shook his head. "You want to say good-bye. Everyone else should have the chance to say good-bye too."

"It's not good-bye," Bea said. "It's simply a transition to a new era. One that respects what has gone before while preserving what we enjoyed."

"I like that," Ziggy said. "I'm in."

Erin frowned. "But what about all the wildlife living there? You can't expect people to actually *stay* there. It's awful."

"I'm sure you and Dylan could help clean it up and move the cats," Bea said. "People don't *have* to stay there, but some people might want to. If nothing else, they'll certainly want to see it, so we should clean it up."

Erin nudged Ziggy, but he didn't say anything. He couldn't possibly think this was a good idea, could he? How were you supposed to *move* cats? "It would take a miracle to make that place habitable."

"Well, then we need to work on that, don't we?" Bea said.

Chapter 7

Women's Intuition

After they were back in the truck and heading north, Erin turned to Ziggy. "Has Bea completely lost her mind? People aren't going to want to come to a reunion, much less *stay* at Dancing Cedars. The idea is insane."

He shrugged. "I get it. If you're two-thousand miles away, Dancing Cedars is abstract. Just a place full of old memories. But if you go there, you remember why it's special."

"I suppose."

"You're a good example. If you hadn't gone out there, would you be on board with the idea of saving it?"

"Probably not."

"I rest my case, counselor."

Erin shoved his shoulder. "Stop saying that."

When they arrived at the end of the road, Ziggy parked in front of the gate. "I don't have the key to the padlock."

"That's okay. I want to walk along the creek anyway."

Ziggy let Moose out, and they went to the trail that followed alongside the creek. It meandered up to the pasture where the Hodgepodge Lodge was located, and they'd followed the route probably hundreds of times. The deer used the trail too, so it was relatively free of debris even after so many years.

They entered the forest where massive cedars and hemlocks shaded the trail. Moose charged ahead of them, having a glorious time sniffing and cavorting his way toward the creek.

"He seems to know the way," Erin said. "Do you bring him out here often?"

"As much as I can." He whistled, and Moose came galloping back toward them. "It tires him out for days."

"He's got acres of trees to run around in at your house."

"It's not the same. Out here, there aren't any rules. He can run where he wants, and no one is around to care." He turned to grin at her. "Kind of like when we were kids."

"People cared. Lots of people."

"But when we weren't in the lodge, we more or less did whatever we wanted."

The creek widened, and there was a clearing where they used to play for hours. Erin sat on a log and closed her eyes. "On Thanksgiving when we were driving along the road, I heard the creek, and I wanted to run down here."

Ziggy sat next to her and whistled for Moose again. "I spend a lot of time here. In the winter, I snowshoe in."

"My therapist told me that I should seek out even the smallest moments of joy. I thought it was stupid because I haven't felt any joy for so long. Then I heard the creek..."

"And you remembered."

"Yes." She turned to look at him. "For so long, I was embarrassed about growing up the way we did. Afterward, I always felt like a small-town hick who couldn't compete with the smart, sophisticated people in the city."

"Hey, be nice. I *am* a small-town hick. And you've never had any shortage of smarts."

"You know what I mean. Being home-schooled confused everybody. When we moved away from Alpine Grove, the school district couldn't even figure out what grade to put me in. I basically skipped two grades, but I had to take algebra in summer school."

"Math sucks."

Erin laughed. "I was so far ahead of everyone in everything except math. I got caught up, but it was another thing that made me feel insecure and uncomfortable about growing up here."

"They didn't know what to do with me either." Ziggy leaned forward and put his elbows on his knees. "Regular public school was incredibly boring. When I wanted to know something, I got books from the library. I made it through high school, but I didn't like it."

"Did you go to college?"

"For a while, I went to community college in Gleasonville. I got an apartment and lived alone for a couple years, but it was a grind because I had to go home lots of weekends to help out. Then Dad fell off a ladder and broke his ankle, so I gave up and moved back home. At the time, it seemed simpler."

"You seem happy."

"More like okay. I've basically accepted that in exchange for being lazy, I have to take care of my parents and help them sell trees." He picked up a branch and pulled off some twigs. "Everything has trade-offs."

"I was thinking the same thing the other day. So is the plan for you to take over the Christmas tree farm at some point?"

"It has been." He threw the stick on the ground. "I don't know."

Erin picked up the stick and poked his foot with it. "It sounds like you have other ideas."

"Nope. That's the problem. All I know is that if I could do whatever I want, it wouldn't involve crowds of people invading my home every year in December. The farm is my parents' dream, not mine."

"What's yours?"

"I'm getting cold. We should walk." He stood up. "Let's go, Moose."

They walked alongside the creek up the hill until it opened up into the pasture. The Hodgepodge Lodge sat on its knoll looking woodsy and rustic in the autumn light, like a tintype of an old homestead. They traversed the pasture, trudging through the tall golden grasses toward the log structure.

Moose caught sight of something ahead and launched forward, galumphing through the grass.

Ziggy whistled, but Moose ignored him. "If that dumb dog finds another skunk, I'm going to kill him."

They increased their pace, but Moose kept running. The distinctive yowling and hissing of male cats fighting came from another direction. Moose abruptly turned around and ran back to Ziggy, who clipped the leash onto the dog. "This year, every time I come out here it seems like there are more cats."

"What are we going to do about them?" Erin asked. "They're everywhere, undoubtedly busy making more cats."

"It sure sounds like it." He tugged on Moose's leash. "Settle down. They were here first. Remember when you messed with that tom and he laid open your nose?"

Erin opened her arms wide. "Bea thinks we're going to *move* a bunch of cats. It's completely nuts. How do you move a feral cat? Even if we could, then what? Are we supposed to find them homes or something?"

"Feral cats aren't like house cats. No one wants to live with a feral. Hunters would probably shoot them."

"*What?*"

"Don't freak out." He waved his arms in surrender. "I'm not a hunter, and I'm definitely not advocating it. Just saying that's a typical way people have done animal control in the past. Another approach is to trap the cats, get them fixed, and then put them back where they were."

"Well that would keep the number of cats from increasing, at least."

They walked up to where the chicken coop had been and Erin crouched down to push grass away from a rotting piece of plywood. "Check it out. Remember when we painted this?"

The wood had faded childish paintings of chickens on it. Erin recalled the hot summer day when Bill had given her and Ziggy paintbrushes and suggested they explore their artistic vision for the chicken coop. He probably sacrificed some of his paint because he was desperate to get the kids out of his hair.

"There's Little Chicken Little," Ziggy said, pointing at a yellowish blob. "He's seen better days."

"Your chicken counting his chickens before they're hatched isn't looking too good either." Erin crouched next to the wood and traced the outline of an egg. "I spent a lot of time wishing I never lived here. And I can't tell you how much I didn't want to visit. The only reason I came was because my mother sent me the plane ticket."

Ziggy crouched next to her. "Your past is part of who you are, Stardust."

They both stood up and gazed down at the wood. Erin turned to face him. "You're the best friend I've ever had."

"Same here. I'm glad you came. I forgot what it's like to have someone I can talk to and say what I really think."

"You always seem so content. Everything just rolls off your back." Erin pointed at herself. "Meanwhile, I'm a total basket case."

He reached to take her hand. "Hey, you're not a basket case. You're working through some stuff. I get that."

"I'm so tired of my own thoughts. I look at you and I think, why can't I just let what happened go and move on?"

"I'll let you in on a little secret, even though I think you already know." He squeezed her hand. "That whole 'I don't care' attitude is fake."

"What do you mean?"

"Hey, when we played with those erasers, I was Joe Cool, remember? At some point, I realized Snoopy was on to something. If you act cool like you don't care, it's harder for people to see they've hurt you, so they leave you alone. That's how I survived school without you."

Erin looked into his eyes. He was right. If she thought about it, she'd always known the laid-back attitude was his defense mechanism. "I missed you too, but I had to move."

"And you moved on. Did your thing. Became a lawyer. Found the guy in your dreams and built a great life." He let go of her hand. "I didn't because like I said, I'm basically lazy and don't like most people much."

"You're not lazy, and let's face it, doing my thing didn't work out so well for me either."

"It will. You're getting there." He gestured toward the Hodgepodge Lodge. "I think spending time here away from everything is helping you forgive him."

"Forgive who? Andy?"

"Once you forgive him for dying, you'll be free again. I think being angry and sad has trapped you in a kind of prison." He smiled. "But the snarky comments tell me that you might be breaking out."

Erin was at a loss for what to say. Was she finally moving on? She stared at his unusual blue eyes and he stared right back at her. Finally she said, "I hope you're right."

"I know I am."

The breeze swirled around them, whipping Erin's hair around her face. She pulled the hood of her coat over her head and tugged the ties down tight. The chill in the air suggested that the odd extended Indian summer everyone had enjoyed was about to relinquish its grip, skip fall, and transition directly to winter.

Although the pines retained their deep dark green, the gold leaves of the aspens and birch were long gone, so they stood bare-limbed on the edges of the clearing. Under that row of trees, she and Ziggy had often made piles of leaves to jump in and throw at each other. They were always disappointed when the inevitable fall rains came and the piles turned to soggy leaf glop.

As they walked around the Hodgepodge Lodge, inspecting the state of the building, Erin reflected upon what Ziggy had said. Was she truly moving on? Part of her was afraid. If she didn't mourn Andy, was it like she didn't love him anymore? Or that she hadn't loved him enough? Actually having a romantic relationship with another man again gave her a sick feeling in her stomach. It felt disloyal to Andy's memory to even consider it.

Ziggy whacked her upper arm with his glove. "Hey! Did you hear anything I just said?"

"What?"

"We need to figure out a plan."

"Right. About the cats. I know." She turned to face the log wall. "So, it's apparent that the cats are getting inside the lodge somehow. We need to look for holes and fix them."

"And get some cat traps." He gestured toward the road. "Somewhere. Maybe the hardware store has them."

"How many do we need?"

"I don't know. We also need to call the vet, Dr. Cassidy, but she might not be up for fixing a bunch of wild kitties. And then who is paying for it?"

Erin gazed up at a second-floor window that was so filthy it looked frosted. "How are we going to clean this place? Somebody must have brought a broom and swept it out before we had Thanksgiving here. But the upstairs is still so gross, I'm not even sure where to start. This is going to be an unbelievable amount of work. What have we gotten ourselves into?"

"It's going to be harsh." Ziggy leaned back against the wall and tugged Moose's leash to bring the dog closer to him. "I need to call the boarding kennel. If we're going to be killing ourselves cleaning and fixing this place, I should board Moose, so I don't have to worry about whatever he's up to."

"At least the kennel is fairly close by."

He turned to look at her. "If we do this, it's going to take some time. More than reading through papers. Are you okay with that?"

"I guess so. If I had another idea, I'd suggest it, but I don't."

"You might have to stay here in town longer than you were expecting."

"I know."

Ziggy pushed himself away from the wall and rubbed his gloved hands together. "It's getting colder. Are you ready to go?"

Erin stepped forward and her right foot caught on a piece of wood. Ziggy lurched forward and scooped her into his arms. "Watch out. Junk is lying around everywhere. We'll need to do some cleanup outside too."

She looked into his eyes. "Thanks for keeping me from face-planting into that pile of dirt that might actually be ancient compost or manure. And for bringing me out here."

"You know I'd do anything for you."

"Apparently so. You even spent hours driving to the airport to get me."

"Hey, I love you." He wrapped her tightly in a bear hug. "I always have and I always will."

Erin's heart lurched in her chest. What was he suggesting? She pulled away. "You're like the best brother anyone could ever ask for. Harry is lucky."

"I doubt he thinks so. Maybe someday you won't find me so brotherly."

Erin took another step backward, glancing down to check for the piece of wood. "I don't think. I mean, I love you too, but not like…you know. We're friends. Beyond that, we're too different. Way, *way* too different."

"That's true, but friends aren't identical twins, parroting each other's thoughts. Friends are people who challenge you and understand you. Seeing you again—it's like no time has passed. You get me. I get you. It's always been that way. Do you know how rare that is?" He opened his arms expansively. "To talk like this? I'm not honest with anyone else like I am with you."

"I'm not either." Erin wrapped her arms around her jacket, suddenly cold. "But I can't. I'm sorry. I just can't."

"I know." Ziggy stepped forward, pulled her arms away, and snuggled her into another hug. "It's okay. But I thought you should know."

Erin closed her eyes and they stood there for a moment, cocooned in the warm embrace. Finally, Ziggy stepped back and shook out his arms. "If we don't get out of here soon, I'm going to get frostbite on my fingertips. The temperature is dropping like a rock."

While they'd been walking around, the sun had dropped behind the hills, and the watery late afternoon light was fading quickly. They hustled down the road back to the truck with Moose leading the way.

After they got into the truck, Ziggy started the engine and fired up the heater full-blast. "Sorry about the smell. The defroster stirs up the stink."

Erin just nodded and rubbed her hands together. Her emotions were tangled into a knot, and the ache in her stomach was worse.

Ziggy put his hand on her leg. "Hey, it's not going to be weird between us, is it? Because we have a crap-ton of work to do."

"I'm fine." Erin said, even though she wasn't. "But since you mentioned being honest, I'm cold, your truck is a hazardous waste zone, and my father bought another puzzle. This one is a picture of a field of wheat, so this evening I have to stare at yellow puzzle pieces, which might drive me ever-so-slowly insane."

Ziggy took her hand and gave it a squeeze. "I know you don't want to miss that kind of fun. Let's get outta here. I have to go rescue Junior Jingle Bear and listen to my parents complain about how he's not family, and my lack of holiday spirit is a huge disappointment to them."

Erin put his hand back on the steering wheel. "Shut up and drive, Ziggy."

He grinned at her. "I'm glad we're cool, Stardust."

~

After she got back to her parents' house, Erin had lots of time to think about the events of the day while placing small yellow pieces into the wheat-field puzzle. She concentrated on ideas for cleaning up Dancing Cedars, rather than on what Ziggy had said about how he felt about her. That train of thought was off limits. He was not her type, even if she were in the market for romance, which she absolutely was not. Unfortunately, although she tried to focus on the cleaning tasks ahead, her thoughts kept straying. The color yellow grew more boring with every puzzle piece she picked up.

Paul looked up from his task and said to Erin, "You're awfully quiet. Is everything okay?"

Erin took a deep breath. Time to come clean with her parents. "I went out to Dancing Cedars with Ziggy. I also agreed to look over some of the paperwork related to Bea's conservation easement idea."

Jennifer looked up. "Oh honey, really? I thought you'd be more supportive of our view."

"It's your view," Paul said. "Not mine."

Erin had no interest in getting in the middle of *that* argument. She was pretty sure her mother wanted her to stay and do women's retreats because it was a way to avoid her father. "I think setting up a conservation easement is a good way to keep the property as it is and fair for everyone who was involved."

"You've always been such an environmentalist," Jennifer said. "I can't fault you for standing up for your beliefs."

"Thanks, Mom. I might end up staying a little longer to help out. I hope that's okay."

Jennifer jumped out of her chair and leaned over to hug Erin around her shoulders. "That's wonderful, honey. Stay as long as you like. I'm loving having you here and being able to share your experiences after so long. I've missed you."

"I've missed you too."

Once everyone retired for the evening, Erin closed herself into her tower room with Casey, who definitely had a preference for spending his nights curled up on her bed. She suspected that Mom didn't let him on the beds, so Erin had vowed the little dog to secrecy.

She opened up the folder of papers about Dancing Cedars and started separating them into piles on the bed. On a yellow legal pad, she carefully logged each item. She wanted a list of what was there, so she could determine what might be missing.

After breakfast the next morning, the phone rang and Jennifer held out the receiver to Erin. "It's for you."

Her mother's disapproving face was reminiscent of the times she'd answered the phone and found Erin's high school boyfriend Joey on the other end of the line. She took the phone and said, "Hi Ziggy, what's up?"

"How did you know it was me?"

"Women's intuition."

"You wanna head out to the commune today? I made a bunch of phone calls after I got home last night. I can get the lodge key from Bea. I want to make a list of what we need to do before it starts to pour this afternoon. The kennel said they've got room for Moose at doggie day care."

"It's hard to imagine an animal that large in day care."

"So are you up for it? I still have to call the vet and stuff, but I can be there in about an hour."

"Okay. See you then."

When Erin hung up the phone, Jennifer put her hands on her hips. "What was that about?"

"Ziggy and I are going out to Dancing Cedars."

"Again?"

Erin hadn't mentioned Bea's big reunion plans, and she didn't want to now. "I want to go for a hike."

"With Dylan?" Jennifer narrowed her eyes. "It seems like you've seen a lot of him since you've been home."

"I'd like to point out that this isn't my home, Mom. And I haven't seen Ziggy in years. We're catching up, that's all."

"I'm a relationship expert, honey. Sometimes ephemeral details drive the flow of my observations."

Erin didn't want to dwell on whatever ephemeral details her mother had conjured up about Ziggy, so she excused herself and went upstairs to change her clothes. Time to raid Mom's closet again because after the temperature plummeted yesterday, it was clear bundling up would be necessary.

Erin watched at the window, so when Ziggy's beat-up maroon pickup pulled up alongside the house, she called to her parents that she was leaving and scurried out the door. The last thing she needed was any more parental interaction with Ziggy. When she was in high school, her mother had given Joey a long, detailed, and tedious lecture about respect and appreciation in a relationship, probably because she despised the guy. Now that Mom was convinced Erin and Ziggy were an item, it would be nice to avoid a repeat of that maternal rant.

Erin opened the door, got into the truck, and shoved the gigantic Moose butt aside. She leaned around the dog to wave at Ziggy. "Good morning."

"Hey Stardust, you're in a hurry."

Erin raised her eyebrows at him. "Are your parents getting along?"

"Nope."

"I rest my case, counselor. Onward."

They went through Alpine Grove and hit the highway going north. The truck bed was covered with a large blue tarp. Erin gestured behind them. "What do you have back there?"

"Dad had a couple of old traps from when raccoons were getting into the chicken coop at Dancing Cedars. Even though the traps are kind of rusty I oiled them, and I'm hoping they're the right size. More or less." He glanced at her. "The price was right anyhow."

"I agree that free is good."

"What's not free is fixing the cats and giving them rabies shots. Assuming we can catch any cats in the first place. Dr. Cassidy is sympathetic and will give us a discount, but it's still going to cost money."

"I hate to say it, but I'm broke." Erin gave him a feeble smile. "You weren't wrong about the state of my employment. Part-time temp work isn't lucrative. That's one reason Mom sent me the plane ticket."

"We'll figure something out. It might not be an issue if the cats are too smart to fall for the traps."

They listened to the radio and chatted about old landmarks on the way to the kennel. Many places had gone through multiple owners while Erin had been away.

As Ziggy turned into the driveway at the Wag On Inn, Erin asked, "How is the trapping going to work? Do we have to check on them every day? We can't just leave the cats in there."

"Nope. I'll drive out and check them." He shrugged. "It might not work either."

"What if we catch the skunk?"

"Don't even think that. As my mom would say, you don't want to put any energy into that idea because the universe might listen."

"That does sounds like something Melody would say."

"She also regularly points out that the universe has a twisted sense of humor."

Erin couldn't argue with that. "Sometimes Moonshadow is remarkably perceptive."

"Mom may be a little odd, but sometimes she surprises you."

Moose stood up and stomped on Erin's thigh. She shoved him away. "Hey, careful with those claws!"

Ziggy unloaded Moose, and Erin peered inside the window of the kennel door. The dogs were barking like crazy in there.

Kat emerged from the kennel, almost smacking Erin in the face. "Sorry. Are you okay?"

Erin waved her away. "I was looking inside. It's a nice setup."

"Thanks," Kat gestured toward the driveway "We might want to move away from the noise.

Ziggy handed Kat Moose's leash. "We're going to be gone for a few hours. I might need to board him again when we figure out exactly how bad this project is going to be."

"We can do day care pretty much any day. If a kennel isn't open, Moose can spend a lot of time out in the yard playing with other dogs, unless it rains."

"Then what?" Erin asked.

"We do a little bit of reshuffling." Kat said. "It's fine. We always figure something out."

"If you do nothing other than keep him away from skunks, I'll be happy," Ziggy said. "We'll be back in a few hours."

They said their good-byes and headed back out to the commune.

It was going to be a long day.

~

Kat brought Moose into the kennel and got him settled. She always tried to keep a space open for day-care dogs because they tended to arrive at the last minute. She'd received many phone calls that began, "I hate to ask, but…." The day-care concept worked out most of the time, except when the kennel was extremely busy. Fortunately, the Australian shepherd that had been occupying the space where Moose was located now had departed the night before.

Kat wasn't sorry to see the long holiday weekend in the rear view mirror. Now a lot of people were busy prepping for Christmas, so they weren't traveling, but the week before Christmas through the new year was already completely booked. For the first time since she'd started the kennel, she felt like the business could actually be successful in the long term.

Joel walked into the kennel building. "I'm guessing this is Moose."

"What gave it away?"

"The fact that if you put a saddle on him, you could ride him through the forest."

"That's not a bad idea. It sure would be easier on my tired feet." Kat gestured toward the door. "I have a call with that new client in ten minutes, but in an hour or so, would you be willing to grab Reggie, so we can take him and Moose out to the yard for a meet-and-greet? I have a feeling those two could end up being buddies."

"Sure." He put out his hand. "Are you done here? Shall I escort you to the house?"

"Yes." She grinned as she clasped his palm. "Thank you, kind sir."

They walked outside into the cold morning air, and Kat looked up at Joel. "I'm not ready for cold weather yet."

"You're never ready. Be thankful you got a reprieve this year."

"I know, but that doesn't make me any happier about having to wear my ugly winter coat again."

"Buy a new one."

"Nice clothes are a waste here with all the dirt, dogs, and disgustingness. I figure I'll wear this coat until it falls apart."

"By the way, next weekend I'll be helping Becca and Jack move out of the Shack."

"Already?"

"Becca is extremely organized. They're moving out a month earlier than they expected."

"I suppose it's easy to imagine her being a little Type A about something like moving to a new house."

"I'll need to ditch the old crappy furniture in the Shack."

"Why?"

"If I'm selling the house, having an ugly old couch sitting in the living area isn't going to enhance the real estate photos. I was thinking I could do a yard sale, but I don't think anyone would be willing to drive way out there."

"You're not *really* selling the Shack, are you?"

He stopped and looked at her. "Why are you so against it? It's just a little cabin."

"But you built it. The Shack has history." Kat let go of his hand and spread her arms wide. "Your history. *Our* history.

Jack and Becca's history. I hate the thought of someone else owning it."

"Everything has a history. With the way the real estate market is heating up, I might be able to get some decent money for the place."

"I know it's your house and your decision, but I don't think it's a good idea." Kat folded her arms across her chest. Selling the Shack felt wrong, but she couldn't explain why. There was no rational reason for her to care so much. But it still felt like the wrong thing to do. "Here's the thing. No one is going to buy it in the winter because it's so far out of town. The access stinks. How about if you wait until spring to make a decision?"

"Then I'd have to winterize it again, like I did before. I'd have to drain all the water from the pipes and get the power shut off."

"Is that a big deal? If you leave everything on and list it with a real estate agent, you'd have to plow the snow out there."

"I suppose."

Kat reached out and took his hands. "You have enough plowing to do here. I think we should think about this for a while."

"All right. I guess it doesn't matter."

She gave him a hug. "Thanks."

They went inside and retired to their respective offices. Joel was working on a programming project, and Kat had to have a conversation with a client about a writing project. It involved interviewing people who had won an award and then writing profiles about them that would be posted on a website.

The new project was a referral from a magazine editor she'd worked with for a while, and she didn't want to screw up the job. The magazine articles were a monthly gig, and she liked the steady income, but this new job involved dealing with a different editor named Sylvia. Trying to talk to Sylvia about the award profiles had not gone well. She seemed to be more than a little disorganized, and Kat was still trying to find out the names and contact information for the people who had won the award. It seemed like an obvious first step, but Sylvia kept putting her off.

Kat gathered her meager notes and took a deep breath, trying to suck up the courage to make the call. Sylvia was one of those one-word emailers who were evidently so busy that they couldn't even make an appointment. After much prodding, it turned out the only day she might be able to muster up five minutes to talk to Kat was on a Sunday. The fact that Sylvia could only talk on the weekend struck Kat as odd, but as a freelancer, she wasn't going to quibble. Money was money. The sound of the phone jarred her from her thoughts. Maybe it was Sylvia.

But it wasn't. Kat's friend Maria said, "Hey girlfriend, what's up?"

"I need to make a call now."

"Like *right* now? What's that about? Are you scheduling calls like an executive or something?"

"Hardly. This woman Sylvia is impossible to reach, and she said I can call her at ten this morning. That's in three minutes, so please talk fast."

"It's about Bob."

Kat suppressed a sigh. Bob Jensen was Maria's current boyfriend. He was a farmer, and Maria was having trouble with aspects of spending time at the farm. "Anything about Bob isn't going to be fast."

"You know how people supposedly change careers three or four times in their lifetime?"

"Yes."

"What's a second career for a farmer? I need ideas."

"That farm has been in Bob's family for generations. You're not going to get him to leave. Two minutes."

"There has to be some alternative, girlfriend. I like him, but the farm life is not for me."

"If you start singing the 'Green Acres' theme song, I'm hanging up."

"Okay, okay. But there's manure everywhere. I mean, how much do cows eat?

"How should I know?"

"You're sure snippy today. I'm having a crisis here. I don't know what to do. I need ideas *bad*. Don't you have any? You must have *something*."

"Nope. I already told you. Bob is a farmer. Deal with it. Thirty seconds. I'll call you back after I find out about this article."

Maria gave up and Kat hung up the phone. Bob had been a farmer his entire life and as she understood it, he loved his farm. Maria would have to either accept the cows and their manure or give up on Bob. Right now, Kat had her own problem to deal with.

She took another deep breath, dialed Sylvia, and left yet another message on her answering machine.

Clearly, this project was doomed.

Chapter 8

Catch Us If You Can

Ziggy and Erin wound their way back along the forested roads to Misty Meadow Lane and took it to the dead end. He had the keys to both the gate padlock and the Hodgepodge Lodge this time, so they wouldn't have to spend as much time in the rapidly chilling outdoors.

Erin got out of the truck, and as she and Ziggy walked around to access the truck bed, a couple of cats shot away from the lodge and across the meadow. Erin pointed at an orange tabby zooming away from them. Cats could move out when they felt like it. "I know the goal is to look for holes in the walls to keep the cats out, but if we do that, they'll freeze to death this winter."

Ziggy undid the bungee cords holding the tarp over the truck bed. "I thought about that. We saw that pieces of the chicken coop are still around. If I make them a shelter, they should be fine. It's not like the lodge has had any heat for them to enjoy all this time."

"I guess that's true. Can you put the coop back together? Will it be enough?"

"If I can build a cocoa hut, I can resurrect an ancient chicken coop."

"I didn't know you made the hut. I'm impressed. It's awfully cute."

"More so if you're ten." He hauled a toolbox from the bed. "Could you grab some of that stuff from the back?"

Erin reached in, grabbed a cloth bag, and peered inside. "What is all this?"

"Trapping supplies. Could you get the traps too?"

After several trips, they had carted everything inside the lodge. Ziggy had also thought to bring firewood for the stove, which was considerate of him. He busied himself making a fire while Erin looked on, eagerly anticipating being warm again.

She crouched down next to him and rubbed her hands together in front of the flames. "If you're trying to attract cats, this should help."

He closed the stove door and stood up. "That's what I was thinking. While we look for holes in the walls, listen for any noise. Even though wild kitties don't like people, all this warmth might bring them inside."

"I guess we should make a list of what we need to deal with here as far as repairs." Erin pulled out a notepad. "Remind me again why we're doing all this?"

"Because we want to get a whole lot of people with different opinions to agree on something for the first time in their lives."

"Well, presumably they agreed to *start* the commune."

"And end it. Everything in between was one long discussion."

"Interspersed with moments of discord." That was an understatement. Erin tried not to sigh. "Okay, looking around this room, there's a big hole next to that window, where the mortar seems to have fallen out."

"And we officially have point number one for the list."

Erin walked around the perimeter of the large kitchen and dining area, poking at the walls with her fingertip. Pieces of mortar crumbled to the floor. "I think we're going to need to do some serious chinking. This stuff is decomposing. Half the wildlife in the forest is going to be enjoying indoor living before too long."

Ziggy crouched in a corner. "I think I found a kitty toilet over here behind the counter. I'm going to have to pull up the floorboards. This is nasty."

"Fixing this up is going to take a lot of work." Erin looked down at the dirty wood in front of Ziggy. "And a lot of wood. That means more money we don't have."

"We've got a lot of scrap lumber at our place, but I'm going to need to set up a workshop in here. And bring the portable generator."

"You have a generator?"

"The tree farm does. It doesn't get much action at this time of year. Right now, Dad is too busy selling trees to miss it."

They went upstairs, noting the various holes in the walls. Erin stopped and grabbed Ziggy's arm. "Do you hear that?"

"Hear what?"

"Shhh. I think I hear something."

They stood still and Erin pointed to the room at the far end of the hall. She moved forward, waving Ziggy to follow and pressing her finger to her lips.

Something small, gray, and furry shot alongside her, and Erin shrieked. "What was that?"

Whatever it was had bolted into the room where the noises had been coming from. Ziggy made a face. "Uh-oh."

They slowly walked toward the door. Low growling came from the far corner of the room. It sounded like a small motorcycle engine. The rrrring increased in intensity as they got closer. A gray tabby was standing guard over three kittens that were huddled in the corner.

Ziggy put his arm out to stop Erin. "Back up."

"I think you're right. Good idea."

They backed out of the room and walked down the hallway. At the stairs, Ziggy stopped and sat down on the top step. "Now we know where some of the cats are."

"What should we do?" She clutched his arm. "And holy adorableness, those little kittens are so *cute*."

"This is like the little chickens." He chuckled. "You are a sucker for baby creatures."

"Oh come on, chicks are sweet. Once they become hens, yes, they are less cute. And roosters are not even slightly cute."

"You just hated Clyde, that's all."

"That bird was evil." She turned to look behind her. "So what do we do about those little bundles of cuteness?"

"I'm thinking we catch the mom in a trap. Take them all to the vet, get Momma Kitty fixed, and get her babies adopted into good homes. From what I read, if they're young enough, feral kittens can be socialized like any other cat."

"Adopted how? There's no animal shelter in Alpine Grove, is there?"

"No, but there's a dog-rescue group now. They might have ideas." He put his hand on her forearm. "You stay here. I'll get the live trap. If we put it in the hallway, maybe we can catch Momma Kitty."

Erin agreed, and she sat at the top of the steps, keeping an eye out for the wily gray feral and listening to Ziggy crash around downstairs. Finally, he returned carrying a trap, a blanket, and the bag of goodies.

He went halfway down the hall and set the trap. The old trap had two doors and a metal trip plate in between. He opened the doors on each end and carefully put food on the metal plate and then covered the trap with a blanket. He snuggled the trap against the wall and walked back to Erin.

She looked up at him as he sat next to her. "Now what?"

"We wait."

"You've got to be kidding. I'm imagining all the cats are in there singing 'Catch Us If You Can.'"

"That's a song by the Dave Clark Five."

She patted his forearm. "Well done."

"Let's leave them be." He got up and descended the stairs. "If the trap gets tripped, you'll hear the clanging. I need to go outside and see if any of that chicken-coop wood is any good."

"I'm going to feel terrible if the kitties freeze." Erin stood next to the stove and rubbed her hands together. "Are we doing the right thing?"

"We need them out of the lodge."

"I know. But they were here first."

"I don't think these cats were here in 1967, Stardust." He gestured toward the windows. "I'm sure some low-life moved away, and it was easier for him to dump his cats at the end of the road than take them with him. Who knows how many generations of cats have lived and died at Dancing Cedars?"

"Okay, you have a point."

"It's not the cats' fault. But they need their own space."

A metallic clang came from upstairs, and Ziggy grinned. "Gotcha."

"I'll get a towel for the babies to help keep them warm." Erin grabbed one of the boxes that held some of the supplies and dumped the stuff on the floor. "Are you sure the vet is going to be okay with this? It's Sunday."

"Dr. Cassidy gave me her home number. She has a soft spot for homeless critters, and she knows me because of Moose. I think that dog has a crush on her."

They went upstairs and were greeted by a low growl. Ziggy moved slowly toward the cage, bent down to push the blanket aside, and grabbed the handle on the top of the cage. The cat thrashed inside, hissing and growling more intensely.

Ziggy held the cage away from him and draped the blanket back over it. "Somebody isn't happy."

Erin took her cardboard box to the room at the end of the hall. The three kittens were making little mewling noises and standing up looking concerned, apparently alerted by their mother's yowling.

Erin got down on her hands and knees and crawled over to the corner with the towel. "Hey, you little fluff balls. We need to take you on a trip."

The largest kitten was black and white and he leaned to sniff her hand. She carefully picked him up by the scruff and put him on the towel. The other two kittens shied away in the corner, and Erin gently moved them to the towel with their sibling.

She scooped up the towel in her arms and the kittens made little tiny meows that tore at her heartstrings. She carefully placed the kittens and the towel in the box and carried it downstairs.

Momma Kitty was still in the cage, but quieter. Erin settled herself next to the woodstove, sitting cross-legged in front of her box of kittens. She opened the top and stroked their tiny heads while cooing what she hoped were comforting words.

Ziggy came back inside and sat down next to her in front of the stove. He peered into the box. "Is there anything cuter than a box of kittens?"

"I don't think so. Nope. I'm sure. There definitely isn't. Look at this little black-and-white guy. He's a total wooly bully."

"Aw, that's an easy one, Stardust. 'Wooly Bully' was recorded by Sam the Sham and The Pharaohs and hit the charts in 1965."

"The DJ on the Oldies Hour was a fan." Erin smiled at him. "I remember sitting right here listening to that song on the battery-powered transistor radio."

He returned her smile. "I think I liked that radio more than I like a lot of people now."

"I know what you mean."

~

Erin remained on kitten-watching duty while Ziggy finished going around the inside and the outside of the lodge. Then he loaded all the supplies back into the truck.

Finally, he picked up the cat carrier and gestured toward the door. "Grab your kittens, and let's get out of here."

Erin took her box of small meowing kitties and got it settled on the floor of the cab.

Ziggy had cleared out some space in the small extended-cab area behind the seats and put the cat carrier back there. Momma Kitty wasn't thrilled by the idea and was yowling her displeasure, which would make the long ride back to town seem even longer.

They left Dancing Cedars, and Ziggy turned on the radio to drown out the feline sounds of discontent. Erin peeked into the box. Even with the music and yowling, the kittens appeared to have fallen asleep, which showed that even youngsters shared the remarkable sleeping ability common to all felines.

After a few miles of driving, either exhaustion or the drone of the radio and the truck caused Momma Kitty to quiet down as well.

Ziggy turned down the music. "Is it okay with you if I stop by the farm and call the vet?"

"Sure. Why wouldn't it be?"

"I was afraid you might want to get home, instead of babysitting kittens."

"You're the one doing all the work. I've just been sitting around petting soft fur."

"Keeping them from escaping is good. And I'm not working. Dad would be the first person to tell you that wandering around the commune land is what I do when I goof off."

"I don't think trapping cats and fixing the lodge counts as goofing off."

"The fact I'd rather trap cats than work is probably me being lazy again, looking for something else to do."

"You said that before—that you're lazy. I'm not buying it. I think you have a mistaken perception of yourself."

Ziggy glanced at her and raised his eyebrows. "Whoa. Way to get all over my case."

"I'm serious." She pointed her finger at him. "You sound so down on yourself. What's that about?"

He raised a shoulder noncommittally, staring straight at the road. "Maybe getting away from the farm made me think about how long I've been doing the same thing because it's easier than figuring out anything else."

"You don't have to."

"I feel like I do. At this point, it's not like I'm going to set the world on fire with some high-powered career. That's not going to happen without a college degree. And my family needs the help." He gestured toward the road ahead. "You've seen how it is there."

"I wasn't talking about a career, but is there something you want to do?"

"Not worth thinking about, and the last time I had a conversation like this, the woman I had it with ran for the hills." He glanced at her. "Since I value your friendship, and I don't want to deal with cats by myself, I suggest we change the subject."

Erin sat in silence for a moment, dying of curiosity. Should she be nice and go for an innocuous subject like the weather? Nah, who was she kidding? "New subject. Tell me more about this woman who ran away."

"No fair. That's a derivative of the first subject."

Erin tapped his shoulder. "C'mon, spill. Who was she? What was she like? How long did it last?"

"She was one of the summer people. Extremely cute. Several summers."

"Okay. Now we're getting somewhere." Erin rubbed her hands together. "Now for follow-up questions. How did you meet? What did you like about her?"

"Give me a break, Stardust. Why are you asking about this? It doesn't matter, and it's old news."

"Because I want to know!" Erin wasn't just saying that either. She couldn't remember the last time she was interested in much of anything. But she was. "What happened with Ms. Cute Summer Woman?"

"It ended like every other relationship. I'm a bizarre small-town hick who lives at *home*. As you might imagine, that's not so great for your social life. My relationship history is like road kill on the superhighway of life, and I try not to think about it too much."

"I understand, but you have good reasons to stay at the farm."

"You get that, but try explaining it to anyone else." He waved his hand in exasperation. "Some people say I'm too lazy or stupid to leave, others say I'm codependent, others say I'm freeloading. I've heard it all."

Erin crossed her arms. "Maybe a little codependent, but I understand why. I'd probably have done the same thing. Your parents are kind people, and I'd want to help."

"That's nice of you to say."

"But you must have thought about leaving."

He glared at her. "Here it comes."

"Well, you have, haven't you?"

"Yes. *Constantly.* So I leave and do what? I know how to raise Christmas trees. Even around here, that's not a particularly marketable skill set."

Erin couldn't help but smile. "Okay, I see your point."

"If you have any bright ideas, let me know." He turned into the driveway and pulled up in front of the house. "In the meantime, keep an eye on those kittens while I run inside and call the vet."

Erin cooed at the kittens and listened to Momma Kitty's low growl for a few minutes. She couldn't remember the last time she'd talked this much with anyone. Okay, yes she could. It was the day before Andy's accident. They'd had a big discussion about her job interview, the direction of his career, and what they wanted to do next. The next day Andy was dead. More proof that no matter how many plans you might make, everything could change in an instant. All too often, the universe was random and tragic.

Ziggy opened the door to the truck, startling Erin from her dour thoughts. He leaned over to look at her face. "What happened to you?"

"Nothing."

"I leave for five minutes and you look like you're going to burst into tears. Did one of those furry monsters bite you?"

"No, nothing like that." She leaned down to peer into the box. "They're adorable. I think they like me now."

He started the truck. "Then what?"

"I was thinking about life plans. It's not just you. Everyone keeps pointing out to me that I should get some too. But the last time I did, it all fell apart. Now I'm half afraid to plan or dream about anything." Erin paused, suddenly feeling guilty. Why was she talking about life plans with Ziggy? She should be making plans with Andy. But why was she even thinking that? She couldn't. She shook her head, as if the movement could clear her addled mind. "I don't know. Never mind. I'll stop rambling at you. Sorry."

Ziggy put his hand on hers and gave it a squeeze. "It's okay. Sometimes rambling to someone is what you need. It makes you feel less alone."

"We're both a little messed up, aren't we?"

"Yeah, probably."

~

Ziggy drove into the parking lot of the Alpine Grove Veterinary Clinic and pulled into a spot. He turned to Erin, "The vet should be here already, so grab your kittens and bring them inside."

"This is nice of her to open the place for us."

Ziggy pulled the cage from the back, which led to an ominous growling from inside. "Momma Kitty isn't going to like this."

A tall woman with curly brown hair wearing a long white lab coat greeted Ziggy at the door. "Hi Dylan. Please take the cage into the back through that doorway."

Erin followed with her box and deposited it on a shiny metal treatment table. The kittens were mewing inside, clearly aware that they were somewhere very different.

Ziggy set the cage full of growling feline in the corner and walked back to the table. "Thanks for dealing with this on a Sunday, Dr. Cassidy."

The vet peered inside the box and smiled at the kittens. "It's getting colder and I want to help you get these guys set up before winter hits."

"We caught these in the lodge, but I think there are a few ferals outside. Like I told you, I'm going to be doing repairs to block them out and then build them a shelter. That means I might be back tomorrow. And maybe the next day. It depends on how smart they get about the traps."

The vet pulled the black-and-white kitten out of the box and held it up to examine him. "Well, this one is a male." She handed the wriggly kitten to Erin and pulled out a small solid black kitten.

Erin snuggled the kitten to her chest. "This guy is the ringleader, I think."

Dr. Cassidy handed the black kitten to Ziggy and grabbed the final kitten from the box. "She's female, and they're all healthy and old enough to be weaned. All they need is some shots, and they'll be good to go. Why don't you wait in the lobby while I get the mother settled into a cage? It will be better if there are fewer people in the room."

Erin and Ziggy hurriedly returned to the lobby, closing the door behind them. Erin made a face at a yowling noise from the other room and Ziggy raised his eyebrows and grimaced in response.

A few moments later, Dr. Cassidy opened the door and walked behind the desk, setting the box of kittens on the counter along with a grocery bag. She leaned over to scribble some notes and then looked at Erin and Ziggy. "You can pick up the cat tomorrow. I'm going to spay her as soon as you leave."

"What about the kittens?" Erin asked as she pulled aside one of the box flaps to peek at the kittens.

"I vaccinated them and packaged up a few supplies to tide you over until you get to the store. Dylan said you're getting them adopted, right? I'm finishing up a couple of notes, but you can take them home now."

Erin turned to Ziggy. "So you're taking them, right?"

"Nope. I can't take them. We have crowds of people at our house getting trees." He patted her shoulder. "I can't even leave Moose there alone, so I nominate you to be the official kitten foster lady."

"Hold on. Don't I get a vote? I can't take a bunch of kittens. My parents will kill me. Plus you know Casey doesn't like cats."

"It's a big house, and Casey is pretty old. I'm sure you'll figure something out."

Dr. Cassidy handed Erin a business card. "Talk to Brigid. She runs the dog rescue in town, but she's great at marketing. She might have ideas to help you find them homes. Maybe they can be Christmas kitties."

Erin glared at Ziggy. "Maybe you can spare a few of those jingle-bear suits your mom is making."

He grinned. "Sure. I have to drive back out and get Moose, but I'll drop you and the wee ones at your house first."

"Drive slowly. I need some time to figure out how to break the news to my parents that they're babysitting kittens. I can't believe I have to have this conversation with them."

"Life is full of choices that might appear to be bad ideas. But at least they make your life interesting."

Erin tried not to roll her eyes, opting instead to simply glare at him. "Thanks for that philosophical interlude."

After they said their good-byes to Dr. Cassidy, Ziggy drove Erin and the kittens back to her parents' house. He waited to make sure she and the kittens got inside okay, but both of them knew it was better if Erin broke the feline news to her parents alone.

Casey ran up to her and jumped up on her, trying to sniff at the exciting box she had in her hands. She shooed him away. "*No* Casey. Where's Mom?"

She wandered down the hall to her mother's office and used her knuckles to tap on the door.

Mom spun around in her office chair and set aside the notebook she was holding. "Did you bring something back from Dancing Cedars?"

With a feeble grin, Erin set the box and the bag of supplies on the desk. "Funny you should mention that actually. I have a little surprise for you."

The kittens rustled in the box and started meowing plaintively. Jennifer widened her eyes and leaned over to peer into the box. "Erin, why have you put a litter of kittens on my desk?"

"Aren't they cute? We need to find them homes." She picked up the bold black-and-white boy and thrust him into her mother's hands. "I've been calling him the wooly bully because he's the bravest one."

Jennifer cradled the kitten and her expression melted. "Hey there little guy. How are you doing?"

Erin mentally congratulated herself. Mom was a goner. These kittens were going to get great homes. The vet had given Erin some cat litter, a temporary litter box, and some food. Jennifer helped Erin get the kitties set up in the half bathroom on the first floor with their supplies and some blankets. Paul pulled himself away from his latest puzzle to see what the fuss was about and he and Jennifer snuggled and cooed at the kittens.

Erin hadn't seen her parents so engaged since she'd been back in Alpine Grove, and it was incredibly sweet. She felt a little mean for assuming they'd reject fostering a trio of innocent homeless kittens. Amid all her hang-ups and drama related to the commune, she'd lost sight of the fact that her parents were extremely compassionate, kind people.

After the kittens snarfed down some food, they fell asleep in a corner of the bathroom on their blanket, snuggling up with one another in a furry pile of cuteness.

All the time they'd spent at Dancing Cedars and then dealing with cats had worn Erin out, so after dinner, she retired to her room to read. She took Casey with her, leaving her parents to play with the kittens, who were wide awake again.

In bed curled up with Casey by her side, Erin settled into her book. She was still working on *Pride and Prejudice* with limited enthusiasm. Occasionally, she heard bursts of laughter from downstairs and her parents exclaiming about various kitty antics. After a while, her head literally started nodding as sleep began to overtake her. It had been a long day out in the cold, and she set her book aside. She closed her eyes and went through her typical routine of counting backward to quiet her mind, loosen her muscles, and relax.

Another peal of laughter echoed, and she turned her head because it didn't sound like her parents. Droplets of water splashed on her arm and in front of her Ziggy was clutching his stomach and laughing so hard he had tears streaming down his face. He was wearing a sky blue t-shirt that was one of the many tie dyes his mom had made during her pastel phase when they'd been about twelve years old. A black-and-white kitten was sitting next to him with a cartoonish Cheshire-cat grin.

The kitten pointed his paw at her and Erin looked down, surveying the long elegant yellow dress, which was covered with mud. She was lying spread-eagled in a puddle and her grimy state of disarray was apparently the source of Ziggy's and the kitten's mutual amusement. What was going on? Why would she wear an empire-waist Regency gown into a mud puddle? Had she tripped? Had Ziggy tripped her? He better not have. She yelled, "Shut up."

He caught his breath long enough to shout, "*You* shut up."

Erin scooped up some mud in her hand and threw it at him. When the clot of grime splattered across the front of his t-shirt, the expression on his face was so classic Ziggy, Erin burst into laughter. The kitten spun around, chasing his tail.

Ziggy ran toward her, slipped, and slid face first in the mud next to her, landing so hard that Erin stopped laughing. "Are you okay?"

He scooped up a fistful of dirt and slapped it on her skirt with a hoot of laughter. "I'm *great*. But we're gonna be in such big trouble. Your mom made that dress."

The rain suddenly increased in intensity and they both looked up. Erin pushed her soggy hair off her cheek and pointed at the sky. "This is the universe punishing you."

"Me? You started it." He slapped his hand on the puddle, splashing her, and somehow making the mud snort under his palm in a rude way. They both dissolved into laughter again.

At a poke on her arm, Erin started awake and found Casey looming over her wagging his tail. Her stomach hurt from laughing so much. She reached up to pet the dog's head. "Did I wake you? Sorry about that."

Seemingly convinced that Erin was unharmed, Casey settled in next to her again. Erin rolled over and stared at the ceiling. When she'd complained about how dirty she'd always been at Dancing Cedars, she hadn't thought about *how* she got so dirty.

She'd forgotten how much fun it was to play in the mud. The dress might be ruined, but the next time her therapist asked about moments of joy, she'd be able to come up with an example.

Chapter 9

Ephemeral Details

Erin didn't remember other dreams she might have had after the muddy one with the waving kitten. Perhaps her addled mind was too exhausted to think up anything more off-the-wall than that one. On a positive note, a welcome benefit of laughing like a lunatic in your dreams is that it left you in a pretty good mood the next morning.

Her parents seemed unusually cheerful as well. When Erin came downstairs for breakfast, they'd been discussing the list of kitten supplies that they needed to acquire at the store.

After Jennifer fed Casey, she handed Erin a mug of coffee. "I heard you laughing last night. Did Casey do something silly in your room?"

Erin set down her mug. "It was probably when I was asleep. I had a funny dream."

"What was it about?"

"Well, it didn't make a lot of sense. I've been having weird dreams since I've been here." Erin made a wry face. "In this one, I fell in the mud at Dancing Cedars when I was a kid. It was raining and the black-and-white kitten waved at me. And Ziggy was there throwing mud at me. It was stupid."

"I don't think it's stupid." Jennifer said. She took a sip of coffee. "You spent all day at Dancing Cedars, so you're probably processing memories, aligning them with what's going on now."

"I doubt it's anything that logical. Although I know why I was filthy all the time when we lived there."

Paul set down his mug. "That's true. But you also were the happiest kids I've ever seen. I talk to parents now who have nothing but troubles with their children. Looking back, I can't believe how easy we had it."

"Your father is right. At Dancing Cedars, you and Ziggy kept yourself amused with all those stories. You were so smart and creative. To be quite honest, I've always been a little envious of your childhood."

"You had a lot of people to help out." Erin said. "But it was a strange way to grow up. After we left, everyone thought I was some kind of freak."

"Maybe, but you turned out fine. Better than fine. I think some kids wouldn't have done well with so much freedom to learn and explore, but you did," Jennifer said. "And now look at you. You're brilliant and successful."

"Well I don't feel like it at the moment," Erin said.

Jennifer shook her head. "You're coming back into your own. I can feel it. I think it has been good for you to get away from your day-to-day life."

"I agree," Paul said. "You'll figure things out. I'm glad you're here taking some time to relax. We've been worried about you, and we're behind you one-hundred percent, no matter what you do."

"Absolutely," Jennifer added.

Erin got up and gave her parents hugs. "Thanks. I appreciate the vote of confidence."

After breakfast, Erin went back to her room to read through documents. She was sorting through more piles of papers when her mother yelled up the stairs that she had a phone call.

She rushed downstairs and her mother handed her the phone. "It's the airport."

Erin had a depressing chat with the airline that despite their very best efforts, they still hadn't found her suitcase. When the polite man on the other end asked how long she'd be in Alpine Grove, Erin said, "Um, I'm not sure."

"Your case was upgraded to an intensive search because there was a little problem with the luggage on several of our flights that day. We need to know when you're returning to your home address."

"What do you mean a little problem?"

"We're working on the issue, and I need to verify your travel plans."

Erin tried not to sigh in the guy's ear. He was being extremely courteous, and it was probably best that she didn't know the details of the airline's little problem. "Please use this address and phone number for the time being. Thank you for following up."

After spending more time raiding Mom's closet, Erin read and sorted through some more papers until Ziggy picked her up for the trip to Dancing Cedars.

When he drove up, Erin dashed out the door and stopped at the sight of the truck. Although the dirty old truck was maroon, Ziggy had acquired a mismatched and incredibly ugly aluminum cap that now covered the bed. The covering was rusty white with blue stripes and so many dents that it looked like it had barely survived a wreck.

She opened the door to the cab and was greeted by the muted sound of yowling feline coming from the bed of the truck. Moose was fogging up the inside of the cab with his panting breath.

"Way to trick out your ride," Erin said with a grin as she shoved Moose over. "Stylish."

"Shut up. It was free."

"I can see why."

"Hey, don't knock it. A few years ago, I had to sweet talk the lady at the dump into letting me have it. When I moved back home, I needed to transport stuff in the rain. I put it back on last night because I need a way to transport Moose and an angry cat at the same time."

"So what you're saying is that necessity is the mother of ugly camper shells."

He laughed. "Yeah, something like that. You're in a good mood for someone who is about to go clean up cat pee."

"Things at home are better. My parents aren't yelling. I think cute kittens helped. They said some nice things to me this morning."

Ziggy glanced at her. "Like what?"

Erin shrugged. "They were supportive. I mean they always have been, but it was the way they said it. I guess I sort of forgot what it's like to be part of a family again."

"Your parents were always there. They didn't go anywhere."

"I know, but I haven't seen them much. It's been a long time since I've been around anyone who knows me and cares how I feel." Erin shrugged. "I'm not explaining it well, but it was different in a good way."

"Does this mean you're rethinking your idea of running back to the empty apartment that 12-year old dream me hates?"

"I don't know about that, but I think I should at least stay through the solstice." She looked up at his face. "I want to see how everything works out with Dancing Cedars."

"If Bea manages to get everyone back for this reunion party, it could be pretty nuts."

"I know. But it's okay. Mom says I'm processing memories. Who knows, maybe she's right. I was thinking that I've spent my whole life since we left the commune terrified of being an outsider, trying to fit in, and always desperate to belong."

"And today your parents made you feel like you belong, didn't they?"

She turned to look at him. "Yes, exactly. Sometimes you're bizarrely perceptive."

"I think being part of a family means being surrounded by people who make you feel welcome and like you belong there." He shrugged. "That's a good thing, but it can be kinda smothering sometimes too."

"I suppose so. And Dancing Cedars was like a gigantic family."

"Taking suffocation to a new level." He sighed. "If this reunion ends up being a perpetual pow-wow on steroids, I might have a nervous breakdown."

Erin patted his hand on the steering wheel. "You'll survive."

"Maybe." He glanced at her. "Speaking of belonging, have you considered the possibility that maybe Alpine Grove is where you belong?"

"What? Absolutely not. Visiting is one thing, but I couldn't *live* here again."

"Why not?"

"What would I do? I definitely do *not* want to do seminars with my mom. Moving here is a ridiculous idea."

"Maybe. Maybe not. Think about it."

~

They dropped off Moose at the kennel, and Erin met Mia, the groomer who had de-skunked the dog. Mia didn't say much, but she obviously liked Moose, even if she was a little shy around Erin and Ziggy.

They got back into the truck and resumed the trek north through the trees and out to the commune. The weather was unsettled with gray clouds that looked like they may or may not have ideas about precipitation. Erin was hoping it wouldn't snow because she was worried about the cats. Ziggy said that the vet wanted them to keep the mother cat in the truck while they worked, then release her right before they left. Ziggy had brought wood to create the feral shelter.

The trees whirred by in a blur of dark green until they turned onto the first of the dirt roads that led out to the commune. Erin said, "You must be sick of driving out here."

"The drive is okay as long as the truck doesn't fall apart on these washboards. Over the summer, I was going to do some suspension work on it, but I never got around to it. I'm afraid the shocks are shot."

Ziggy parked in front of the Hodgepodge Lodge and they began unloading stuff from the back of the truck and bringing it inside. He had brought a wide range of tools, stepladders, lumber, the generator, and boxes of hardware and cleaning supplies. They were ready to attack a wide range of problems, and Erin was more than a little daunted by how much they had to do. But there was no turning back now. The more time she'd spent at Dancing Cedars, the more Erin felt Bea was right about the conservation easement. The land here was special, and Erin wanted to be part of helping to keep it that way.

She gathered the pile of rags and towels, along with a bucket, and filled it with water from the old, rusty pump. "I'm going to tackle the disgusting corner near the counter."

"Sounds good." Ziggy was holding the stepladder and a caulking gun. "I'm heading upstairs to fill holes. I dug up the old radio and put new batteries in it, if you want some tunes. It's in the box over there."

Erin turned on the radio and set to work. She started by sweeping up disgusting residue that was better left unexamined and then moved into the realm of scrubbing.

She sang along when a good song came on the radio, but the mindless cleaning also gave her a lot of time to think. What Ziggy had said about staying in Alpine Grove nagged at her.

It wasn't like she'd been living some fabulous dream life for the last two years. The work she did as a temp had nothing to do with anything she cared about. It was simply a means to pay the bills.

She hadn't done anything she cared about for two years. Mostly she'd slept, trying to escape thoughts of Andy. Oddly, letting herself dream about him again had helped her grief. She still missed him desperately every hour of every day, but part of her had let go of a little bit of the anger.

Inexplicably, talking to Ziggy about TASTE had helped more than talking to a therapist ever had. In the beginning, talking or even thinking about TASTE led to crushing waves of sadness. But since she'd been in Alpine Grove, talking about it as part of her past made the pain a little less visceral.

Was she finally moving on? Letting herself dream of doing something different? Something beyond simply existing? What if she worked at something she loved, instead of killing time at a temp job for a paycheck to buy groceries? Maybe starting over required figuring out what she cared about now. Could she face trying? She wasn't sure, but she was grateful no one was pressuring her to make any hard decisions. After her mother's initial bout of questions, she'd left Erin alone. And at the moment, all she had to deal with was what was right in front of her. Which was dirt. A whole lot of dirt.

Ziggy came downstairs for their lunch break, and Erin pulled out the sandwiches Jennifer had made for them that morning. They sat at the old wooden table quietly eating.

Erin put down her sandwich. "You've been awfully quiet up there. How's it going plugging the holes?"

"There's not enough caulk in the world to patch the stuff falling out between the logs. All the ancient chinking crumbles if you touch it." He raised his eyebrows. "I know what you're going to say. Don't touch it. But I did. Oops."

"I did too. It ends up all over the floor."

"I decided to focus on holes that are actually in the wood, not between the logs. I need to find out from Dad what they used to chink this place."

"Did he do it? I thought the building was already here."

"I'm not sure." He shrugged. "Dad might have done repairs, so he might know what that gray filler stuff actually is. Dad has all kinds of obscure knowledge socked away in that head of his."

Erin giggled. "Remember when he showed us how to make candles?"

"Otherwise known as The Dipping Disaster of 1973. After that, he bought candles at the store and vowed never to let us near melted substances ever again."

"I know. What a mess. I scraped some wax off the floor over there a little while ago. It seemed fitting, since I'm the one who probably spilled it."

After lunch, Ziggy put on his coat and went outside to rehabilitate the former chicken coop and turn it into a shelter for wayward felines. He told her to listen for the sound of the cat-trap door slamming shut upstairs.

Erin moved on to sanding with the goal of removing some of the most egregious smells from the floor in the corner that had been the kitty toilet. She grabbed sandpaper and a rubber sanding block and set to work.

As she sanded the old wood, she reflected on the various dreams she'd had about Andy. What was with all the snow? She never could see him clearly, which was incredibly frustrating and mysterious. In the dreams, she was always chasing to catch up with him.

She sat back on her heels, grabbed the scissors, and cut a new piece of sandpaper for the block. Racing through the snow wasn't that different from real life. She'd always been chasing Andy, figuratively speaking. He was such a hard worker and so smart, he drove her to be her best. It was like they'd had an unspoken contest. Who could work harder, get the best job, make the best grades. No wonder she did so well in college. In terms of career, Washington, D.C. was all about work. The first thing anyone asked was what you did for a living.

It was funny that when Ziggy had asked about Andy, he pointed out that he didn't ask what Andy did, he asked what he was like. No one ever said anything like that back in DC. Everyone was trying to place people on a little ladder of status. But with Ziggy there was no pretense. He knew the person she truly was. And let's face it, feigning a cultured, cosmopolitan persona with a guy who'd seen her covered in mud would be difficult.

If she were being brutally honest with herself, being here and hanging out with Ziggy was a heck of a lot easier than rushing back to D.C. to find a job. That probably made her a lazy slob, but at this point, competing against a bunch of high-powered workaholics sounded far too exhausting.

The lodge door opened with a whoosh of cold air and Ziggy slammed it behind him. He shook his arms, throwing his coat on the floor.

Noting the furious expression on his face, Erin stood up. "What happened? Are you okay?"

"No, I'm *not* okay."

~

Ziggy held out his right arm, then clutched it to his chest with his other hand. "I put the chicken coop back together, but I tripped on a roll of wire and sprained my damn wrist *again*."

Erin walked to him and tried to reach for his hand. "What do you mean *again*? Were you hurt before?"

"It's not a big deal." He stepped backward away from her. "Almost every year, I fall off a ladder or trip and land on my hand. It pisses me off that I keep re-injuring the same ligament. I suppose it's better than landing on my head, but it still hurts."

"Let me see." Erin reached out and he let her pull his arm away from his chest. "This whole side of your hand is bruised, and I think your wrist is swelling up. You need to go to a doctor."

"No I don't. It will be fine in a couple days." He pulled his hand away. "But I do need ice, which we don't have here."

"Mom suggested bringing a cooler, but I didn't think we needed it for sandwiches."

"Could you drive us back to town? It's hard to drive one-handed. I've tried before, and shifting gears is a problem."

"I don't have a license."

He squinted at her. "You don't have a driver's license? Are you kidding me?"

"I didn't have a car. My license expired, and I didn't get around to getting a new one. My passport proves to anyone who cares that I am who I say I am. I was in a city with good public transportation, so I rode the subway and buses a lot." She ran her fingertips along the top of his wrist and held out her other hand below his. "Try to grip my hand."

"No. And ow, would you cut that out?"

"I can't tell if you've broken something or not. We should leave everything here. You need to see a doctor."

"No I don't. It's a sprain."

"Let's release the cat, go get Moose, and get you home."

Ziggy grumbled something under his breath as he bent to pick up his coat and put it back on. "I need to unplug some stuff from the generator and bring it inside."

Erin tidied up her dusty workspace, dumped her nasty bucket of cleaning water outside, and ran upstairs to check the cat trap. It was empty. Maybe the cats were getting wise to the situation. When she went outside, Ziggy was pulling the second cat trap and blanket out of the back of the truck. Momma Kitty was growling ominously.

She ran over to him and took the trap. "I can do that."

"Let's take it over there near the coop." He strode away from her. "The stupid roll of wire I tripped over is out of the way."

Erin set down the trap and pulled the blanket off the top. They crouched next to it, and Ziggy pointed at the release lever and explained how to open the trap door.

Erin let Momma Kitty out, and the cat launched into the chicken coop shelter. Erin picked up the trap by the handle. The blanket smelled extremely bad, so she plucked it off the ground with two fingers and held it out away from her. "Let's go. I'm worried about your wrist."

When they got to the truck, Erin opened the shell door and the tailgate and heaved the blanket and trap into the bed. Ziggy waited with his left wrist trapped under his right arm. He had a pinched, miserable expression on his face.

Erin reached for his arm again. "Let me look at it."

"Why? It's swelling up, okay? You already know that. When was the last time you drove a truck?"

"It's been a while." Erin paused. She'd never driven a truck, but she wasn't worried about that. It was time to come clean. "There's another little problem. I've never driven a vehicle with a manual transmission before. You'll have to teach me."

"Oh jeez. It figures." He stomped over to the driver's side and got in.

Erin stood at the window and waved at him. He shook his head, so she ran around to the passenger side, opened the door, and leaned her head in. "What are you doing? I'll drive. How hard could it be? The clutch is on the floor, right?"

"Get in. I'm not letting you trash the transmission. This truck has enough problems. We'll tag team."

"What are you talking about?"

"Just get in. I'll work the clutch, you operate the gearshift. I'll tell you when to shift gears."

"I doubt this is legal." Erin got in and looked down at the gearshift. "How is this supposed to work?"

He leaned around and put the key into the ignition with his left hand and moved the gearshift. "Well, for one thing, you're going to have to scooch over closer to me."

Erin moved across the bench seat and Ziggy lifted his right arm, laying it across the seat back. He reached across with his left hand to tug on her sleeve. "Oh come on. I don't have cooties. You need to be able to reach the gearshift."

Erin was uncomfortable with the close proximity. She felt like she was practically in his lap. She pointed at the gearshift. "So the little diagram says first is up. Do I just move it?"

"Not before I put in the clutch. Try turning the key first. Driving works better when the truck is running."

"Oh yeah. That would help." She twisted the key in the ignition and the old truck coughed to life.

"Now put it into reverse. It's in neutral now, so move it to the right and down."

Erin leaned over and tried to follow his instructions, but something was wrong. "It won't go down."

"This truck is old. You have to put a little muscle into it. Shove it hard to the right and down. It doesn't like reverse."

"It doesn't *like* it." She glanced at him. "Really?"

"Did I mention the truck is old? It's set in its ways."

Erin yanked the lever right and struggled to get it to go downward. "It won't work."

"Use both hands."

Erin took a deep breath, grabbed the gearshift with both hands, and jammed it right and down. "I did it."

Ziggy steered the truck backward in a large circle and stopped. "Forward ho."

Erin yanked the gearshift out of reverse and rammed it into first. "Go!"

Fortunately, they didn't need or want to go fast down the rutted dirt road, so Erin was able to relax for a moment. In his big ugly work coat Ziggy was warm, and the body heat was comforting. It was cold out there.

He stopped and got out to close and lock the gate behind them. He handed Erin the keys. "Put it in neutral and fire it up."

The truck didn't seem to enjoy the process of Erin and Ziggy figuring out how to shift through the gears together, but they got into a rhythm, so by the time Ziggy said, "Fourth," it was relatively smooth.

They picked up Moose from Mia the groomer, who had brushed him out and cleaned him up a little. The dog seemed proud of his newly fluffed-up fur and was clearly thrilled that

Erin was now in the middle seat, so he could score shotgun and drool on the window.

When they got on the highway, they successfully got the truck up to fourth gear and Erin was able to relax while they cruised back toward town. Driving a manual transmission was a lot of work. What a pain. She nudged Moose, who was taking up more than his fair share of real estate on the bench seat, but he was fast asleep and didn't budge.

Ziggy glanced down at her. "What's wrong?"

"Let me see your wrist again."

He moved his arm from the back of the seat over her head and put it in front of her. "Ta-da."

She touched it gently. "It's swollen. Maybe you can leave the truck at our house, and Mom can drive you home."

"She's not going to want to do that."

"I'll talk her into it. This is an emergency."

"No it's not. She can follow us and take you home. You can take a few days off."

"But what about trapping the cats and all the stuff we left?"

"I'll get Dad to take me out. Downshift, please. We need to slow down."

Erin shifted and sulked as they entered Alpine Grove. She wasn't going to let the parental dispute keep her from going back out to Dancing Cedars. There was still so much to do.

Ziggy parked in front of the house and he turned to her. "Okay, I'll hang out here while you talk to your mom about following us."

"No, this is stupid. You're coming inside."

"Why?"

She tugged at his coat. "Don't be stubborn. I want her to look at your wrist. We can put some ice on it. Then I'll get her to drive you home."

He twisted and leaned back on the door and tucked his right wrist under his arm again. "Nope. I'm not getting in the middle."

Erin pulled her knees under her and used both hands to try to pull him away from the door.

He laughed and flailed his arms in mock helplessness. "You do realize you can't force me to move. Even moving Moose would be easier."

"I can't believe how stubborn you are." She tried to shake him loose from his recumbent position, but only shook his coat, which had zero effect. "Would you move?"

"Not gonna happen. Your parents don't want to lay eyes on me, and that's fine with me."

"Don't be such a jerk." Tired of shaking, she collapsed onto his chest. "I'll sit on you like I did when we were twelve."

He wrapped his long arms around her. Their faces were inches apart, and he raised his eyebrows. "That might not work out so well. We're not little kids anymore, Stardust."

"No we're not." She acknowledged the question in those amazing blue eyes by kissing his lips softly. "We're not."

❧

A few intense minutes later, Erin finally pushed herself away, and she and Ziggy stared at each other for a moment. She wasn't sure what had come over her, and now she had no idea what to say or what he might be thinking.

He traced her jawline with his thumb. "What are you doing?"

"I don't know. Your lips looked so soft, and I wanted to… um, well, I don't know. But they *are* soft. Really nice."

"Thank you, I guess."

She looked behind her and turned back to offer a weak smile. "Moose is literally breathing down my neck. Will you *please* come inside?"

He tried to sit up straighter and held his injured wrist above his head, so she could maneuver. "All right. But you need to move over."

She scrambled toward the passenger side of the truck and shoved Moose aside so she could snake around the dog and get out the door. This was so weird. What *was* she doing? Throwing herself at Ziggy, of all people? Had she completely lost her mind? What about Andy? Didn't she still love him? Ziggy was, well, Ziggy. He was her friend. Probably the best friend she'd ever had. But now she'd found out that among his other skills, he knew how to kiss. Really well. Wow.

She wasn't lying about his lips. After all the time she'd spent with him, watching him talk, eat, smile, and laugh, somehow she'd never thought about what his lips might feel like before. But now it would be difficult *not* to think about his lips and that kiss again. And again and again, pretty much whenever she was around him.

She got out of the truck and stood next to Ziggy, who was staring up at the pretty house and holding his wrist under his arm again.

Grabbing his free hand, she dragged him up the steps to the door and pulled him inside. Casey rushed into the hallway with a great clattering of claws and Ziggy crouched down to say hi. "Hey there, Casey. You're supposed to be watching your speed, remember?"

Erin said, "The kitchen is through here. Let's get you that ice."

She threw some ice into a plastic bag and handed it to him. "Mom is probably in her office. Don't run off."

Ziggy took off his coat and sat at the table, but didn't say anything. He arranged the bag around his wrist, looking irritated.

It didn't seem like he was going to make a break for it, so Erin went down the hallway and found her mother in her office, talking on the telephone. Erin waved to get her attention, and Jennifer smiled at her. "I have to go. My daughter is here. I'll talk to you soon."

Once the phone was in the cradle, Erin blurted out, "I need your help."

Jennifer got up. "Why are you all flushed? Is something wrong? Are you sick?"

"I'm fine, but Ziggy hurt his wrist."

Jennifer furrowed her brow. "Is he all right?"

"He's in the kitchen."

Jennifer started toward the door, and Erin followed her. "I was hoping he could leave his truck here and you could drive him home and then pick him up tomorrow morning so we can drive back out to the commune."

Jennifer strode to the kitchen table and Ziggy looked up. "Hi Saffron…Jennifer…um, Mrs. Quinn."

"Let me see." Jennifer sat next to him and held out her hands. Ziggy removed the ice and held out his arm.

Jennifer ran her fingertips up along his wrist. "I don't think anything is broken, but you're all bruised. The wrist has a lot of small bones. How does it feel?"

"I told Star—Erin—that it's no big deal. I sprain my wrist almost every year." He pulled his arm away and put the bag of ice back on it. "Right now it hurts, but it will be okay in a couple days."

Jennifer looked up at Erin, who was hovering over her shoulder, and turned back to Ziggy. "Erin wants me to drive you home."

A corner of his mouth turned up in a half smile. "Yes, she does. Sometimes she can be a little bossy."

"That's an insightful observation," Jennifer said. "Are you in a rush? I was about to call for a pizza. Would you like to join us for dinner?"

Erin said, "Please stay."

He smiled. "Thanks. Pizza sounds great. Mom mentioned some casserole thing with brown rice and Brussels sprouts. I'm okay with missing it."

Paul walked into the kitchen. "What's all the commotion about?

Erin and Jennifer stepped aside and Ziggy waved. Although Paul was clearly surprised, he managed to sound unconcerned. "Hello Dylan. I didn't know you were here."

"He's joining us for dinner," Jennifer said. "I'd like to talk to you about my phone call from Donna. I also need to call in a pizza order. Let's go to my office."

Paul followed Jennifer out of the room, and Erin raised her eyebrows at Ziggy. "Do you ever feel like we're in the middle of a party where everybody knows something you don't?"

He laughed. "All the time."

She sat next to him. "For the record, I'm not bossy."

"Not lately, but you used to be. I'm glad to see you being you again."

Erin looked down at her hands in her lap. "So, about earlier, um, I don't know what happened."

"What do you want me to say?"

She looked up. "I'm not sure."

"You know how I feel. I'm already dreading you leaving Alpine Grove."

"I'm not leaving immediately. The main thing is that I don't want to screw up our friendship.

"Not going to happen, okay? Spending all this time with you has been…well, I'm not sure how to explain it. Kind of a relief, I guess." He rearranged the bag of ice on his wrist. "I haven't had anyone I could talk to in a long time. Maybe I can stop pouring out my guts in writing all the time."

"You write?" She pointed at his wrist. "That's not going to help."

"I can't believe you forgot I'm left-handed."

"Oh yeah, we both are." She raised her left fist. "Lefties unite! We're going to take over the world."

"I'll settle for a tiny corner, thanks."

"Is your wrist feeling better? I'd like to show you some of the Dancing Cedars documents." She leaned over to examine his wrist. The side of his hand below his thumb was turning purple, and she ran her fingertips over the area. "This looks painful."

"Stardust, please…"

"What are you two up to?" Jennifer said as she returned into the kitchen.

Erin and Ziggy lurched away from each other and Erin said, "Mom, don't sneak up on me like that."

Jennifer narrowed her eyes. "I know that look. It means you're doing something I wouldn't like, if I knew about it."

"We're talking about Dancing Cedars. There's a lot to do," Erin said.

Jennifer looked unconvinced. "What do you mean *do*? I thought you were going for a hike."

"We did," Erin said.

"Your father has gone to get the pizza. While we wait, would you like to honestly share what you're doing out there?"

Erin glanced at Ziggy, "We're cleaning it up a little."

"Why? When we went out for Thanksgiving, it was the first time anyone had been there in a long time." Jennifer raised her eyebrows. "What's going on?"

Erin still hadn't mentioned Bea's big reunion idea because as far as she was concerned, telling people was Bea's responsibility, not hers. But it didn't explain why they were cleaning up the Hodgepodge Lodge. "I um, I…"

Ziggy said, "You saw that there were cats inside the lodge. We're fixing holes to keep them out and trapping them and taking them to the vet to get them fixed. I'm making the cats a shelter for the winter."

Erin nodded vigorously. "Yes, that's what we're doing. We need to go back out because we left everything there."

"Like my tools," Ziggy added.

Jennifer crossed her arms. "I'm sensing that this isn't the full story, but it's nice of you to help out. And I'm glad you saved those innocent little kittens. Winter would not be kind."

Erin nudged Ziggy and pointed toward the ceiling. "So about that stuff?"

"What?" He looked up, then back at her. "Oh yeah, okay."

"Let us know when Dad gets back with the pizza." Erin got up and Ziggy followed her upstairs.

Erin shut the door behind herself, pulled the brown folder off the dresser, and started spreading documents on the bed.

Ziggy leaned over her shoulder. "What am I supposed to be looking at here?"

Erin pointed at a pile of papers. "That one is the forestry plan. That's the conservation easement information. That's tax information going back for years. That's a list of recent land sales in the general area. And that one is miscellaneous stuff like photographs."

"Okay." He picked up a photo of the meadow in springtime. It was covered in wildflowers with the evergreens lining one side. "This looks familiar."

"Where's the legal information? The deed? Proof of sale? I mean has anyone done a title search?"

"How should I know?" He set the photo back on its pile. "Why are you asking me?"

"Did Bea give you any more stuff? Is this it?" Erin shook the folder to emphasize it was empty.

"I can't help you." Ziggy sat down on the bed, holding his wrist. "You'll have to ask her."

"I was hoping maybe she told you that there was more information coming."

"Nope."

"I thought this would be easy." She sank down onto the bed next to him. "Go over some documents and say, 'looks okay' and move on."

"Nothing with Dancing Cedars is ever simple. Even your mom thinks we're up to no good."

"It's probably her analyzing more ephemeral details of our relationship."

"What?"

"Never mind." She waved her hand dismissively. When she looked at him, their eyes met, and the way he was staring at her made her stomach go all fluttery. "What? Is something wrong?"

Without saying anything or averting his eyes from hers, he leaned over and kissed her slowly and deliberately.

Erin put her arms around his neck, accepting the moment because after all, she had started it.

Jennifer shouted from downstairs, "Erin, the pizza is here!"

Erin let go of Ziggy, and exhaled a breathy, "Wow."

"I know. We can't keep doing this." He picked up the ice pack and put it back on his wrist. "It's my fault. While you were talking, all I could think about was kissing you again. Then the word ephemeral sounded sexy and I couldn't help myself."

Erin laughed. "My mom *is* a relationship expert. We'll blame it on her."

He put his hand on hers and said quietly, "No, I'm serious. I can't do this. We need to stop, or it's going to wreck me."

Taken aback, she turned her hand over and interlaced her fingers with his. "I don't know what you mean. We're fine."

"You can have anyone you want. And I know that's not someone like me. So let's not do this anymore. Pretend it never happened, okay?"

Erin nodded, feeling a little sick. What did they just decide? "Okay."

Chapter 10

Nobody Does It Better

After the pizza, Jennifer drove Ziggy home, and Erin retired to her room with Casey. She put the piles back into the accordion folder. If Bea didn't have any other documents, somebody would have to go to the county offices and do a title search. Odds were good that she'd be nominated for that task.

She lifted Casey onto the bed and got under the covers. Reaching for her book, she changed her mind, left the book alone, and rolled over on her side. After the long day, she was exhausted and reading nineteenth-century fiction seemed to mess with her dreams.

She closed her eyes, and although her body was physically tired, her mind was extremely and annoyingly awake, busy dwelling on the day's events. She opened her eyes and stared at the ceiling. What was Ziggy thinking right now? Was he thinking about her as much as she was thinking about him? He'd said that they should pretend that they'd never kissed. Yeah, right. That was like showing someone a piece of chocolate and saying, now don't think about chocolate. What's the first thing that pops into your mind? Luscious, sweet, gooey, chocolate goodness.

She rolled back onto her side and squeezed her eyes shut, then counted backward from ten a few times. It wasn't working. All her thoughts kept going back to Ziggy.

Was there something in particular about warm milk that helped you sleep? Warm milk always sounded revolting. But hot chocolate was basically warm milk with cocoa, and it was yummy. Did the jingle-bear guy drink lots of hot chocolate? Probably everyone out at the tree farm did, including Ziggy. Ugh, stop it. Shut up, brain. Don't think. Count back from ten.

Ten, nine, eight, seven, six, five, four, three. And we have ignition. Two, one. Liftoff.

Erin screamed as g-forces slammed her against the side of the cocoa hut she'd painted at the Bryant tree farm. She hung onto the green window trim, hoping that it would support her weight and not tear off, sending her hurtling to the ground. The farm disappeared beneath her, the Christmas trees shrinking to little dots on the landscape below. Her hands hurt, and she couldn't hold on much longer. What if she simply let go? At least it would be quick, if not necessarily painless.

The window of the hut opened and large hands clasped her wrists tightly. She let go of the window trim, and her body was momentarily floating free, but then she was yanked through the window into the small building.

She landed in a heap on the floor and looked up at a man with long gray hair and a grizzled beard. He said in a gravelly voice, "What are you doing out there?"

"I don't know." She scrambled to her feet to look at him more closely. "Ziggy?" The brilliant blue eyes were the same, but how did he get so old?

"No one calls me that anymore. I'm Dylan Bryant. Who are you?"

"Ziggy, it's *me*." Erin placed both hands to her chest. "Stardust."

He frowned and shook his head. "I don't know you."

"Of course you do." When she reached for him, she was sucked out the window again, the air rushing by her as she screamed.

At a wet poke in her ear, Erin sat bolt upright. Her heart was racing, and her cheeks were wet with tears. Casey looked up at her with a furrowed brow, and she stroked the fur on the top of his head. "Okay, that was horrible. I'm sorry, Case. I'm afraid staying in the same room with me might have some down sides."

The next morning, Erin was out of sorts, tired of the bizarre dreams messing with her head. She made herself some toast and coffee and sat at the table, trying to make sense of her mind's festival of weird.

Jennifer walked into the kitchen with a mug, "Ah, I thought I smelled coffee. I could use a refill."

"I made a new pot." Erin took a sip. "When are you picking up Ziggy this morning?"

"I'm not. When we got to the tree farm, he asked me to wait for a second while he talked to someone in a bear suit. He came back and said that the bear would drive him out to the commune to get his stuff."

"What about his truck? It's still sitting out there in front of the house."

"He said he'd get someone to bring him over here in a few days, once he can drive again." Jennifer poured coffee into the mug. "He's certainly very polite. It's interesting that he's become so shy, considering what a wild child he was."

"He's not shy. Or at least not around me." Erin never would have thought to use the word shy to describe Ziggy. He always said he didn't like being in groups, so he might be introverted, but he didn't strike her as shy.

Jennifer sipped her coffee. "Well, he knows you better. Maybe you bring him out of his shell. I always used to think he inherited Melody's creative spirit, but he's much more subdued as an adult."

"I should call him and find out when we're going back out to Dancing Cedars."

Erin ended up leaving a somewhat cryptic message on the Bryant Tree Farm answering machine. Presumably Ziggy would get it eventually. Preferably before he had gray hair and no longer remembered who she was. Suddenly cold, she wrapped her arms around herself. Some dreams—or more accurately nightmares—were best forgotten. The vague unsettled haze of this dream didn't want to leave her psyche anytime soon. It might be silly, but she desperately wanted to talk to Ziggy to make sure he was okay.

After eating breakfast and loitering around for a while hoping for a call from Ziggy, Erin needed to get out of the house. She had to talk to Bea about the commune anyway. If she didn't have more paperwork, maybe she'd walk down to the county offices, since it was likely she was going to have to do a title search. Fortunately, Alpine Grove was so small, she could walk anywhere she needed to go to get property information.

Because she had to go into the store and potentially a few government offices, Erin left Casey behind. He watched her put on her coat, looking offended. She apologized, but he wasn't having any of it. He turned and clattered down the hall toward Jennifer's office.

Without the slow dog, Erin was able to swiftly walk through the residential areas to the main street of town. At Bea Haven Gifts, she opened the door, which sported jingle bells that greeted her merrily. The bells made her think of jingle bears, which made her think about Ziggy and her awful dream again.

Bea came out from behind the counter and gave her a hug. "How are you?"

"I'm fine." Erin picked up a small crystal frog from the counter and examined it. "I sorted through the papers in the folder you gave me and there's no ownership information. Is there more stuff somewhere?"

"No, everything has always been in that folder." She leaned back against the counter. "Are you saying we have no proof we actually own the land?"

"There's lot of tax statements, so somebody knows. I can look up title information at the county offices, but I wanted to check with you first. No matter what everyone decides to do, the first thing anyone is going to ask is if the title to the property is clear."

"I trust you to figure it out," Bea said with a smile. "But you look upset. Don't worry. I'm sure everything will be fine."

"Ziggy and I went out to Dancing Cedars and started cleaning up." Erin set the sparkly frog back on his mirrored lily pad. "I don't suppose you'd like to adopt a kitten, would you?"

"I can't, but I have talked to a couple of people about the reunion, so I'm glad to hear that you're working on removing the cats." Bea put her hand on Erin's forearm. "Did something happen? You look upset. Is there anything I can do?"

"It's stupid." Erin looked into the older woman's face. As one of Erin's many "aunts," Bea had been the recipient of countless confidences, so Erin continued. "I had a dream, and it upset me, that's all. I can't stop thinking about it."

Bea looked toward the front of the store. It was early, and no one else was there. "What was the dream about?"

"I was falling and Ziggy pulled me up, but he had gray hair and didn't recognize me."

"If Dylan rescued you, that doesn't sound so terrible." She smiled. "And I hate to tell you this, but he'll have gray hair someday like the rest of us. Well, assuming he still has hair at all, of course."

"But he didn't know who I was. He had this look on his face like he'd never seen me in his life." Erin picked up the frog again. "I know it doesn't sound like much, but it broke my heart. I was crying and I couldn't convince him he was my friend, and I felt so alone again."

"Did you have an argument while you were out at the commune?"

"Not really. Since I've been back, we've talked about anything and everything. It's been sort of intense really—like we had to catch up with everything that happened since I left. We've talked about memories, feelings, and even the mistakes we've made over the years."

"Well, I'm certainly not a psychiatrist, but why would your unconscious mind be saying that he doesn't know you?"

"I have no idea." Erin spun the tiny frog in her fingers. Okay, maybe she had an inkling. "Well, he did say that he's always loved me. But he didn't see me for twenty years, and I told him all about my fiancé. So how could he feel that way? He doesn't truly know who I am now."

"I don't know about that, but you were inseparable when you were kids. It does sound like you've shared a lot recently. I also know that all of you kids had some issues adjusting when the commune broke up. Tracy was younger, so I think she adapted more easily than Ziggy did. He lost the extended family we had at the commune and his best friend. I don't know the details, but I think he went through some difficult times."

"He said something about getting expelled from school. I think he's not particularly happy right now either." She shook her head. "I still don't see what that has to do with my dream."

"I'm not sure, but over the years I've come to appreciate how rare it is to find people who will keep loving you even when times change and you change. Maybe you aren't the same as the person he used to know, but it's not impossible to believe that he cares about you."

The bells on the door jingled, and Erin set the frog back down. "I'm sorry to go on like this about a silly dream. I should let you get back to work."

"Why don't you take this little guy? Consider it my gift to you for helping with Dancing Cedars." Bea wrapped the little frog and the lily pad in tissue paper, put it into a bag, and handed it to her. "Promise me you'll talk to Dylan."

"I will." She took the bag and gave Bea a hug. "Thanks."

~

Erin always felt better after she talked to Bea. Something about her kind, thoughtful way of conversing made Erin feel heard and appreciated. Once she got back to the house, she'd call Ziggy again. But first, she had bureaucracy to deal with.

After two hours of talking to quite a few employees at the county assessor's office, the good news was that Erin had found out everything she needed to know about Dancing Cedars. The bad news was that a corporation had put a lien on property.

As she walked back to the house, her mind was flooded with questions. Did Bea know about the lien? Did her mother? Without clear title, nothing could happen with the property. Was the lien tax-related? Everyone seemed to complain about the taxes. Maybe someone involved with the commune had gone bankrupt.

Back at the house, she checked on the kittens and went to the kitchen to make herself a sandwich. Her parents left her a note that they had gone shopping in Gleasonville and would be back later. Erin set the sandwich on a plate and sat down at the table to review the copies she had of the documents she'd found. She handed a piece of crust to Casey, who was being the perfect well-behaved dog sitting at her feet, wagging his tail and hoping for handouts.

Although Erin wasn't an expert in property law, she knew a lien on Dancing Cedars wasn't good. A lien basically meant that someone involved with Dancing Cedars owed someone else money. Voluntary liens were the most common. Every mortgage was essentially a voluntary lien, giving a lender a lien on the property. If the homeowner didn't pay, the lender could foreclose. But Bea had said that the mortgage had been paid off years ago. Involuntary liens included judgment liens where someone filed a lawsuit. Bea would have to know about something like that, wouldn't she?

There also were property-tax liens, IRS liens, and child-support liens, but those would be obvious. In this case, a *corporation* had placed the lien against the property. Erin chewed thoughtfully. It was possible that someone had used the commune property as collateral. Then they didn't pay, and a lien was placed on the property. The lien should have been recorded, but the county records office couldn't find it. They knew the number of the recorded document, but the document itself was missing and with it the details of the lien. They promised to search for it and let her know. Maybe it had fallen into the same black hole as her Samsonite.

She handed Casey a final piece of crust. Whatever had happened with the lien, it probably involved some serious interpersonal drama from twenty years ago. Ugh. What had she gotten herself into?

Erin washed her plate, put it in the drainer, and tried to call Ziggy again. Maybe he was out collecting his stuff from Dancing Cedars. Or maybe he was avoiding her. All she knew was that she wanted to see him and talk to him about the latest commune problem.

Being alone with her thoughts was never a good idea, so she took Casey out for a short walk around the block, returned him to the house, and set out for Bea Haven Gifts again.

The store was mobbed for some reason. Maybe everyone had decided that Tuesday was a big day to do early Christmas shopping. She managed to pull Bea aside long enough to ask her if she'd ever heard of a company called Ignite Enterprises, LLC. Bea shook her head, shrugged, and returned to the line of customers.

Without any way to get more answers, Erin left the store and went to the library. Maybe she could get information about the corporation. The first obvious step was to contact someone at the company and find out what was going on with this lien.

Erin spent the rest of the afternoon in the library at the reference desk, working with a librarian whose name was Jan. The woman was a researching machine, and after poring over lots of reference books and online databases, the only thing they learned was that Ignite Enterprises, LLC didn't want to be found. The corporation was registered in Delaware, but it was an anonymous limited liability corporation, or LLC, which meant that the owner or owners names weren't listed anywhere.

The fact that the corporation was registered in Delaware didn't mean it was located in that state either. As Jan pointed out, many people registered corporations in Delaware because you didn't need to have residency in Delaware, and the state had no corporate income tax.

By the time she left the library, Erin was confused and depressed. Some anonymous person behind a corporation had something going on that could prevent anything happening with Dancing Cedars. She had no idea who it was, but it pretty much had to be someone who had been involved in the commune back in the seventies. Who else would know about the place, much less care?

When she returned home, her parents were back with approximately three-thousand kitty toys. Dissatisfied with the shopping options in Alpine Grove, they'd gone to the mall in Gleasonville and acquired everything a discriminating young feline could possibly need.

she concluded that Ziggy was avoiding her and that the situation couldn't continue. He was her friend, and she was going to talk to him whether he liked it or not.

After breakfast and kitty play time, her parents had a call with their booking agent about more events. Dad was resisting the travel and Mom wasn't. Odds were good it would be an acrimonious call.

At loose ends, Erin stood in front of the living room window looking out at the pretty yard and Ziggy's truck sitting at the curb. A few cars drove by, and Erin couldn't help but notice that Dad's SUV was just sitting there in the driveway looking lonely.

She went to the kitchen, where Casey was snoozing in his dog bed. He lifted his head and gave her a hopeful look. Grabbing the keys to the SUV from the drawer, she held her index finger to her lips and whispered, "Shhh." Casey wagged his tail, which Erin hoped meant that her secret was safe with him.

She exited the house and closed the front door as quietly as she could. Yes, driving without a license was illegal, but how many officers of the law could Alpine Grove possibly have? She'd been here for a while now and had never seen a patrol car, so odds were good she wouldn't get stopped.

The fifteen-minute drive to the tree farm was largely free of any other cars. It was such a pretty morning that for the first time, Erin wished she had a license again so she could drive around whenever she liked. Maybe it was time to finally deal with that little administrative detail.

When she drove up to the farm, Ziggy was standing outside near the fence in the middle of a pile of split wood. He had a wrist brace on his right arm and held an axe in

Erin had fun playing with the kittens, watchi
tumble over each other in glee, chasing a feather
parents were laughing at the antics, and Erin was bet
they'd adopt at least one of the adorable little balls
The cuteness was hard to resist.

After the kittens collapsed into a pile of fur for
Erin called Ziggy again.

"When he answered, she said, "I've been trying t
you. Did you get my messages?"

"I was busy." There was a pause and she could he
say, "Mom, that's not cocoa."

"Are you making cookies again?"

"Yeah, we ran out. Kids are pigs."

"I thought you were out of the Christmas prep game
Barry the jingle-bear guy was doing it."

"He is, but there's still a lot to do. I had to shear
trees that were missed. Then I had to cut branches
unsellable trees to make wreaths. Then I helped Mom n
some wreaths to sell to florists."

"You did all this with one hand?" Erin scowled. "W
are we going back out to Dancing Cedars?"

"I'm not sure. I'll give you a call, okay? Wait, Mom, d
do that. I mean it. I'm absolutely *positive* that's not coc
Um, Erin, I've really gotta go. Bye."

Erin stared at the phone as if it could give her answe
Ziggy had more or less hung up on her. What was that abou

~

That night Erin didn't have any strange dreams, but she kep
waking up, so maybe her mind simply didn't have enough
time to get creative. While lying awake staring at the ceiling,

his left. He set the axe aside and placed a log on end onto a tree stump. He picked up the axe with one hand, swung it over his head, and whacked the log. Moving to the side, he whacked the log a couple more times, and the log fell into three pieces.

She parked the car off to the side of the driveway and walked over to him. "Who splits wood one-handed?"

He put down the axe again. "Who drives without a license?"

"Someone who wants to talk to you." She spread her arms wide. "Do you *ever* return phone calls? Or am I so special that I have to drive illegally to talk to you?"

"Not to mention that you don't own this car." A corner of his lips turned up in an ironic half smile. "I'm guessing you didn't mention this trip to your parents. They're going to be so pissed."

"We have work to do. What happened to the bear guy?"

Ziggy tugged at the wrist brace on his arm. "He'll be here when we open at ten."

"Can't someone else chop wood? Where's your father?"

"Helping with breakfast."

"I thought you could get away and help fix up Dancing Cedars. We promised Bea."

"Things got busy here."

"It's the holiday season, so it's going to be busy. We both know that, but you said you were taking this year off." Erin put her fists on her hips. "What happened?"

He set a log on the stump and picked up the axe again. "Nothing I want to get into, okay?"

"When you didn't agree to be the bear, that was the first time you ever said no to your parents, wasn't it?"

"I don't know." He swung the axe high and brought it down, so it hit the stump with a loud thwack. "They want me around here. It's complicated."

"How about what *you* want? Doesn't that matter? I'm talking about you living *your* life, not theirs." Erin crossed her arms across her chest. "Are you going to help me or not? Because if you're not, I need to know."

He set down the axe and turned to face her. "I don't get it. Why do you care so much about going out to Dancing Cedars?"

"We're talking about you, not me."

"Not anymore. Now we're talking about you."

"I'm not sure." Erin dropped her arms and kicked at a piece of kindling with her shoe. "I guess it feels good to care about something. I haven't cared about anything at all in a long time."

Ziggy picked up the axe again and whacked the log on the stump with it. The wood shattered into four even pieces that fell to the side. He dropped the axe on the ground, sat on the stump, and looked up at her. "I'm glad to hear that. I really am. But maybe you should find someone else to help out at the commune."

"Your parents can live without you for one season." She waved in exasperation. "It's time for you to figure out what *you* want to do. You know this, and you more or less told me so."

"You're right. I should do that." He leaned over to pick up an errant piece of wood and threw it on the pile. Looking up at her again, he said, "But the other problem, if you want the whole truth and nothing but the truth, is that it's getting too weird between us."

"What's weird? We're friends."

"That's true. But if we keep seeing each other, I'm not going to be able to stop thinking about you or stop wanting to kiss you or stop loving you."

"I love you too." She walked over and put her hands on his shoulders. "You know that."

He took one of her hands off his shoulder, kissed her palm, and looked into her eyes. "The problem is the whole lovable-brother thing isn't going to work for me, Stardust."

"I had a lot of time to think about that because I couldn't sleep." Erin gazed into his eyes, squeezed his hand, and then sat on his knee. She put her arms around his neck. "And maybe it's not that kind of love for me either. Maybe it's a sneaky kind of love."

He chuckled. "That sounds sexy."

"Stay with me for a minute here." She gave him a quick kiss on the lips. "What if you've known someone for so long that you don't have to go through all the steps?"

"What steps?"

"Well, normally when you meet someone, you have attraction, then maybe some infatuation. Then you go on a date and maybe you find out if you have chemistry. After that, you go through the whole does-he-like-me stuff. Then you worry that maybe the person is actually a jerk or has some terrible vice, but you don't know it yet. And on and on as you spend more time with someone and decide to stay together or break up. Or maybe even fall in love if you're lucky. But in our case, I already know you. I know who you are deep down like I've never known anyone else. I know your heart and your mind. And now I know that you don't kiss like a mutant platypus or worse, so the chemistry question is out of the way."

"How reassuring."

"We didn't go through the normal steps, but I do love you. And not in a 'I put up with you like an annoying brother' kind of way, but in a 'I want to see you so badly that I stole my parents' car' kind of way. I can't stop thinking about you. And how I feel may have metaphorically tiptoed into the room, but it's here to stay. I love you. And right now, I'd like it if you could kiss me again. Nobody does it better."

"Carly Simon. No one does it half as good as you either, so I'm happy to oblige. But only if you're sure."

"Very sure."

He wrapped his arms around her and kissed her, and for the first time in what felt like forever, all her worries about Ziggy simply melted away.

Their romantic interlude among the firewood was interrupted by Greg yelling for Ziggy from the door of the house.

Erin didn't let go. "Now that we're clear on what's going on with us, I still need to talk to you about the commune."

Ziggy waved his hand at his father and then placed it on Erin's cheek. "Don't go anywhere. I'll be right back."

He jogged up to the house, said something to his father that didn't seem to get a positive response, and returned to the pile of firewood.

Erin stood up. "So have you freed yourself from wood-splitting duty?"

He walked to the driver's side of the car. "I told him you're here so we can go retrieve my truck."

"We should do that. Did you ever pick up your tools from the commune?"

"No, but my wrist feels okay, so I can work again tomorrow." He got into the SUV and examined the dash. "This is a nice rig."

She flashed him a grin. "Hey, I've got standards. I only steal the highest quality automobiles."

On the drive back to her parents' house, Erin told Ziggy about the mysterious corporation that had placed the lien on Dancing Cedars. "It has to be someone who was at the commune."

Ziggy glanced at her and raised his eyebrows. "That includes a lot of people. Do you remember how many random friends of friends crashed there? It was like a free hippie hotel."

"We need to talk to Bea. She's never heard of the corporation, but maybe she'll remember if there's someone who has a grudge."

"You'll have to do it. I have to get that firewood under cover before it rains." He pulled into the driveway, parked, and handed her the keys to the SUV. "Maybe you should do something about your driver's license."

She put her hand on his wrist brace. "Maybe you should tell your parents you're taking me to Dancing Cedars tomorrow."

They got out and walked to the truck. Ziggy took her hand. "Thanks for coming to talk to me."

She looked up at him. "I think I had to work through a lot of anger and guilt. Maybe the bizarre dreams helped. I know Andy wouldn't want me to be miserable forever."

"Did he say that in one of your dreams?"

"No, but I was thinking that might be why he wouldn't stop when I was chasing after him. Maybe my subconscious is telling me that it's time for me to let go. I was so angry at how unfair TASTE was, and I was afraid if I let go of the grief, Andy would disappear completely. But he's gone and me being miserable doesn't change anything. Everyone suffers in some way or another."

"Bad things happen." He pulled her close to him and swished her hair behind her shoulder. "But so do good things. When Bea asked me to pick you up at the airport, I did it because I wanted to get away from the farm, and I was curious to see you again. But when I saw you at the airport, I couldn't believe how beautiful you are. It was like I could barely breathe."

"I didn't recognize you." Erin leaned back to grin at him. "The last time I saw you, you had no facial hair, and you were about three feet shorter."

"I was the shortest boy in eighth grade, then the tallest in tenth. They tried to recruit me for the basketball team."

"I get the impression you declined."

"After years of being picked on by jocks, no thanks. I hate team sports."

"The closest I got was being on the debate team."

"That's probably different. A lot of fake camaraderie with a bunch of jerks I hated wouldn't have worked out. I think my parents were hoping if I got good at shooting hoops, I'd get a scholarship. I doubt that would have happened though. Being tall isn't enough. I'm kind of a klutz."

"To hear you tell it, you do trip and fall off ladders a lot." Erin smiled. "That surprises me, considering all the trees you used to climb."

"Remember when they couldn't find me for two days? That was awesome." He cupped her cheek with his hand and leaned down to kiss her. "I need to go. See you tomorrow."

"Not if I see you first."

Erin went inside and scurried to the kitchen to put the car keys back in the drawer. Her parents were in her mother's office having an argument, so maybe no one had noticed her absence or the disappearance of the SUV. That would be nice. But the timbre of the raised voices made her think she should go in there and try to help neutralize the situation.

She went down the hall, and when she got to the doorway, Dad slapped his palm on the desk. "I don't want to do it. We just got back from Japan, where I saw the inside of a hotel room, a conference center, and then spent an extra day waiting around at an airport hotel. That's not seeing the world. We don't stay anywhere long enough to *see* anything. We spent a ton of money restoring this beautiful house, and now we hardly ever get to enjoy it."

"But this trip could be huge for us. Donna said Eleanor has scouted twelve locations."

"That's eleven too many. I don't want to do this, Jennifer. I *don't*. I need a break."

"You rejected my idea of staying here and doing women's retreats. You're stifling me!"

Erin cleared her throat and Jennifer looked at her. "Oh, I didn't see you standing there."

Although she wanted to say "obviously," Erin refrained and instead said evenly, "Is everything okay?"

"Your father and I disagree on a fundamental priority," Jennifer said.

"Having a life should be a priority," Paul said. "At this point, another one of my goals is to spend a lot less time in airports."

"Did you need something, Erin?" Jennifer asked.

Erin clasped her hands together in front of her. It was a long shot, but she needed to ask. "I was wondering if you know anything about a company called Ignite Enterprises, LLC?"

Neither Paul nor Jennifer had heard of it, and Jennifer asked, "Why do you ask?"

"The company has put a lien on Dancing Cedars."

Paul crossed his arms and glared at Jennifer. "That sure complicates your women's retreat idea. It figures someone slapped a lien on it. That will be yet another mess we have to deal with."

"Don't be negative," Jennifer said. "The lien would also be a problem for the conservation easement, I assume."

"It is," Erin said. "I'll talk to Bea about it. I'm sure we'll figure it out. Maybe it's some type of misunderstanding."

Neither of her parents seemed to have any more feedback or interest in talking about Dancing Cedars, and when Dad resumed sniping about how much he hated airports, Erin left the room, glad to be away from the strife. Yikes. She wasn't sure how they'd find a way to resolve this problem. The fact that they were partners in a business that was all about helping people create harmony in their relationships was a little ironic at this point. At the moment, harmonious was one thing her parents definitely were not.

She called Bea to let her know that Ziggy was better, and that they were going back out to Dancing Cedars the next day to trap cats and resume their cleanup. Bea was thrilled because she'd been busy working on inviting people to the big reunion to talk about the conservation easement.

Hopefully, they'd have a property to save. If Erin didn't figure out who was behind this mysterious corporation, legally they couldn't do much of anything with Dancing Cedars.

Chapter 11

The Thinking Spot

Erin spent way too much time fruitlessly going through the paperwork again to see if there was any reference to the lien, the mysterious corporation, or an angry or deadbeat owner. All she got for her efforts was a paper cut because there was a big fat nothing in that pile.

After an unusually restful sleep, she was feeling better than she had in months. When she saw Ziggy's truck in front of the house, she practically skipped down the sidewalk and hopped into the cab.

Ziggy leaned around Moose, grinning at her enthusiasm. "What happened to you? And can I have some?"

"Sleep!" She shoved Moose aside so she could give Ziggy a big smacking kiss. "No dreams of any kind. For the first time, my mind apparently couldn't think of anything creepy, scary, or weird to keep me awake."

Moose licked her cheek and Erin wiped off the slobber. "I'm glad to see you too, Moosie. So is he going to doggie day care?"

Ziggy pulled away from the curb. "Yep. He gets to see all his buddies again. It's a good thing too because he's been making a nuisance of himself at the farm. Maybe he's jealous of junior jingle bear, but this dog has been beyond obnoxious.

Yesterday, he ate half a batch of cookies and threw them up in Dad's shoes."

Erin stroked the dog's giant head. "Oh Moose, you didn't."

"He did. When Dad discovered what was in his shoes, I thought he might blow out an artery or something. And then we had to make more cookies, which as you know can be tricky on a good day. And yesterday definitely wasn't a good day."

"My parents spent most of yesterday fighting or sulking. I holed up and looked through paperwork again."

"Did you find anything?"

"Nothing. Maybe on the way home, we can catch Bea at the store before it closes. She's so busy, I don't know how she's going to manage a reunion with everything else going on."

"Christmas is coming." He patted Moose's head. "Those of us who deal with holiday retail will be glad when the shopping is done."

They dropped off Moose at the kennel and had a short conversation with Mia, who clearly was developing an affection for the big dog. She volunteered that her dog, Gizmo, and Moose were friends now, and it was great for her because it meant Gizmo did nothing but sleep after a long day of romping with his new best buddy.

Ziggy continued on the back roads, heading out to the commune property. The air was crisp, but the gray clouds on the horizon gave some credence to the predictions of rain. Erin was glad they still weren't talking about snow. She wasn't prepared to deal with Alpine Grove winter weather yet. Her years in the mid-Atlantic states had made her wimpy when it came to the harsh reality of frigid temperatures, slush, and snow.

On Misty Meadow Lane, not too far from the end of the road, two men were hauling furniture out of a small rustic cabin.

"Looks like someone is moving out." Erin pointed at the motley collection of old furniture. "Was that ugly couch at Dancing Cedars?"

"If so, it didn't get far." Ziggy slowed, "Hey, I know that guy. The one on the left is from the kennel. That's Joel, Kat's husband."

"She's married?"

"Yeah, they seem happy together."

"Nice." She patted the back of his hand on the gearshift. "I saw what you did there. That's The Turtles. I think we heard that song about a thousand times."

"I wonder what they're doing with that stuff." Ziggy pulled to the side of the road across from the cabin. "Maybe they're ditching it."

"If people are staying for this reunion, it might be nice if they have something to sit on other than those hard wooden chairs."

"Even an ugly couch." He got out of the truck. "It doesn't hurt to ask."

They walked across the gravel road to the grassy driveway that led up to the house. The two men were facing the house and gazing down at the plaid couch, chatting.

Joel kicked a leg of the couch. "I know. The stupid thing weighs a ton."

The other man said, "Still don't want it. Becca will kill me if I come home with that couch in my truck."

Joel turned and waved at Ziggy. "Hi. You have the big dog, right? Did you miss the turn for the kennel?"

"Nope. Moose is there. I'm Dylan, and this is Erin." He gestured toward the road. "We're working up at the commune property."

Erin said, "You took care of my parents' dog, Casey."

"Casey was with us for quite some time. He liked hanging out in Kat's office." Joel nodded at the other man. "This is my friend, Jack. He did some work up at the commune too."

"Jack Sheridan?" Erin asked.

He raised his eyebrows. "Yes. Do I know you?"

"No, but I read your management plan. It's well thought out in terms of habitat restoration and forest health."

"Thanks. I spent a lot of time out there. Probably more than I needed to, but it's a beautiful place. Did Bea get the conservation easement set up yet?"

Erin shook her head. "There are some issues that need to be resolved."

"A lot of people are involved who have to agree," Ziggy added. "People who historically haven't agreed on much of anything in a long time."

"But we're going to make it happen somehow," Erin said. "We want to make sure the land is preserved. It's a special place to us."

"Yeah, we lived up there when we were kids," Ziggy added.

"You must have known Tracy then," Joel said.

"We did. Little Rainbow was spoiled rotten because she played all the adults off each other," Erin said. "Not that I'd ever tell Bea, but that kid was a master manipulator."

Ziggy laughed. "She was the youngest, so she got away with everything. What a brat."

Erin pointed at the couch. "I don't suppose you're selling any of this furniture, are you?"

"I can't imagine anyone driving all the way out here to pay me for it, so Jack is helping me drag it to a thrift store," Joel said.

"We'll take it." Ziggy said. "Some people will be coming out to the commune, and it would be good if there is more than a beat-up table and chairs there."

"Are you sure?" Joel gazed down at the couch. "A lot of it still sort of smells like smoke."

"That's better than what the rest of the building smells like right now," Ziggy said. "With three trucks, we can get it all up there in one trip."

"Works for me." He pointed at Jack, "Grab that end."

"All right," Jack said. "But you still owe me a beer."

~

Everyone loaded up furniture into the trucks and drove up the road to the commune. Ziggy opened the gate, and the parade headed up the hill to the Hodgepodge Lodge.

Once everything was unloaded and inside, they stood in front of the lodge.

Joel shook Ziggy's hand. "Thanks for taking this junk off my hands. I think Kat was worried I might drag it all home."

Jack scanned the pasture and the woods beyond. "I'm glad you're working to preserve this parcel. There aren't many open spaces like this anymore."

Erin clasped her hands together as if she were praying and gave the two men an imploring look. "I don't suppose either of you would like to adopt a kitten, would you?"

"*No,*" they said simultaneously.

"We have five cats already," Joel said. "And they don't always necessarily get along."

"We have two dogs and, well, no," Jack said. "We're not up for a cat."

"Oh well, I had to ask," Erin said. "The kittens are adorable."

Joel and Jack agreed that they probably were, but made a hasty exit.

Ziggy hauled the generator out of his truck. "Time to get to work."

The cleaning stuff was all exactly where Erin had left it. She used the old pump to put some water in a bucket and went up the stairs to pick up where she'd left off. Ziggy had sealed most of the largest holes, and it appeared that none of the local felines had figured out a way inside.

The plan was for Erin to hose down everything and then they'd go through and sand or replace the flooring that was too far gone. So Erin had the lovely task of removing things like the headless mouse carcass, suspicious feathers, ancient excrement, and various forms of forest detritus and filth. It was a disgusting, dirty job, but ultimately rewarding in some ways because her efforts made such a visible difference.

By the time she broke for lunch, she felt like the smell of cat pee was etched into her nostrils. She went downstairs and found Ziggy sitting at the table with his head resting on his crossed arms, fast asleep.

She walked up behind him leaned over, kissed his cheek, and whispered. "Hey, wake up. It's lunchtime."

"Guess I was tired." He sat up, stretched his arms above his head, and pulled off the rubber band holding his ponytail together.

Without thinking, Erin reached out to touch his long, wavy brown hair. She'd never seen it loose before. It was thick, and the way it was surrounding his face, the contrast intensified the blue of his eyes. "Are you okay?"

"Yesterday, Dad was convinced it was going to rain, and getting all that firewood under cover wiped me out." He moved his head to the side. "What are you doing to my hair?"

"Taking out the tangles." She ran both hands through his hair and pulled it back, away from his face. "It's so soft."

"Combing my hair is more fun when you do that than when I do." He closed his eyes and smiled. "That feels amazing."

"So what are your parents going to do when you aren't there anymore?"

He opened his eyes. "I have no idea. It's part of why I keep hanging around."

"Have they considered retiring?"

"With what money? They have no savings and they're too young to collect Social Security."

"They could sell the farm, couldn't they?" She curled his hair behind his ear. "A house, land, and a profitable business has to be worth good money, right?"

"Every time I've hinted at the idea, my father loses it." He looked into her eyes. "He's been selling trees so long, I think he can't imagine doing anything else."

"But you're doing most of the work. It's not fair."

He pulled her into his lap. "I can't believe that I'm pointing this out to *you*, but life isn't fair. You can't always get what you want."

"The Rolling Stones." She gave him a quick kiss. "Come on. That's an easy one. And yes, I'm the first one to complain about the unfairness of life. But I want to know. I keep asking this question, and you never answer me. What do you want?"

He reached over her shoulders and gently removed the band holding her messy ponytail before threading his fingers into her hair. "You mean other than you?"

"You keep changing the subject when I ask you what you would do if you weren't at that farm twenty-four seven, doing all the work your parents either can't or won't do."

"Once you figure out what you're doing next, maybe I'll tell you." He ran his thumbs down the sides of her neck and kissed her. "What happened to lunch?"

What a pain. Ziggy was nothing if not stubborn, and he wouldn't say anything if he decided not to. Giving up on the question for the time being, Erin got up and retrieved the sandwiches from a cooler that they'd brought. That morning at her parents' house, she'd dug up a cooler because there was no way she was letting Ziggy near another ladder without having a lot of ice nearby.

She set out the sandwiches on paper plates, and Ziggy settled into his lunch.

Erin walked to the couch and pulled a legal pad from her bag. "When you mentioned all the people who came through here, I tried to list everyone I could think of."

"Like I said, Dancing Cedars was the Alpine Grove hippie hotel. I think anyone who was a member of any commune in the West passed through at one time or another."

She laid the pad in front of him. "Can you help me fill in some of the blanks?"

He flipped up a piece of paper. "This is quite a list."

"I started with the owners, then everyone who lived here at least semi-permanently, then those who were here for only a few days or weeks. Most of those are just impressions."

He pointed at a line. "Guy with the leather fringe jacket doesn't narrow it down much."

"I know. But I plan to go through it with Bea as well. Those are more like notes for me."

Flipping the page back, he ran his finger down the list of owners. "It will be a miracle to get these twelve people on board with a single idea. I mean, look at this list. My parents, your parents, the Sullivans, and then Summer, Topaz, Bear, Meadow, Willow and River. They've never agreed on anything."

Erin pointed at the pad. "I wrote down their real names. Kristin, Lila, Dean, Leah, Emily, Kevin."

"Okay, whatever. No matter what you call them, could you find twelve more different people?"

"Probably not." She put her elbows on the table and rested her chin on them. "Is anyone else still living around here other than the people who were at Thanksgiving?"

"I don't think so. She's not an owner, but remember Gardenia? She and her daughter, Heather, were at Dancing

Cedars for a while. Gardenia's name is Gwen, and she lived in Alpine Grove for a long time. I heard she moved though. Heather was a couple years behind me in school."

"I'm getting depressed here." Erin let out a sigh, picked up her sandwich again, and took a bite.

He grabbed her hand and dragged her up. "Let's go."

"Go where?"

"Isn't it obvious? We need to go to the thinking spot."

She laughed as she grabbed her coat. "You're absolutely right."

~

Erin followed Ziggy outside, and they crossed the meadow to the forest to the creek trail. Clouds were gathering above, but the air was still, which made the forest seem cloaked, dampening any sound. It was almost silent, except for the occasional angry squirrel chattering at them as they walked by.

They walked down an incline with the sound of water rushing over rocks burbling below them.

Ziggy leaned against an enormous rock and held out his hands with his fingers interlaced. "Up you go."

Erin stepped into his hands, put her hands on his shoulders, and launched up to the top of the boulder. Ziggy climbed up and sat next to her, putting his arm around her.

She leaned her head against him. "How many crises have we resolved here?"

"We were pretty sure that all the problems of the universe could be fixed at the thinking spot."

Erin closed her eyes and let her mind wander, listening to the sound of the rushing water and Ziggy humming something that sounded suspiciously like "Love Will Keep Us Together" by the Captain and Tennille. She was too relaxed to comment on it, but he probably knew she knew anyway.

Ziggy stroked her hair. "So what are you going to do?"

She moved to look at him. "I don't know. We need to clean up the lodge, have a reunion, straighten out the mess with the title, deal with the lien, and convince twelve people that a conservation easement makes sense. I'm taking it one day at a time. Today, we clean."

He kissed her. "That's not what I meant. Are you going back to Washington, D.C.?"

"It's where I live."

"Why?"

Erin paused, not sure what to say. "Well, I went to law school there because Andy and I were living there. And I had a job. Then I passed the bar. I told you all this already. Washington is where my life was…*is*."

"Does it have to be? Do you like it there?"

The creek babbled below them, making all the hustle and intensity of D.C. feel far away, almost like a dream or a life that had happened to someone else.

Erin looked at him. "I did enjoy it at one time, but not as much anymore."

"I was just thinking that you said I'm still living my parents' life. Maybe you're still living Andy's."

"It wasn't only his life. It was mine too. I was there because I wanted to be."

"Are you now?"

Erin frowned. Ziggy had a habit of asking hard questions. "Not really. No. When I think about getting a job at a law firm there, it makes me want to crawl under the covers. Everyone is so power hungry. It's all about status. Working for the right firm. Being on the fast track."

"Then you went off the rails."

Erin laughed. "God, I can't believe you made me laugh about my current crap-tastic life. How twisted is that? What's wrong with me?"

"You need to lighten up on yourself, Stardust." He gave her a hug. "We should probably get back to work."

"Wait! I answered the question, so now you have to tell me what you want to do."

"You didn't answer. 'I don't know' isn't an answer."

"No fair." She shook her finger at him. "And don't get on me about life being fair again. I want to know what you want. For *you*, not your family."

"To be with you."

"Oh come on. That's not an answer."

"It's all I've got. All I know is that I'm not letting you leave again without a fight. If you want me to move across the country, I will."

"Are you nuts? You can't do that."

"Why not? You keep telling me I need to do something that I want. What I want is to be with you." He ran his fingertips along her cheek. "I want to see your face every day for the rest of my life."

Erin was dumbfounded. "You can't mean that. We've barely spent any time together."

"What's to know? I love you. You love me. As you pointed out, we already know each other, having spent every single day together for years running around here."

"We were kids. And then we didn't see each other for decades."

"Doesn't matter."

Erin shook her head, confused. "What are you saying?"

"Don't leave." He gestured toward the creek. "Or more accurately, leave Alpine Grove if you want, but don't leave me behind again."

Erin looked into his eyes, and the intensity scared her. She turned aside and gave him a hug, pressing her cheek into his chest. He was completely serious, but committing herself to someone again terrified her. She told him she loved him and she did, but she hadn't thought this through.

This wasn't just some random fling or one-night stand. He was talking about a whole lot more. But what if something happened to him? The next time he fell off a ladder he could break a leg. Or snap his neck. Damage his spine and be a paraplegic. Or die. She knew better than anyone that stupid accidents happen all the time. How could she possibly go through that again?

Ziggy moved and Erin sat up straight, wondering what he was thinking. How could anything work? She couldn't imagine Ziggy in DC. Could she move here? Wouldn't that be going backward? She'd been so desperate to get away from Alpine Grove and her oddball hippie roots. How could she return?

Erin glanced up at Ziggy and their gazes locked. He grinned at her. "We need to get outta here. Now you're thinking too much. Damn this rock."

He launched off the boulder and held out his arms. "Let's go."

Erin smiled and let him help her down. He grabbed her hand and set off running toward the lodge. "Race ya."

By the time they got to the Hodgepodge Lodge, Erin was too out of breath for her brain to chew on their conversation. But what Ziggy had said was unforgettable, sitting in the back of her mind, waiting for her to come back to it.

They checked the traps and found a gigantic orange tom cat in one and a smaller black cat in the other. The sleek black cat was likely a male, given the overt spraying motions he made to express his displeasure at being confined.

Ziggy stayed outside, returning to the chinking program. He'd made remarkable progress spreading cementitious goo in and around the decomposing chinking that remained between the logs.

Erin went upstairs to work on another bedroom. She ran an extension cord through the window, and Ziggy fired up the generator so she could use the electric sander on the floor. It was loud, dirty work, but like the cleaning, it was satisfying to see the bright, bare wood emerge from under the filth.

Several hours of sanding later, Erin unplugged the sander, shut off the generator, and went back inside to collapse on the ancient couch they'd gotten from Joel. Ziggy was still working, but she wasn't used to so much physical exertion, and she was absolutely positively done.

She stared at the wooden ceiling. What *was* she going to do with herself? Maybe she kept hammering Ziggy with this question because she wanted the answer herself. But she had no clue what she wanted. Right now, it felt like she was at some type of crossroads. She had killed herself studying for a law degree, and now she wasn't sure she even wanted to be a lawyer.

When she'd moved to DC with Andy, she'd gotten a job as a court reporter, and then she became a paralegal. Her boss encouraged her to go to law school, and against all odds, she got in and got a scholarship. She'd worked so hard, studied so much, and even passed the bar. After all that, why wasn't she interested in practicing law?

She closed her eyes and flopped her arm over them. Staying in Alpine Grove was appealing in some ways. The most obvious draw was that Ziggy was here. Part of her understood how he felt. The idea of leaving him and going back to DC alone made her stomach hurt. She couldn't bear the thought of not seeing him again. But becoming so attached to him so quickly became more alarming every day. She had to make a choice. Loving someone was scary, but sometimes love wasn't enough. How could he be so sure it would work out?

She'd been positive everything with Andy would be perfect. On June twenty-third, 1996, they were going to become husband and wife, their whole lives ahead of them. And look how well that turned out. They'd been engaged for years, then finally set a date. She'd always wondered if things would have been different if she hadn't been so insistent on the perfect wedding. She'd expected that being engaged would be fun, with lots of bridal showers and celebrations. Except none of those things happen when the groom dies six months before the wedding.

At a touch on her arm, she leaped up and almost toppled off the couch. Ziggy moved to grab her, then sat down and put his arms around her. "I got you, babe."

"Sonny and Cher. Thank you." She wrapped her arms around his neck and kissed him. "I got you too. We'll figure something out."

"Good." He hugged her hard and nuzzled her neck. "Because I love you."

"I know. I love you too."

~

Ziggy announced that he was done for the day, and after bringing his tools inside, he loaded the cat traps into the back of the truck. Erin put the cooler behind the seats in the extended cab.

A black-and-white cat barreled across the meadow followed by a gray tabby that overtook the tuxedo and tackled the larger cat, rolling the two of them end over end. The tabby emerged from the fray and took off running.

At the feline screeching and yowling, Erin made a face at Ziggy. "I think there might be a few more cats that need to be fixed."

"There's a lot of testosterone out in that meadow."

She got in and looked through the back window at the truck bed. "Not to mention in the back of your truck."

"It reeks. I'm going to have to paint it or something. I know this truck looks like a hunk of junk, but it always starts and doesn't seem to care how badly I beat it up."

A total of four cats were now running around outside the truck. Erin pointed in front of them. "What are they doing?"

"Maybe they know we're taking their friends away?" He revved the engine. "Get out of the way. I promise. We'll bring them back. Go on."

The cats scattered and Ziggy carefully turned the truck around and slowly went down the driveway.

The cats in the back were yowling loudly. Erin turned on the stereo, and "Waterloo" by ABBA blasted from the speakers, startling both of them.

Erin pointed at the back. "I think neutering at the vet counts as the feline Waterloo."

"It's their destiny, and they aren't escaping, that's for sure."

They sang along loudly and badly to more ABBA, effectively drowning out the sounds of unhappy felines. By the time they got to the kennel, Erin was practically hoarse and exhausted, but it was a happy tired. Belting out loud music with your best friend in the world was good for the soul.

Ziggy pulled up in front of the kennel, and a black-and-white dog leaped next to the truck, trying to see inside the back window of the ugly camper shell.

As Erin got out, Joel emerged from the kennel. He pointed at the house, "Lori, go home."

The dog turned and ran up the driveway toward the log house.

Joel peered in the back, "Wow, those are some angry cats."

"I'm taking them to the vet to be fixed," Ziggy said. "We keep seeing more out there. At this rate, I'm going to rack up some serious vet bills."

Joel smiled. "I know how that goes. Did you get the furniture set up okay?"

"Yes!" Erin said. "It was so nice to have a place to relax after working all day."

"Let me know if you need help reassembling the bed. Jack and I might have lost some screws when we brought the pieces down from the loft." He turned toward the door. "I'll go get Moose."

Ziggy pointed at the kennel. "Did he ever say why they were moving all that stuff? He lives here."

"It looked like they were emptying it out. Maybe he's selling the cabin."

Joel returned with Moose, who launched toward the truck, dragging him behind. The dog put his front paws on the back bumper, peering in at the cats.

Ziggy took the leash from Joel. "Sorry about that. Now you know why he's here and not out with us while we work."

"Moose doesn't seem to understand cats," Erin added. "He's convinced they want to play and they never do."

Joel reached into his pocket and pulled out a piece of paper. "Kat said you agreed to a weekly bill, so here's the bill including tomorrow."

"Okay, I'll bring a check with me in the morning." Ziggy pocketed the paper, and they said their good-byes.

Once Moose was successfully stuffed into the extended cab, next to the cooler, they hit the road again. Erin gazed out the window watching the evergreens go by. All the physical labor was catching up to her, and now every muscle in her back hurt to some degree. Tomorrow was likely to be ugly.

Ziggy put his hand on her leg. "Are you okay? You're awfully quiet all of a sudden."

"I think I overdid it on the cleaning. And now I have to deal with my parents."

"What's going on?"

"They had a huge fight, and the tension at the house is bad again." Erin sighed. "I don't see how they'll resolve it either."

"Why not?"

"Dad is sick of all the travel and hotels. Mom loves it. They're supposed to be talking to people about successful relationships and listening skills, but they're not doing it themselves."

"Can't they do their thing from one place?"

"Maybe when they were living in LA, but not here. They set up at convention centers and huge hotels." Erin gestured toward the window. "That's part of what my dad hates. He says he never sees anything except the inside of hotel rooms. And now their booking agent has lined up twelve potential new dates."

"Is he going to do it?"

"I don't know. He claims he's sick of airports."

"What if they traveled, but stayed in one place for a while? They could do multiple events or different types like the retreats your mom wants."

Erin looked at him. "I'm not sure if anyone ever suggested that before. They've always traveled like bands do, going from one gig to the next."

"There is a place here that does retreats now. Remember the North Fork Lodge that had the big Halloween haunted house? They did hay rides, pumpkin carving, and bobbing for apples."

"Yeah, remember that kid who completely lost her marbles after eating a caramel apple?"

He laughed. "Everyone called her the sticky kid. I've never seen anyone have a temper tantrum like that. She was hard core."

"No kidding, she was lying on the floor and kicking her arms and legs. I remember that my mother was appalled. Can you imagine what people at Dancing Cedars would have done if we'd pulled crap like that?"

"It's bad enough having two parents lecturing you. Try twelve."

Erin put her hand on his and they interlaced fingers. "They would have had one of those perpetual powwows where they sat us down and tried to discover the root of our discontent."

"Don't harsh on the harmony, man." He squeezed her hand. "Gotta radiate positive vibes."

"Wait! I just remembered the name of the guy with the fringe jacket!" Erin let go of his hand and reached for her notepad. "Phoenix."

"He always said you were uptight. Hey, mellow out, girlie."

"I don't think he ever even knew my name." She took his hand in hers again. "I want to hold your hand."

"The Beatles. Jeez, that's way too easy. You're not even trying."

"Hey, mellow out, dude. It's been a hard day's night."

~

Kat looked up from her notes at the sound of the door opening and the resulting dog barking. Joel walked into the kitchen, peered into the refrigerator, and closed the door.

Kat said, "If you're looking for the leftover stuffing, I ate it. Thanksgiving is officially over."

"It's been a week, so I hope so. I feel like I need to eat salad for the next six months."

"You'll change your mind when you're standing in front of the wilty lettuce at the grocery store. Winter isn't great for vegetarian eating."

"How's your article coming?"

"I hate it, thanks."

"That well, huh? I dealt with Moose. He'll be back tomorrow."

"Thanks." Kat stood up and stretched her arms above her head. "I've been sitting up here at the table because I couldn't stand looking at my computer anymore. My notes from talking to these award-winning people are lame. Why did I take this project?"

"Because you never say no."

"Did you get everything moved out of the Shack this morning? Do the local thrift stores hate you now?"

"Yes and no."

Kat walked over and put her arms around his waist. "Care to clarify?"

"Yes, the furniture is gone. No it's not scattered throughout thrift stores in Alpine Grove. It's at the old commune."

"You mean the property at the end of the road? I thought there was nothing up there."

Joel leaned to kiss her and went back to the refrigerator. "There's an old log building. It might have been a barn originally, but it's more finished. Well, sort of."

Kat followed him and gazed at the shelves in the fridge. She pulled out a package of tofu. "*Sort of* doesn't sound good."

He closed the door. "It's made of gigantic log timbers, but it's so old, the wood is all weathered and gray. The chinking isn't looking too good either."

Kat opened the freezer and grabbed a bag of frozen spinach. "I've always wondered what the commune was like. Tracy told me there's a big meadow and a creek."

"The land is beautiful." Joel went to the pantry and reached for a can of coconut milk. "Imagine a meadow surrounded by the type of huge trees we have here. Part of the creek flows alongside the driveway."

"The area near the Shack is gorgeous." She moved around him to grab a bag of rice. "Could you get the carrots?"

"Yeah, we need those." He walked back to the fridge. "I can tell by your voice that you still don't want me to sell the place."

Kat set the bag on the counter. "I know you think I'm not being sensible and responsible about it, but selling feels wrong."

"You said that before. Is this you resisting change again?"

"No. Maybe. I don't know."

"I'm going to make some repairs and drain the water this weekend. Then it can sit for four or five months under a mountain of snow, so you can forget it exists." He put his arms around her. "Don't worry."

"Worrying is what I do."

"Mostly when you don't want to write something."

"Yeah, yeah."

After dinner and the final dog walk of the day, Kat couldn't stand thinking about her pathetic article anymore, so she gave up on work, grabbed her novel, and settled into bed to escape into something that had nothing to do with awards given to egotistical workaholics who had trampled the competition in the exciting realm of insurance. Ugh.

She woke up when Joel crawled into bed. He gave her a kiss and curled up alongside her.

Putting her arms around him, she asked, "Did you finish what you were working on?"

"No. Did you?"

"No. I stared at my notes, called Maria, and read my book. I wish I'd never taken this project."

"I know. Can you get out of it?"

"I can't. Tomorrow, I need to write it, send it, and forget about it. If I do a crappy job, it might be a blessing because they'll never ask me to write anything for them again. Even if they do, I'll never agree to another assignment from them. The editor is making me insane."

"You may have mentioned that once or twice. How's Maria?"

"Not handling life at the farm well. I think she's going to break up with Bob. It's a shame because he's a nice guy. But if you hate farm animals and growing vegetables, a relationship with a farmer is going to be problematic."

"That's too bad."

"She's trying to convince him to change careers, which is unfair. He's a third- or fourth-generation farmer, I think. It's who he is, and he loves it. We should all be so lucky."

"I can relate to career angst."

"You're feeling better about your work now, aren't you?" Kat ran her hand across his chest. "You've been doing less programming and more work around here. The new cabinets in your workshop are looking great."

"This spring you should be able to get your dishwasher, assuming we still have the money for it."

"You aren't worried about the lack of rent from the Shack are you?"

"I'm not making much these days either, since I've been working on the new kitchen."

"It doesn't matter. Thanks to word of mouth, the kennels are booked solid through the new year. Overbooked, even. We have a waiting list. And then people are going skiing and then President's Day. Then you're close to spring break with still more vacations."

He stroked her hair. "If we're that busy, I think you should stop taking writing jobs you hate. What if you write about something you're interested in or care about?"

"No one will pay me to do that. I'm a technical writer."

"You *were* a technical writer. That doesn't mean you have to write about technology forever. Much less insurance awards." He kissed her. "I believe you are the one who said that I didn't have to be a programmer forever if I don't want to."

"I'm confused. On the one hand, you say you're worried about money. Then you suggest that I turn away money."

"I want you to be happy, not angry and pissed off like you've been with this last article."

"I see your point. Money isn't everything."

"No, it's not."

Chapter 12

Wild Thing

For Erin, Friday was scheduled to be a repeat of the day before. Ziggy picked her up after breakfast, they got the cats from the vet, dropped off Moose, and drove back out to Dancing Cedars. The clouds were such a dark looming gray that it was as if sunrise had been a silly myth.

By the time they got to the commune, snow flurries were whirling around the meadow. Erin hauled the cooler inside, while Ziggy released the angry cats near their remodeled chicken-coop shelter.

She was starting a fire in the old woodstove when the front door opened with a whoosh. Ziggy hauled in the 8-foot stepladder he'd been using for chinking and slammed the door behind him.

He leaned the ladder up against a wall. "It's crowded in here. Maybe we should spread out some of this furniture."

"I finished sanding and wiping down the front bedroom. We could move those bed parts out of the way. That would help."

Ziggy stood in front of the window with his hands in his coat pockets. "It's swirling around like a snow globe out there. The first snow often seems confused, like it doesn't know how to be a blizzard yet."

231

Erin walked over to him. "Snow seems to learn quickly. Remember when we got lost in that whiteout?"

"Playing arctic explorer wasn't one of my better ideas. Good thing your dad found us when he did."

Erin put her hand on his arm. "We probably shouldn't stay out here too long today. Maybe do a little cleaning and go back home early."

"It's probably not even snowing in town, but out here at this elevation, who knows what might happen. Let's get this stuff upstairs."

Erin picked up a pair of the old metal bed rails and went toward the stairs. Ziggy followed with more parts. They dropped them in the room and went back for the mattress.

Ziggy walked to the wall where the mattress was leaning. "You get that end."

"But then I'll have to go backward up the stairs. I hate that."

"If you don't, you get the heavy end. Pick one."

"Fine. Backward it is."

After a lot of wrangling and demands for rest on Erin's part, they managed to drag the old mattress up the stairs. Ziggy flipped it onto the floor of the bedroom, and Erin flopped down on top of it.

She rolled onto her back and stretched out her arms. "Ouch. That was horrible. I'm still sore from yesterday. I hate moving mattresses. The last time I…oh no." Erin curled herself into a fetal ball, hugging her knees to her chest and squeezing her eyes shut.

"Stardust?" Ziggy kneeled down on the mattress and ran his thumb across her cheek, wiping away tears. "What just happened?"

Erin pushed herself up to a sitting position and wrapped her arms around her knees. "Don't mind me. It's me falling apart *again*."

"Did I do something?"

She wiped her eyes. "No. My brain flashed on moving a mattress with Andy. Sometimes, tears have this way of coming out of nowhere. It's like I get punched in the gut with a memory."

He put his arms around her. "I'm sorry."

"When I got back to the house last night, Mom told me my stupid suitcase showed up yesterday. I finally have my ELFs again."

"Elfs? Take it from someone who has seen more of Santa's little helpers than the average person. The plural of elf is *elves*."

"I don't mean elves as in Christmas or the little guys on packages of cookies. I mean Erin's Little Friend. ELF. My yellow pills."

"What yellow pills?"

"The ones that help me sleep. I didn't take any last night. I thought about it, but I didn't." She slapped a palm on the mattress. "But this crap is why I took them for so long. Feeling nothing was better than the crying jags. I'm so tired of this. I should be past all the crying by now."

"Is there anything I can do?"

"You already are." Erin rested her cheek on his chest, listening to his heart beat.

He ran his hand across her hair, but didn't say anything for a moment. Finally, he said, "I don't think there is any 'should' when it comes to sadness and grieving. When something bad happens, it takes as long as it takes to deal with it."

"But it's been years, and I still burst into tears at random moments. Like moving a mattress. How stupid is that? What is wrong with me?"

"Nothing." He kissed her temple. "I used to think that life would be this linear progression with a straight line from school, job, marriage, kids, whatever, on and on until you die. But I think it's more like a zigzag. Or a really messy scribble."

Erin leaned her head back to smile at him. "If that's true, I think I broke my crayon."

"That's how it goes. In my case, it was go to college, Dad breaks his ankle, so I give up, drop out, and come home supposedly temporarily. But the next year, a tree falls on the roof. Then there's the year with the needle blight when we had to apply a special fungicide we couldn't afford. Then the tractor dies. And then another year, Harry melts down in school. Then one year, Mom gets a cold that turns into pneumonia. Oh, and then Harry thinks his girlfriend is pregnant."

Erin sat up. "Hold on. Does Harry have a kid? Are you an uncle? Or maybe technically, I'm an aunt."

"Nope. It's a long story, but the ending is that he's an idiot. I told him to buy some condoms." He stretched his arm out. "I mean sure it's a cliché, but if you're that horny, put one in your wallet, for God's sake. It's not that complicated."

Erin giggled. "Way to offer some sage brotherly advice."

"Sorry to get off track, but what I'm getting at is that I think your crayon is fine. You're going through a major scribble, that's all."

Erin rested her cheek on his chest again and closed her eyes, visualizing colorful artwork and enjoying his warm embrace. She jerked backward when Ziggy leaped away from her, scrabbling backward like a crab across the mattress.

His eyes were wide. "Holy crap. That was huge."

"What?" Erin looked around and ran her fingers through her hair. "Is there a spider in my hair?"

"I don't know, but I'm pretty sure a possum ran out of the room and down the hallway. Or maybe a gigantic pack rat. Whatever it was, it wasn't a cat, that's for sure."

"How did it get inside?"

"I thought I patched all the holes." He stood up and shook out his arms. "Maybe we should assemble the bed frame. The floor is a little too crowded and action-packed."

Erin shuddered involuntarily. "At least I'm not thinking about death anymore."

"Nothing like large varmints to shred thoughts of anything else." He went to the doorway and turned to look back at her. "You're okay, right? I need to get a cat trap out of the truck."

"I'm fine. Thanks for talking me down off the ledge."

"Always. Be right back."

Ziggy set up a trap in the hall and baited it with some of the food they'd brought. He took a flashlight and started investigating the lodge, looking for more holes.

While Ziggy was varmint-hunting, Erin got the toolbox and set to work assembling the metal bed frame. Anyone who stayed here definitely would want to be up off the floor. And that nasty varmint had better not crap all over her newly sanded floors either.

When Ziggy returned, they dragged the mattress onto the frame. Erin sat and surveyed the room. "I'm guessing from all the hammering I heard, you found a hole."

He sat next to her. "All patched up now. Hopefully the varmint ran back outside, so we're not sharing the lodge with him anymore."

"You'd think we'd hear something that large."

They sat quietly for a few minutes, staring at the room and listening for varmint movement. The silence was broken only once by the sound of a piece of wood clunking into pieces in the woodstove downstairs.

Erin raised her eyebrows. "I think we're alone now."

"Tommy James and the Shondells." He flopped back onto the bed. "I swear this building has more holes than a cheese grater."

She lay alongside him and ran her fingertips across his wrist. "You took off the brace."

He turned his head to look at her. "It gets in the way."

"Thanks again for doing all this work."

"I want to." He rolled over and pulled her close, lifting her arms up around his neck and sliding his hands along her back. "At first it was to spend more time with you, but now I'm determined to make this lodge habitable in time for Bea's reunion. It feels like some sort of test. Us against the elements and every form of vermin imaginable."

"I think the vermin are increasing in size." She moved her hands from his neck and placed her palms on his chest with a smile. "So you wanted to spend time with me, huh?"

"What do you think?" He chuckled and kissed her in a way that melted her bones, leaving no doubt about his answer to the question.

Erin unbuttoned his flannel shirt and ran her hands over his chest. She moved her head back, so she could see his face. "All that one-handed wood chopping seems to be good for you."

He laughed. "I need to work off stress somehow. Did I mention I haven't had a girlfriend since the last one ran for the hills?"

"Well, you haven't chased me off yet."

"Are you sure you don't want to leave?" He smiled as she maneuvered to pull off his t-shirt. "Because this is your last chance. When you start taking off my clothes, you're making a statement."

She threw his shirt on the floor and kissed his bare chest. "I don't want to go anywhere. I want to stay right here with you."

~

Later, Erin was enveloped in a blanket and Ziggy's long arms and legs, feeling more relaxed than she had in an extremely long time. Even after prolonged inactivity, her body seemed to remember how sex worked, which was a relief. Other than a few bouts of awkwardness, she didn't feel like she'd been a total clod anyway.

Both of their ponytails had fallen out at some point during the action and Erin traced a strand of his long hair with her fingertips. "I'm glad you took your own brotherly advice."

"I was starting to wonder if the Condom of Hope would ever make it out of its foil wrapper." He twirled her hair around his finger. "But it was worth waiting for."

Erin snuggled the blanket closer to her neck. "I'm glad not every blanket in this place smells like cat pee."

"This blanket wasn't near cats. I had it stowed in the cab for emergencies." He propped himself up on his elbows. "Like getting stuck in the snow."

Erin admired the view as he strode to the window. He turned to look at her. "We need to get out of here. It's starting to seriously come down out there."

Erin dragged the blanket off the bed with her as she went to look outside. "You have chains, right?"

"Part of the emergency kit." He grabbed his jeans and tugged them on. "Time to roll. Take me home, country roads."

"John Denver. Have you seen my sock? I can't find it."

"Maybe the possum ate it."

"That's not funny." Erin looked under the bed. "My foot is going to freeze."

Ziggy yanked a sock off one of his feet and held it out. "It might be too big."

"Ya think?" Erin laughed. "That's terribly gallant of you, but I'll tough it out."

The trap in the hall was empty and Erin fervently hoped that the varmint had dodged it and scampered off to the great outdoors. They hurriedly gathered up their things and carried them to the truck. Ziggy checked the outside traps, which were free of any possums or felines. He threw the traps into the back of the truck and set to work putting on the tire chains.

After Erin finished loading the cooler and various other supplies into the cab, she sat with her arms crossed, trying to warm her hands under her armpits. The multiple trips to the truck had chilled her to the bone. It was snowing with the type of fat, splatty, soggy flakes that she loathed because they often slid down your neck.

Early snows could be extremely wet and unpleasant. Although the odds were good that the storm would only be rain in town, getting there was likely to involve a white-knuckle ride. Today, she was feeling better about not having a license.

It was a slow trip down the icy driveway and along the back roads through the forest. By the time they got off the hill and back to the kennel, they'd dropped in elevation enough that the snow was more like semi-frozen slop, rather than fully formed flakes. The precipitation streamed down the windshield, the wipers whapping heavily in their effort to move the slushy gunk out of the way.

Erin waited in the truck while Ziggy handed Kat the check. They appeared to exchange only about three words, and after handing off Moose to Ziggy, Kat retreated into the kennel.

Ziggy stuffed Moose into the extended cab and got in, rubbing his hands together. "The snow floor is getting thin, so I need to take off the chains. I hate this type of weather."

Erin patted Moose's huge head, glad to be inside. "We'll be here."

The drive south to town was downright scary. After years in Washington, D.C. where snow flurries could constitute a state of emergency, seeing real snow and slippery roads was a stark reminder of how treacherous winter driving could be. It didn't help that people who could navigate bad road conditions in spring apparently lost all those skills by the following fall. Every single year, it was like over the summer everyone forgot how to drive in snow. Fortunately, Ziggy seemed to have nerves of steel, calmly and patiently navigating the highway and avoiding fellow drivers and the various cars that had pulled off to the side, either intentionally or not.

Finally they made it back to Alpine Grove, where the weather had segued into a noxious brew of freezing rain and semi-frozen glop. At least in town, the pavement was still visible. Having traction on the road was a welcome relief after skating through the icy hinterlands.

Ziggy pulled in front of the house and turned off the truck. He leaned forward, put his arms on the steering wheel, and rested his forehead on them.

Erin leaned close to him and realized he was shaking. "Are you okay?"

"Give me a second." He lifted his head. "I'm so grateful to be off the highway."

"You're a good driver. I wasn't worried."

"It's not me I'm worried about. It's the random guy in a rusted-out 1972 Ford Torino with bald tires sliding over the center line into my lane that I'm worried about."

"That guy must have stayed home."

"I kept thinking about how my mother says the universe has a twisted sense of humor." He pulled off his gloves and flexed his fingers. "We finally get together, then I go and kill us on the highway. I suppose at least I'd die happy."

Erin's heart lurched. "Don't even kid about something like that."

"I'm sorry. I wasn't thinking. It's been a complicated day."

"You seemed perfectly calm."

"Getting there." He held out a hand that was still shaking slightly. "Better anyway."

"Why don't you come inside for a minute?"

"I should get home. Plus, your parents are going to grill you on what you were up to with me. No thanks."

"How do you know that?"

He tilted his head and gave her a half-smile. "Look in the mirror. You look like you just had a lot of great sex."

Erin grabbed the rearview mirror and tilted it to examine her appearance. Okay, her hair was a disaster, and maybe she looked a little disheveled, but that didn't mean anything. "I do not. I look like I was out in the weather, which I was."

"If you say so. Maybe it's just me." He leaned over and gave her a smoldering kiss. "You're okay with what happened, right? We're still good?"

"Of course. Nothing's different."

"Yes it is. Sex changes things. It might be worse or it might be better, but it's always going to be different."

Erin pulled him close. "Stop worrying. Everything's good and I still love you. Please come inside for a minute."

"I need to go. It's only going to get colder and icier. I should make sure everything is okay at the farm."

"Call me when you get there to let me know you made it home. Tomorrow, after the plows have been out, I want to see if I can get Bea to set up some time to talk. Will you come with me?"

"Why do you need me there?"

"You have a different perspective and remember different things than I do."

"All right." He held up a hand, which remained still this time. "See ya tomorrow."

"Not if I see you first."

Erin waved as Ziggy drove off down the street, then she went inside. The house smelled like herbal tea and yummy baked goods. The sound of her parents laughing came from the living room. She walked in and found them on the floor playing with the kittens.

Jennifer looked up at Erin. "Good heavens, honey, what have you been up to? Did you and Dylan finally consummate your relationship?"

Erin looked down at herself. Was she wearing a sign or something? "We were at Dancing Cedars, and it started to snow. The roads are bad up north, so I hope you're not going anywhere."

Paul picked up the black kitten and snuggled the small purring beast to his chest. "Nope. When it's nasty outside, we try to stick close to home."

Erin went to the kitchen to make herself some tea. The phone rang and when Erin answered, Ziggy said without preamble, "Moose and I are here."

"Thanks for calling. My mother thinks we had sex."

"Told ya."

~

After hanging up with Ziggy, Erin took a shower in the hope that her mother would ease off on the comments about her appearance. To be fair, her hair was startling, but it had been a busy day, what with the furniture moving, sex, scary weather, and varmints.

Nobody made any comments at dinner, and afterward Erin declined an opportunity to work on her father's latest puzzle, preferring to retire to her room with Casey. The fact was, she was exhausted.

She went to the dresser and pulled the container of yellow pills out from under her pile of socks in the top drawer. Did she need ELF? Fingering it in her hand, she scanned the label, tucked it back into the dresser, and closed the drawer.

She walked to the bookshelf and scanned the titles. *Wuthering Heights?* Tortured, obsessive love. Nope. *The Lion, the Witch and the Wardrobe?* Narnia: a land frozen in eternal winter. Definitely no. *A Clockwork Orange.* Absolutely not.

Giving up on edifying classic literature, she pulled out a skinny Harlequin romance that had been tucked behind *War and Peace.* At least it was short, and it had to have a happy ending.

She placed Casey on the bed and he happily curled up into a furry pile. Tucked in with her book, Erin dug into reading and determined pretty quickly that the studly billionaire had some serious issues. What a jerk. For one thing, he was incredibly impatient, always checking his Rolex. Get over it, dude.

Finally, she couldn't stand any more of Reginald's arrogant behavior, so she set the book aside. She closed her eyes, and her mind immediately started analyzing every word she'd exchanged with Ziggy, ending with his comments about how sex changed things. Was he regretting it? It didn't seem like it at the time, but now she wasn't so sure.

After years with Andy, she knew all his likes and dislikes. Now everything with Ziggy was new and confusing. She'd even thought about Andy a few times and felt guilty about being with Ziggy. What if she was bad, compared to other women Ziggy had been with? It couldn't have been that terrible though, or she'd know, wouldn't she?

She flopped over on her side and stared at the dresser. It was if the yellow pills were calling to her, asking her to open the bottle and take them. She flipped back onto her back and tried to find a more comfortable spot, doing the counting backward thing again. If she got from one hundred all the way down to one, she was giving up and taking a pill.

The scent of gingerbread cookies caught her attention. Fluffy, picturesque snow swirled around her and the radio was playing "Wild Thing" by the Troggs. A giant possum dressed as Santa Claus waved at her and pointed at the meadow beyond. "Hey you, check it out. It's groovy."

Erin looked across the field and saw Andy, wearing the same long wool coat that he'd been wearing in Georgetown. Why was he at Dancing Cedars?

She moved through the snow, wondering how she could still hear that crummy little transistor radio out here in the meadow. Not to mention a giant possum. Well, crap. This was another of her weird dreams, wasn't it? Oh well. Best to go with it.

Andy said, "You're late. We have to get over there. Did you bring my notebook?"

"What notebook?" She looked around, and the possum was waving at a Holstein cow that was sitting on a rock smoking a hookah. The possum certainly was friendly. Was the cow stoned? On a stone? She giggled.

"What's so funny? I don't see anything over there. Why are you staring?" Andy grabbed her hand. "Come on, Erin.

Stop stalling. You were supposed to bring the notebook with all my notes. My promotion is riding on this. Hurry up."

She let Andy drag her across the meadow. He'd always been in a rush, looking forward to the next big event. It was always something. Sometimes she felt like she couldn't keep up. She wasn't a slacker, but his unrelenting ambition was a driving force that she didn't always share.

He dragged her past a flock of chickens that were doing a fowl conga line, twirling in the snow to "Dizzy" by Tommy Roe.

"Wait." She pulled on Andy's hand. "You have to look at that—there are dancing chickens!"

"Erin, would you stop dawdling? We're *late*."

Erin dug her feet into the snow. "No! Wait a minute. Where are we going?"

"I told you. Weren't you listening?"

"No, you didn't. Don't lecture me like I'm a child."

He stopped, and she scanned his face. Suddenly, the snow she was standing on dropped out from beneath her and she screamed as she fell down into a black cavern.

She opened her eyes and stared up at Casey's panting face. She reached to ruffle his ears. "Well, that one went beyond bizarre. A stoned cow? Yeesh. I'm sorry I woke you up, Case, but you should be getting used to this by now."

Shadows danced across the ceiling as a car went by outside. Yes, the dancing chickens and the Santa possum were off the wall, but the conversation with Andy wasn't terribly different from some she'd had in real life. She loved him with all her heart, but he hadn't been perfect. When he was stressed or anxious, he could be bossy and demanding. She wasn't perfect either. Sometimes she did dawdle when his impatience pissed her off, saying she wanted to 'stop and smell the roses' for a change.

No matter how much she wanted her old life back, they both were human with flaws and foibles. The idea that their life together had been all rainbows and unicorns every single day was a wishful fantasy borne out of grief and nostalgia.

Although she'd do anything to see him again, Andy was gone. She'd never be able to apologize or take back any of the things she wished she'd never said. If only she'd told him how much she loved him one more time.

She rolled over onto her side and started counting backward. To help relax, she envisioned herself cocooned in Ziggy's warm embrace again. How could two such wildly different men profess to love her? The two were practically polar opposites, and yet she loved them both. It didn't make any logical sense at all. Love was hopelessly confusing.

Maybe Melody was right, and it was the universe's twisted sense of humor having another laugh at her expense. She couldn't wait to tell Ziggy about her whacked-out dream. He would laugh and inevitably make some silly comment that would make her join in.

Imagining his expression when she told him about a giant Santa possum grooving to "Wild Thing" made her battered little heart sing.

~

A dog barked, jolting Erin out of a deep sleep. She sat bolt upright in bed and reached for Casey, who was facing the window with all the fur on his back standing up. She reached to rub his head between his ears. "Hey, shhh. Are you having weird dreams too?"

Erin jerked, her attention focused on a movement outside the window. Was she dreaming again? If there was a giant possum out there, she would not be amused. Enough with the dreams already.

A gloved hand tapped on the glass, and she leaped out of bed, looking frantically for something to defend herself with. Grabbing her shoe from the floor, she peeked around the window frame holding the shoe in front of her.

Ziggy waved from a perch on a branch in the massive oak tree next to the house.

Erin threw open the window and a frigid gust of air blew into the room. "What are you doing out there?"

"Freezing. Could you let me in?"

"Meet me downstairs. Don't you dare fall out of that tree!"

Erin shut the window and hustled down to the front door as quietly as she could. What kind of demented lunatic climbed trees in a snowstorm at two in the morning?

She opened the door and found a frosty Ziggy on the doorstep. She hissed for him to come in, and he followed her up the stairs. She went into her room and picked up Casey off the bed. The small dog wagged in her arms at the sight of the late-night visitor.

Shutting the door, she lowered Casey to the floor and faced Ziggy. "What are you doing here in the middle of the night?"

He took two steps toward her, placed his gloved hands on either side of her face and kissed her thoroughly.

When he finally released her, Erin was breathless. Wow. She made an effort to collect her wits. "Did you come here to kiss me?"

"No, but that's a bonus. I need a place to stay tonight. I have the key to Dancing Cedars, but there's no way I want to deal with the roads up there. There could be a foot of snow at the commune by now."

She pulled off his snow-covered coat, dropped it onto the floor, and tugged him toward the bed. "What happened?"

"It's kind of a long story." He sat next to her and pulled the comforter up around his shoulders. "I'm cold."

Erin got up and yanked the covers down off the bed. "Get in. Then tell me."

"You don't need to ask me twice." He pulled off his shoes, stripped down, and leaped into the bed, yanking the covers up to his chin. "I think I froze some vital body parts."

Erin crawled in next to him and snuggled up. "You *are* cold. Tell me what happened. Why are you here?"

"After I dropped you off and went home, my parents were fighting again. I headed for my room and hid out for a while writing some stuff, then Dad pounded on the door."

"What did you write?"

"Nothing interesting. Anyway, Dad storms in and tells me Barry quit."

"You mean Barry, the jingle-bear guy?"

"He got fed up with it. Took his check and hit the road."

Erin had a bad feeling she knew where this was going. "So then what happened?"

"Dad starts saying it's good Jingle Barry is gone because they're in debt, so paying him was a problem. I pointed out that he wasn't paying me during my time off, so it evens out." He scowled. "That didn't go over too well."

"Is the tree farm in trouble?"

"Yeah, it barely scrapes by. My parents aren't great with money." He ran his fingers through the hair behind her ear. "You're beautiful, you know."

"Don't change the subject. What happened?"

"Don't bring me down."

"Electric Light Orchestra. A little out of our time period, but I'll give it to you."

"Thanks. Can't get it out of my head."

"More ELO. Very funny. No more songs. Stop evading." She gave him a kiss. "The argument got worse, didn't it?"

"A lot worse." He took a deep breath and closed his eyes. "Huge fight. Massive. I totally lost it."

"What did you say?"

"Jeez, I don't even know. Dad started talking about how I needed to buckle down and work harder. Not to mention dress up as a bear. He said the farm was my legacy. I remember saying, 'I don't want this albatross.'"

"Wow. You actually said that?"

"Then he went off on how he *forbids* me to go back to Dancing Cedars. I yelled that he can't forbid me to do anything. I yanked open the closet door so hard I pulled it off the frame. Then I grabbed a suitcase and started throwing clothes and notebooks into it."

"I don't think I've ever seen you that angry."

"I hope you never do." He closed his eyes. "I don't think I've ever *been* that angry. Everything I've been thinking for years came out. Everything."

"So you came here?"

He opened his eyes. "I could have gone to a motel I guess, but I didn't want to show up at the H12 in the middle of the night, mostly because I know Jon and Annabelle. I was so furious I could barely think. I came here and sat in my truck for a while watching it snow until I calmed down."

"Then you climbed a tree." She grinned at him. "How typical. Some things never change."

"I suppose." He rested his head on her shoulder. "I know it sounds sappy, but while I was sitting out there in my truck, all I wanted was to talk to you. I decided to see if I could reach your window from the tree. Good thing I have long arms."

"I'm glad you're safe." She ran her fingertips across his temple. "We should go to sleep."

"Your parents are going to freak when they find me here tomorrow."

"They're not going to mind. Whatever problems they have are with your parents, not you. Mom thinks you're shy and polite."

"You've got to be kidding."

"Don't worry about it. We'll deal with them in the morning."

He rubbed her shin with his toes. "Hey, I'm sorry to barge in on you like this, Stardust."

"It's no big deal. I've been having more strange dreams, so in a way, I wasn't that surprised. It's like you said before. We should be grateful for all the things that didn't happen. At least it wasn't a giant possum in a Santa suit knocking on the window."

He raised his head to look at her with wide eyes. "No way."

"Yes, way!" She laughed. "He was in the meadow listening to 'Wild Thing' on the radio."

"That's totally groovy." He chuckled and wrapped his arms around her. "Thanks for putting up with me."

"I love you." She gave him a kiss. "I know you're upset now, but maybe this is for the best. You've been taking care of everyone else for a long time. Maybe it's time you take care of you."

"I doubt Dad would see it that way, but you're probably right. It's way past time for me to figure myself out."

"Me too. Now go to sleep."

Chapter 13

Pyro Zeppelin Fan

The next morning, Erin opened her eyes and determined that she was effectively trapped by Ziggy and Casey, who were both sprawled all over the bed. It was a little crowded, but they looked so content that her heart melted a little and she couldn't bear to wake them up. Instead, she reached for her book and read a few more of the adventures of Reginald the arrogant billionaire.

As she flipped a page, she looked up and discovered Ziggy was watching her. He smiled. "A guy could get used to waking up like this."

"I hate to break up this cocoon of warmth you and Casey have created, but I need to run down the hall to the bathroom."

He relocated to set her free and then hunkered back under the comforter. Casey stood up and spun around a few times before resettling into a tight ball in almost the same spot.

When Erin returned, it appeared no one had moved. She peeled the covers back from Ziggy's head. "Where's Moose?"

"At the house. I couldn't take him with me because I wasn't sure where I was going. As a final jab, Dad said that Moose is going to be spending a whole lot of time in the barn if I'm not there to watch him."

"You need to go back and get your dog."

"I know. I was waiting 'til the morning comes."

"Oh please. Grateful Dead. American Beauty." She slapped his arm. "That's too easy. You're not even trying."

"It's early."

"Get up. You need to face the day."

He sat up and wrapped his arms around his knees. "This day is going to be brutal for a lot of reasons. Denial has been glorious."

"Go take a shower. I need to break the news to my parents that we had a slumber party."

"We did!" He laughed. "And it was excellent."

She leaned over to give him a kiss. "Yes, it was."

Erin went downstairs with Casey and made a pot of coffee. She heard the shower running upstairs. Maybe Ziggy had actually listened to her. Wouldn't that be nice?

Her mother came into the kitchen, poured herself a cup of coffee, and sat down at the table. "I thought you were showering."

Erin wrapped her fingers around her mug more tightly. "Um, we have a house guest."

"Let me guess." Jennifer turned her gaze toward the ceiling. "Why is Dylan here? He wasn't here last night."

Erin explained about the fight, the bad roads to Dancing Cedars, and the late-night visit. She left out the tree-climbing details. Mom didn't need to know everything.

"He's planning to *live* out at the commune?" With a look of consternation, Jennifer took a sip of coffee. "Technically, he shouldn't stay there without getting everyone's permission first."

"I don't know what he's planning to do. But all the work we've been doing out there has made it a little better. We even got some free furniture." She gestured at the windows. "He has nowhere else to go until he finds a place to live. And maybe a job." Erin shrugged. "I can relate to being in transition. My life has been in flux for a while."

"I'll talk to your father. Unless he objects, Dylan can stay here for a few days. I'm sure he just needs to work things out with his family."

Given what Ziggy had told her, Erin didn't think he and his father were going to work out much of anything, but she nodded gamely. "Thanks, Mom." Most people their age weren't dealing with their lives crumbling into rubble like this. Maybe she should go to the mall, sit on Santa's lap, and ask for a life plan for Christmas. Clearly, she wasn't doing too well on her own.

Jennifer got up, poured a cup of coffee for Paul, and left Erin alone in the kitchen with Casey and her thoughts. She looked up when Ziggy walked in. His smile and wet hair reminded her of her muddy laughing dream.

She pointed at the pot of coffee. "Over there."

He grabbed a mug and sat next to her. "Where is everybody?"

"Mom took some coffee and went to talk to Dad."

"Yeah, Arrow is gonna love this. Running away from home at my age is pretty lame." He took a sip of coffee. "Your parents must think I'm a serious loser."

"If you think about it, our parents running away to a commune in 1967 wasn't all that different. Plus putting aside everything else, we're friends and have been forever. Friends help each other out. You'd do the same thing for me. In fact, you did when you picked me up at the airport and let me stay in the Kris Kringle barf room."

"I suppose I did. Well, I'll do my best to get out of here ASAP. I'm going to call Joel and see if that little cabin is available for rent."

"It's pretty remote. If you get a job in town, that's a long drive."

"I can live off my savings for a while."

"You have savings?"

"I haven't had any food or lodging expenses for years, remember?" He gestured toward the windows. "All that time, I watched my parents spend money on stupid things like a bear suit. Did you know that a bear suit costs three hundred dollars? How many trees do you have to sell to pay for that? It's nuts. The numbers don't work."

"I thought you said you were bad at math."

"Heck, even *I* can add. I've put half of what I earned into savings." He shrugged. "I only get paid seven-fifty an hour, but I've saved what I could."

Erin furrowed her brows. "Tree farming certainly doesn't pay well."

"It's fifteen thousand a year, which totally stinks. But with minimal expenses, it's not as bad as it seems."

Erin did some quick mental calculations. "I'm getting the impression you might have more money than I thought."

He grinned. "Compound interest is cool. After taxes, I make about a thousand bucks a month. I use half for stuff like clothes, truck repairs, gas, and insurance. The other five hundred I save."

"I guess that would add up."

"The average return over time has been about seven percent, so over the last ten years, I've put aside about sixty thousand, but I've earned about twenty-five more in interest."

"Holy crap." Erin gaped at him. "You're saying you have eighty-five *thousand* dollars in savings?"

"More or less. It changes depending on what my portfolio is doing."

"I can't believe you have a portfolio."

"Well, duh, obviously. Did you think I put the money under my mattress or something?"

"Did you share any of this financial wizardry with your parents? It sounds like they could use it."

"Early on, I tried. I set a budget and spending guidelines for them, but it didn't work. Mom would get some brilliant new idea and Dad would go buy some expensive piece of equipment or decorations. I gave up and told them to talk to a CPA. That guy set me up with a salary, so the farm wouldn't get in trouble with the IRS. After that, I only focused on the trees. If Mom and Dad bankrupted the farm, it wouldn't be my fault. I'm just the dumb employee."

"Not so dumb." Erin put her elbows on the table and rested her chin on her hands. "Financially speaking, if you're going to live off savings, Alpine Grove is a far better place to do it than Washington, D.C. At least you can afford rent. I've got almost nothing left."

He put his hand on her forearm. "All the more reason for you to move here."

Erin wasn't ready to make that decision. "We'll see what happens."

They both looked up as Paul and Jennifer returned to the kitchen. Paul set his mug in the sink and turned around, crossing his arms. "Hi Dylan. It sounds like you're staying for a while."

"Just a day or two. Thanks for letting me crash here."

Jennifer said, "I think you should talk to your parents, honey. Melody must be frantic by now, wondering where you are."

"Once the plows are out, I need to go pick up Moose. I'll tell them where I'm staying," Ziggy replied.

"Are you bringing the dog here?" Jennifer frowned and turned to raise her eyebrows at Erin. "You didn't mention that. As I recall, Moose doesn't like cats, and you've already saddled us with kittens."

"You love those kittens, and you know it," Erin said. "Casey has adjusted fine."

Ziggy said, "I'll take Moose out to the kennel. It's no big deal. I need to call them this morning anyway."

"We're meeting Bea today before the store opens," Erin added, giving Ziggy a significant look. "Maybe we should get going."

"Yup, let's do that. Thanks again for letting me stay."

They scurried up the stairs and Erin shut the door behind them. "Why do I feel like we got bawled out by my parents?"

He laughed and wrapped her in a hug. "They're a heck of a lot more polite about their disapproval than my parents are."

"Let's get out of here. Since you're loaded, I think you should take me out to breakfast."

"All right, but I'm also a cheapskate, so keep that in mind. I mean, you've seen my truck. I paid two hundred bucks for it fifteen years ago, and it was old *then*."

She giggled. "Good point. Bargain-basement breakfast it is."

The sun had come out, and the weather was in a sparkly post-snowstorm mode that was absolutely stunning. They walked through the glittering side streets to town, holding hands.

Ziggy turned, gave her a wide-eyed look, and said, "Hey, we're walking down a street." He then launched into a loud rendition of the Monkees' theme. Erin joined in, and they twirled down the sidewalk through the residential area, enjoying the pretty morning and getting a few funny looks.

Erin was out of breath by the time they got to the main street of town. "You are such a goofball."

"Takes one to know one."

❀

After a hearty breakfast at the deli near the H12 motel, they met Bea in front of the gift store. They had a half hour before the store opened, and Erin hoped it would give her enough time to interrogate Bea about anyone and everyone who might have a claim on Dancing Cedars.

They sat in chairs behind the counter, and Erin went through the list of owners to see if Bea remembered anyone being in debt. After a lot of conversation, they learned little.

Although almost everyone involved had various financial issues over the years, Bea had talked to them all about the reunion and asked about the corporation. No one had heard of it. Bea added that no one should have been able use the property as collateral without everyone's agreement.

Erin pointed out, "That might be true, but it seems like someone did. Legally, any of the owners has a one-twelfth interest. But without more information, it's impossible to know what happened."

There was a lull in the conversation. Ziggy looked depressed and Erin figured he had to be worried that his parents were the ones who had sold out.

Bea said, "I have to open the store in a couple of minutes. What do you think we should do?"

Erin said, "I need to find out who owns this mysterious corporation. So far, I've got nothing, but I'll start making calls. Someone has to know. If we can figure that out, next we need to determine that the debt the lien represents is actually valid. If it is, that person needs to pay off the debt. The lien holder then signs lien revocation paperwork."

They all stood up and Bea gave Erin a hug. "I know you'll work this out. I have faith in you."

Bea unlocked the front door and went outside, greeting two women who were standing at the window and chatting.

Bea grabbed Erin's sleeve to stop her. "Wait. It's Gardenia and Heather."

"Welcome back." Ziggy said and turned to Erin. "Gwen and Heather used to live out near the dog boarding kennel."

"A nice woman named Mia took the trailer off my hands," the older of the two women said. "We're just passing through town, but I had to stop by here."

Erin hadn't seen Gardenia or her daughter Heather since they'd lived at Dancing Cedars, and now she wouldn't have been able to pick either of the two out of a crowd. Heather was three years younger than Erin and back then had been close friends with a girl named Harmony. While Ziggy was dragging Erin all over the forest on their adventures, Heather and Harmony had been at the lodge playing games with their dolls.

Bea briefly gave the two women an overview of what was going on with the commune and the conservation effort.

Erin chimed in, "Have you heard of a corporation named Ignite Enterprises? It could be owned by someone who knows about Dancing Cedars for some reason."

Gwen said, "Never heard of it. Is it local?"

"No, it's a corporation registered in Delaware. It's an anonymous corporation, which means the filing doesn't list the owners."

"That's suspicious." Gwen scowled. "Ignite. Fire. Blaze. Inferno. Maybe it's that jerk who was the pyro."

Bea shook her head. "I don't remember anyone like that."

"Me neither," Erin said. "What did he set on fire?"

"Nothing critical. He was a little too into fireworks though." Gwen waved off the comment. "That summer probably fifty people passed through that place, and he was one of them. I barely remember what he looked like. He wore the same Led Zeppelin t-shirt the whole time he was there. By the time he left, he was ripe."

Erin remembered more than a few stinky people, particularly in the summertime. A firework-loving dude in a Zeppelin t-shirt wasn't much of a lead. She would have to set aside a lot of time to call anyone she could think of in Delaware.

A man approached the group. "Is the store open?"

Bea stepped aside so the man could go inside, and Gwen gave her a hug. "We need to get going."

Bea stopped before going inside. "Will you be in town on the solstice? A bunch of people are getting together at Dancing Cedars for the thirtieth anniversary."

Gwen and Heather declined the invitation, but said they'd stop by again before they left town.

Ziggy and Erin said their good-byes and started back for the house. He took her hand. "How are we going to find out who owns this corporation if they want to keep it secret?"

"I'm not sure. Any ideas? I don't think the pyro Zeppelin fan is much of a clue."

"Maybe not, but I think it's the guy we were talking about the other day. The guy with the fringe jacket wore a Zeppelin t-shirt under it."

Erin let go of his hand stopped to face him. "Phoenix. Fire."

He grinned. "Exactly."

"That's great, except does anyone know what his real name was? The fact that a hippie named Phoenix was at the commune doesn't get us very far."

Their gazes locked, and they simultaneously turned around and went back to the store.

Bea was behind the counter, pulling items from a box and unwrapping them. She looked up in surprise. "You're back already?"

"Do you remember a guy named Phoenix?" Erin asked. "He's the guy Gwen was talking about. He wore a leather jacket with fringe."

Bea looked down at the crystal in the tissue paper. "I think…yes, I'm sure. That was Spencer."

Erin put her palms together, as if in prayer. "Last name?"

Bea bit her lip. "I can't remember. Wait! Yes, I do. Spencer Widman. He said you could remember because he was a wild man."

"Do you know what happened to him?" Ziggy asked.

"I have no idea," Bea said, turning to smile at a customer who was approaching the counter.

"Okay, we'll let you know if we find anything," Erin said, grabbing Ziggy's hand. "Library. Now."

They hustled down to the library, galloped up the steps, and went inside. Ziggy greeted Jan, the librarian Erin had worked with when she researched the company. They acted like the best of buddies, which they probably were, given how much time Ziggy spent here reading and checking out books.

Erin mentally acknowledged a flash of jealousy. Jan was rather pretty with curly reddish-blonde hair and a body that probably attracted some serious male attention.

Although Erin didn't often focus on what Ziggy looked like because she'd known him so long, objectively speaking he was handsome, tall, and in incredible shape from the physical labor he did at the farm. And of course he had those amazing, expressive eyes that were startling even to her.

Ziggy might be the smart, funny guy who'd been her best friend since forever to her. But to other women, he was probably considered a high-quality dating prospect, particularly in Alpine Grove, where pickings had always been notoriously slim.

He shoved her shoulder, "Yo, Stardust. Were you listening?"

"What?"

"Spencer is a developer."

"You mean like a software developer?"

"No. Land. According to this article Jan found online, he speculates in land development. Mostly in Las Vegas, but he's bragging about expanding into California."

"Wow. As Gwen said, that's suspicious."

"Yeah, it is." He took her hand and gave it a squeeze. "Now what?"

She turned to Jan. "Could you help us dig up everything you can on this guy? Let's start with his business interests and contact information."

Jan grinned widely, obviously embracing the research challenge. "I'd love to."

~

After they got home from the library, Ziggy called the kennel and after much negotiation, he convinced them to house Moose for a few days. Erin was relieved that she didn't have to have the homeless-dog conversation with her parents.

She offered to go out to the tree farm with Ziggy, but he claimed it was probably better if he had the inevitable argument with his parents without her there.

He was probably right, and she had to see if she could track down the elusive Spencer Widman by phone anyway. Assuming she managed to reach the guy, it was likely to be an awkward conversation. "Hi, you don't know me, but do you own a corporation that you obviously don't want anyone to know about that happens to have a lien on a commune that you reportedly visited more than twenty years ago?" Ugh. During her career, she sometimes had to make unpleasant calls, but this had the potential to be particularly embarrassing.

Mom and Dad had gone to Gleasonville, probably to shop for more kitten supplies, so after tending to the little felines, Erin settled in her mother's office with all the copies and printouts that Jan had given her at the library. Casey had taken on canine supervisory duties and was snoring in the dog bed near the desk.

The first few numbers she tried were either dead ends or disconnected. Finally, she got a hit. When she asked for Spencer and stated her name, the prim voice on the other end said, "May I ask what this is regarding?"

Startled, Erin paused for a bit too long, then said, "I'm inquiring about his interest in a property in Alpine Grove."

The snippy receptionist put Erin through and a man said in a gruff voice, "Widman."

Erin gulped. How should she phrase her question? Her mind raced, scrambling for words. She was rusty at sounding like an articulate professional. In her most lawyerly voice, she said, "Hello. My name is Erin Quinn and I represent the interests of the owners of a property in Alpine Grove. I'm attempting to determine if you are an owner of an LLC with the name Ignite Enterprises."

"Who did you say you are?"

"Erin Quinn."

"Are you a lawyer or something?"

Although Erin had passed the DC bar, she'd never practiced, but he didn't know that. "Yes sir, I'm an attorney. Do you own the LLC?"

"Who wants to know?"

Erin's irritation level rose and she said more curtly. "The people who own the land I mentioned have discovered that

Ignite Enterprises, LLC has placed a lien against the property. We'd like to discuss the nature of the obligation."

"When you owe money and don't pay it back, that's what happens. What's it to you?"

"We'd like to have the lien removed because we are looking into protecting the property with a conservation easement through a land trust. It's an equitable solution for the owners, but we need to remove the encumbrances on the title."

"We'll that's too bad, girlie. You can't do any conservation crap without my say-so. And I've got other plans."

"It has come to my attention that you're a land developer."

"Yep, which means I know that much acreage could be worth some bucks."

"I'm hoping that we can reach an amicable solution to this situation. I'd like the details of the obligation. What is the amount in question?"

"I'm sure it's more than you can afford."

Erin would have loved to reach through the phone line to smack him, but stifled her anger. "I've had difficulty determining the details of the lien. I know it's a non-purchase money security interest lien, but the record of it has been difficult to access." Try impossible.

"So what?" he snarled. "That's not my problem."

"I'd appreciate some details. You have attached a lien on the property and we'd like to work out a mutually amenable solution to satisfy the obligation."

"Nope. I've got plans and they aren't any of your business. Hey girlie, gotta go. I got a meeting."

Before Erin could say anything else, he hung up. She hadn't learned much beyond the fact that Spencer made the Grinch who stole Christmas seem like an easygoing, fun guy. And after all these years, he *still* referred to her as girlie, which made her want to throw something against the wall.

Disgusted, she stood up and raised her hands over her head in a long stretch. It was Saturday. She'd talked to a receptionist, so it appeared she'd called Spencer's work number. Why was he working on the weekend? And making his staff work too. What a tool.

Erin scooped her papers into a pile, stuffed them into a folder, and clutched it to her chest. She was heading for the stairs, when her parents came in the front door. They were holding folders too. It was like an office-supply family reunion.

Erin stopped in front of them. Mom's eyes were red and she looked upset. "What's going on? I thought you were going shopping."

"I thought you told her," Paul said.

Jennifer offered a watery half smile. "We went to visit a lawyer."

"Why? I'm a lawyer. I might be able to help, and I'm free," Erin said. She had a bad feeling she knew why they didn't ask.

Jennifer held out her file. "These are separation papers, honey."

"We went to Gleasonville because we didn't want to use that guy here," Paul added. "He spends half his life chatting up the hostess at the Italian restaurant, and who knows who'd find out."

Erin sat down on the bottom step, laid her folder on her knees, and looked up at them. "Wow. Are you sure you want to do this?"

"Your mother wants to set out on her own, so it makes sense to divide our assets," Paul said.

"But you still love each other, don't you?" Erin looked down at the papers, then looked up again. "You've been together for so long."

"Of course, we love each other. But I'm not ready to stop doing events," Jennifer said. "Our paths are diverging."

Erin stood up again, gripping her folder tightly and hugging it to her chest. "This doesn't make any sense. I don't see why you can't work something out."

"I'm sorry, Erin. But I want to retire," Paul said. "To be honest, I didn't think you'd care so much."

"I don't think you've looked at all the options. All the variables. What if you compromise?" Erin said.

"We've talked this out, honey." Jennifer said. "I'm sorry if it upsets you. I hear what you're saying, but this makes financial sense for us. We've worked out an agreement, so we don't have to sell the house."

Paul said, "Your mother loves this place and doesn't want to part with it, and I respect that."

Erin couldn't believe they were being so reasonable when this was so wrong. She pointed at her father. "What if you didn't have to travel as often?"

"As I said about a hundred times, that's what I want," he said. "I'm done with weekly or daily stints at airports. Life is too short. I'd like time to relax."

Erin pointed at her mother. "What if you could still travel?"

"That's exactly what I'm talking about doing, honey. What are you suggesting?" Jennifer said.

"Don't do what you've been doing. Stay in one place for a month. Or six months. Or a year." Erin spread her arms wide, gripping her folder in one hand. "Do a bunch of seminars in one central location, so you can spend enough time to see the place and relax. Make people come to you. Then go to another location or go home for a period of time."

Paul said, "That a good idea, but what about the house? And Casey. We can't leave him alone here for months."

"I don't want anything to happen to the house," Jennifer added. "And Casey is getting older. We can't board him for an extended period like that. It's not fair to him."

"Get a caretaker," Erin said. "Ziggy is homeless. How about him?"

"What about you?" Jennifer said. "I'd love it if you were here taking care of things."

"Me?" Erin wrapped her arms across the folder on her chest again. "I don't think that's a great idea."

Jennifer grinned at Paul. "What do you think? This feels better than what we were considering."

"I agree. Tomorrow, let's call Donna and see if there's any way we could switch the scheduling around."

Jennifer looked at the folder in her hand. "Maybe we'll set these aside for the moment and see what the universe holds for us."

Erin stepped forward and hugged her mother. "Obviously, the universe doesn't consult me often, but if you two love each other, I think you should stay together."

"I hope you're right." Paul laughed and put his arms around the two women. "Group hug for luck."

~

As minutes turned to hours and afternoon turned into evening, Erin wondered what had become of Ziggy. She thought he was just going to go get Moose and take him out to the kennel. Yes, it was a bit of a drive to get there, but he'd been gone for *hours*. He could have made five trips back and forth by now. What if something had happened to him on the highway? The roads were fine in town, but plowing sometimes was delayed or nonexistent out in the boonies. What if he'd decided to go to Dancing Cedars to get his tools and gotten stuck up there? He was an adult and certainly could take care of himself, so she didn't want to be an alarmist, but she couldn't stop herself from inventing tales of doom.

After dinner, she grabbed her book and parked herself in a chair in the living room so she could see outside. At every car going by, she looked to see if it was Ziggy's junky old truck pulling up to the curb. The little pit of worry in her stomach had turned into a sickly crater of quasi-nausea. She couldn't lose another person she loved. The universe wasn't *that* unfair, was it? If something had happened to him, would anyone think to call her?

Erin was setting her book aside to get up and look up the number of the tree farm when a truck pulled up outside. The wave of relief that flooded through her made her feel almost lightheaded, but she leaped out of the chair and ran out the door.

Ziggy was reaching for a box in the extended cab and looked up in surprise. "Hey, get a coat. It's freezing out here."

Erin wrapped her arms around him. "Where have you been?"

"I dropped off Moose, then went back to the farm, tried to fix some stuff, put the blade on my truck, and plowed." He moved away from her and picked up the box. "You're shivering. Let's go inside."

Back in her room, Erin closed the door behind her and launched herself into Ziggy's arms, hugging him hard. "Where were you?"

"I told you. I went home. Or not home anymore, I guess. I had to plow. The hydraulics on the blade for Dad's truck are shot, and people don't buy Christmas trees when they can't get to them."

"I was worried. It probably won't surprise you to hear that when I don't hear from you, my thoughts tend to travel down dire pathways."

"I suppose that makes sense, but I was outside all day and couldn't get away. Too much working and fighting." He moved away and sat on the bed. "Right now, I need a minute to decompress. I'm so tired I can barely see straight."

"I have so much I have to tell you."

"Can it wait? People have been talking at me all day." He flopped backward on the bed. "I need some quiet."

Erin crawled alongside him. "I hate to ask this, but your father has had all summer to get someone to fix the plow. Why didn't he?"

"Logic rarely comes into play." He sat up and gave her a hug. "I don't want to talk about this now. I'm going to take a shower. I feel like I'm covered with oil."

He grabbed some clothes from a duffel bag and disappeared down the hall. Erin was relieved he was okay, but alarmed that he didn't want to talk about whatever had happened at the farm. He *always* talked to her. Well, except when he was off climbing trees. Maybe all those times he'd disappeared, he wasn't only getting away from the adults. Hmm.

When Ziggy returned, his hair was wet and he was squeaky clean, but he looked no less exhausted and disturbed. He jammed the dirty clothes into the duffel, and a few spiral notebooks thumped onto the floor.

Erin pointed at them. "What are those?"

"Nothing." He sprawled out on the bed on his side with his arm under the pillow. "I should have left them there. But then my parents would read what I wrote and think I'm more of a lazy, lunatic freak than they already do."

Erin lay on the bed facing him and rubbed his arm. Whatever argument he'd had with his parents must have been bad. "You're not lazy. I'm sorry you had such a terrible day."

"I tried to fix Dad's plow and if the repair holds, it will be worth it. The truck itself doesn't sound too great either, so it will probably fall apart next."

"What if you gave him money to fix it or bought him a new plow rig? Then you'd be done with the whole mess."

"I've tried that type of thing." He ran a finger along her temple, moving her hair back from her face. "The problem is that if I give them money, they'll just piss it away. So I give them my time instead. Or I did. They're freaking out that I don't want to anymore."

"You have the right to live your own life."

"So I've heard."

"And for the record, you're not a lunatic. Don't say stuff like that. Having an active imagination and original thoughts is something to be proud of." She kissed him. "Even my mom said you always had a creative spirit."

"That's probably mom-speak for lunatic freak. Having a pile of notebooks full of random scribbles doesn't make me Hemingway."

"What do you write about?"

"Random stuff. Thoughts and ideas mostly. Sometimes just words. For a while, I'd come up with a string of adjectives to describe what happened during the day and how I felt."

"It sounds like *tired* would be the word for today, since you're so worn out."

"Also frustrated, disappointed, discontented, discouraged, baffled, defeated, disillusioned, disgruntled, exasperated." He waved his hand. "Ugh. None of this is new, and I'm sick of it. Can we talk about something else?"

"Do you ever write down your stories? You used to make up the most fantastic adventures."

"Nothing that organized. Most of it's short, like snippets of text about what I'm thinking. Or poems, lyrics, and that type of thing."

"Hold on. You write song lyrics? That's so *you*."

He grinned. "I love that you think that, but it's no big deal. Just basic song structure and some rhymes."

"Do you play an instrument?"

"Sort of. I taught myself guitar from a book from the library. I can play basic chords, but I'm terrible. Nobody is going to confuse me with Jimmy Page or Eddie Van Halen."

"How come you didn't bring your guitar here with you?"

"I don't have one. I used to borrow Dad's when I had a tune in my head that I wanted to work out with the lyrics."

"That's wonderful! Did you write down the songs?" Erin gripped his arm. "I *really* want to hear a song you've written."

"I can dig them out sometime, I guess. Some of the chord charts are sort of wonky, but I could probably figure them out again." He smiled. "To be honest, I didn't think I'd ever play them for anyone, so I didn't worry about it too much."

"I want you to play your songs for me. Consider it my Christmas present."

"I already got mine. Spending all this time with you has been the best present I've ever received." He wrapped his arms around her. "I know my life is kind of a mess right now. Thank you for being a friend."

"Andrew Gold. But the song was re-recorded in the eighties by someone else for the TV show 'The Golden Girls.'"

"Impressive."

Chapter 14

Time in a Bottle

The next morning, Erin woke up next to Ziggy, snuggled like a small spoon nested next to a much larger one. He had his arm around her and was still fast asleep. She remained motionless, listening to the sound of his breathing and thinking about what he'd said the night before.

For quite some time, spending time with her hadn't been much of a gift to anyone. Because she and Ziggy talked about a wide range of random things, it startled her when he indicated how much he cared about her. It had been a long time since she'd been close to anyone who felt strongly about her, and she'd been so busy grieving that she'd forgotten what it felt like to be important to another person.

Andy had loved her, but because he had a lot of his own stuff going on, their relationship had had a different dynamic. When she was around Ziggy, she felt sexier and more fun than she had in years. No wonder she'd freaked out when he'd disappeared. She couldn't let herself think about how she'd feel if something happened to him.

He moved his arm, took her hand, and interlaced his fingers with hers. "I know you're awake. What are you worrying about?"

"I'm not worrying." Okay, she was. "Just thinking."

"I can think of a way to get you to stop thinking."

Erin giggled. "So it seems."

Quite a bit later, Erin finally related the events of the prior day to Ziggy. He agreed that Spencer was a first-class jerk and was pleased that her parents might not split up.

They finally meandered downstairs seeking coffee and found Casey snoozing in his kitchen dog bed. A note on the counter said that Erin's parents had gone to buy some more kitten food, which was kind of a relief to Erin. She still wasn't sure if they were completely okay with Ziggy staying there or not.

Ziggy made coffee while she checked on the kittens, who were fast asleep in their room. Jennifer had said that they made a point of playing with the feisty little felines at least three times a day so they'd sleep more when people weren't around to keep an eye on them. The plan seemed to be working.

Erin returned to the kitchen and Ziggy handed her a mug. "I feel way better than I did yesterday."

Erin took a sip and grinned at him. "Sleep and sex seem to agree with you."

"Definitely the way to start the day." He wrapped a long arm around her shoulders, "Not thinking about broken machinery, bills, and bankruptcy has a lot to recommend it too."

She looked up at him. "Is it really that bad?"

"Yeah. When you and I were talking about how they need to sell out, that's pretty much the best option, unless I take over the farm."

"And you don't want to."

"No, and I feel guilty about it." He leaned down to kiss her. "Have I mentioned I don't want to talk about this? Let's do something fun today."

"I need to call Bea and ask her to see if she can find out who owes Spencer money. It has to be one of the landowners. None of them had heard about the corporation, but maybe they know Spencer. She's been in touch talking to them about the reunion anyway."

"After you do that, let's go somewhere. We've never actually gone out, well, anywhere."

"You mean like a *date*?" Erin grinned. "This is us doing everything out of order again, isn't it?"

"At least I don't have to worry about whether or not you'll be willing to give me a good-night kiss."

"If you take me out, I'm pretty sure you're going to score."

"This idea gets better all the time."

After showering and getting organized, Erin called Bea, who promised to track down the person who was in debt to Spencer. She also encouraged Erin to talk to the local land trust about the conservation easement. "There's a lot of legal stuff to understand. I've been working with a woman named Joanna, and I told her to expect your call."

"Bea, I told you before, I can't practice law in this state."

"You're not. You're talking to people we're working with to set up the easement. I'm sure you'll have a better idea what she's talking about, legally speaking."

Erin acknowledged that her years of law school might help and promised to call first thing Monday.

When she got off the phone, Ziggy grabbed her hand and pulled her to him. "Ready for your date?"

"I guess so. Where do you want to go?"

"Let's go to the Italian restaurant for lunch. That's where half of Alpine Grove ends up on first dates."

Erin raised her eyebrows. "So how many times have you been there?"

"Never even once with you. Let's pretend we've never met."

"What?"

He tilted his head and gave her a quizzical look. "So where did you grow up?"

Erin laughed. "I lived at this whacked-out hippie commune outside of a little town in the middle of nowhere."

He put his palm on his chest and widened his eyes. "Wow, that's so interesting. What was it like?"

"Well, living without electricity has some challenges. Have you ever had to visit an outhouse when it's two degrees outside?"

"At least the spiders would be dead."

"That's *amazing* that you mentioned the spiders." Erin grabbed his hand and dragged him toward the door. "How did you know?"

"Lucky guess."

"Well, I can tell you stories about spiders. The big, scary ones like to hang out in outhouses. It's like a spider breeding ground."

He held the door open for her. "Really?"

Erin locked the door behind them. "But there was this kid who used to try to trap them and set them free, so I wouldn't be scared."

"What a weirdo."

"Actually, it was sweet." She squeezed his hand. "Your turn. Where did you grow up?"

"Near a forest filled with gigantic ancient cedars. I spent lots of time playing by a creek. My best friend and I used to lie in the sun and listen to the water flowing over the rocks. We stared up at the sky, watched birds fly through the trees, and made up stories about the shapes we saw in the clouds."

"That sounds lovely." Erin knew it had been, but was surprised he remembered it so clearly.

"When things get me down, I think back on it. Lying on the moss was one of those perfect peaceful moments that's locked in time. Nothing else mattered in the world, except being there with my friend, soaking up the sun, listening to nature, and enjoying being together."

"It was wonderful, wasn't it?" Erin stopped and faced him. "I think I didn't let myself remember for a long time."

"That probably made it easier to leave." He pulled her close. "It wasn't all good, but there were some perfect moments like that when I wish I could have saved time in a bottle."

"Jim Croce. And yes, that day was magical wasn't it? I'm so glad I spent it with you." She rested her cheek on his chest. "Thanks for being my spider defender too."

"I hope all the work we're doing out there will be worth it."

She leaned back to look up at his face. "Now that you've got the plow on your rig, we should probably get back to it."

"Hey, we're supposed to be on a first date. Enough work talk. What's your favorite color?"

Erin laughed and started walking again. "Green. The deep green of cedars in the springtime."

As promised, Erin called the Cedars Land Trust the next morning and had a long conversation with an extremely helpful woman named Joanna about the proposed conservation easement. The land trust was a nonprofit organization focused on conservation. The landowners all had to agree to sign papers that transferred the development rights for Dancing Cedars to the land trust, which would effectively extinguish those rights and protect the land. The easement was perpetual and would have to be adhered to by any future heirs or owners of the land. The landowners would receive tax benefits and the reassurance that the land would stay the way it was permanently.

Bea had done a lot of the preliminary work to establish the value of the land by getting a forestry management plan done. The forester Erin had met, Jack Sheridan, was the one who had done the work. His girlfriend Rebecca Mackenzie had also performed an appraisal of land values in the area. Joanna had been working on the paperwork that everyone would need to sign. Erin hoped that the work the land trust was doing wasn't going to be for nothing. She'd told Joanna that they were working on getting the title issues figured out. "Working on" sounded better than "grasping at straws."

The rest of the week passed in a blur. Every morning, Erin and Ziggy went out to the property, set up the cat traps, and got down to work cleaning, caulking, and repairing. They did pause for lunch and a bit of afternoon delight on the creaky old bed, but mostly it was a whole lot of work.

Every night, they returned to the house and helped Erin's parents with dinner. It turned out that Ziggy was a halfway decent cook, undoubtedly from all the years he'd spent preventing his mother from creating inedible or potentially poisonous food.

While they were cooking, Jennifer and Paul even chatted with Ziggy about the old days out at the commune. Erin was a little surprised at how well they got along, given the bad blood between his parents and hers. It reminded her that even though they sometimes drove her nuts, at heart, her parents were extremely kind people and she was lucky to have them in her life.

Late Saturday afternoon, Erin crossed off the last item on the to-do list they had created. She held up the legal pad. "That's it. We did it. There's nothing left."

"And outside, all the cats I'm seeing have tipped ears. I think twelve was the magic number." Ziggy said, referring to the fact that when the cats were under anesthesia being fixed, Dr. Cassidy put a small notch in an ear to indicate that the cat had been fixed. It was easy to tell, even from afar.

"I'll check the traps one more time."

Ziggy wrapped her in a hug. "Then I think we should go celebrate. We can pick up all the stuff tomorrow. I have to take the generator back to the farm."

When they got back to the house, Jennifer pulled Erin aside. "Bea called. She's talked to everyone and no one remembers Spencer lending them money."

"And he didn't lend it to you and Dad. Are you sure she talked to the Bryants? I'm pretty sure Ziggy hasn't asked."

"She said they don't remember anything."

"I need to dig up the paperwork for the lien. Technically, we don't have complete legal ownership of the property until the lien is removed." Erin sighed heavily. "The land trust won't touch it without a clear title. I checked the county offices, where the lien was recorded. All they have is a number, but no document. They're looking for it."

"What does this mean?" Jennifer asked.

"I suspect that Spencer is looking to collect the debt when the property is sold."

"Why?"

"He's a developer." Erin scowled. "And if my impressions are correct, a despicable one. I'm guessing he could get a rich friend with high-powered lawyers to help him get the land. Then turn it into a strip mall or something."

"Back to the strip mall idea?" Jennifer smiled. "That's a rather negative assertion."

"As a paralegal, I talked to some fairly repulsive people, but he was worse." She shrugged. "Even during our short conversation, he came off as an insufferable, greedy misogynist."

"Well, I think that's all the more reason for you to kick his ass. Legally speaking, of course."

Erin laughed. "Thanks, Mom. I'll work on it."

When Erin woke up the next morning, Ziggy was already out of bed. She could hear him talking to her parents downstairs. Way to sleep in. All the cleaning must have caught up to her.

After dealing with her morning ministrations, she went downstairs. Ziggy and her parents were sitting around the table drinking coffee and chatting.

Jennifer said, "I can't believe it's only a week until everyone arrives."

"I can't believe Bea got so many people to show up," Paul added.

Ziggy said, "I can't believe we caught all those cats."

Erin placed her hand on his shoulder. He looked up at her with a warm smile, and she gave his shoulder a squeeze in reply. "You'll be glad to hear that the lodge smells a lot better too."

"I still haven't finished my Christmas and solstice shopping," Jennifer said. "I want to pick up some things for the gathering."

The phone rang and Paul got up to answer it. "Yes, he's here." He pointed at Ziggy, "It's your father."

Ziggy locked his gaze with Erin and frowned. "Um, I should probably take this in the other room. Is it okay if use the phone in the office?"

Jenifer nodded and Ziggy disappeared. Paul listened for a moment and hung up.

He sat down, "Zappa's sure pissed about something."

Erin was afraid whatever it was wouldn't be good news for Ziggy. When he walked back into the kitchen, she knew from the stormy expression on his face that he was leaving.

They went upstairs and Erin shut the bedroom door behind her. "Why do you have to leave?"

"It's ten days before Christmas. They need my help. It's an emergency."

"Is it? You told me it's *always* an emergency with them."

"How should I know if it is or isn't? Dad said it was. I have to believe him."

Erin sat on the bed. "I had a feeling this would happen. You're going back, aren't you?"

"I can't stay with your parents forever, and boarding Moose has cost me a fortune. I was picking him up today anyway."

"What about renting the cabin?"

He jammed clothes into the duffel bag. "When I dropped off Moose, I asked Kat, and she said it might be available, but she said it's Joel's place, and I need to talk to him. He hasn't gotten back to me."

"Does he know you've been staying here?"

"Maybe. I'm not sure." He zipped up the bag and threw it over his shoulder. "I have to get Moose and the generator. Then go back to the farm for a while."

"How long is a while?" Erin stood up and crossed her arms. This had to stop. "You're never going to leave them, are you?"

"What are you talking about?"

"You say you want us to be together, but how is that ever going to happen?"

"A lot of that depends on you."

Erin uncrossed her arms and took his hand. "Well, I can tell you I'm not ever living with your parents. And if you refuse to ever set yourself free, it means I'm never living with you."

"Like I said, I'm not planning on living with *your* parents either." He let go of her hand and grabbed a shirt off the back of a chair. "I don't even know that you want to be with me long-term anyway. After the reunion, then what?"

Erin paused. "I, well, I could stay here in Alpine Grove. I haven't decided."

"And that right there is the problem. If you honestly wanted us to be together, whether it's at the cabin or *anywhere*, you'd say so."

"It's complicated. I'd have to move and well, I've been busy. We've both been busy."

"We have. But I'd love you to want me."

"Are you talking about the song? You're throwing in Lobo *now*?"

"The stage name for Roland Kent LaVoie. And yes, because it fits. The real problem is that you don't."

"Of course I do. I love you."

"You say that, but I don't think you want me like I want you, or you'd make a decision about being together. At this point, I don't know if you ever will, which is a decision in itself. Maybe all I did was help you work through your grief."

"What are you saying?"

"I keep thinking that maybe you can't commit to us because you already had the love of your life. The brilliant sophisticated professional. As the loser townie community-college drop-out, I'm always going to come in second."

Stunned at the forcefulness of his words, Erin put her palm to her chest. "You can't be serious. I don't think that at all. You're two incredibly different people."

"It sounds like it. And there's no way I can compete with memories of the perfect man." He picked up the box from the floor. "I have to go."

He left the room and Erin stood there aghast. She heard the front door close, went to the window, and watched as he drove away.

What had just happened?

~

After a long and exhausting crying jag, Erin went downstairs to get some food. All she'd had was coffee, and because her stomach was tied in knots, she was afraid she might be sick. Maybe a sandwich would help.

When she walked into the kitchen, her father was sitting at the table reading a newspaper. He looked up and immediately stood. Opening his arms for a hug, he said, "Hey, what happened?"

Erin hugged him and managed to mumble, "Big fight… so stupid. Dumbest fight ever…I don't understand."

"Sit down and I'll make you some tea. Tell me what happened."

Erin did as instructed and rested her elbows on the table. "Ziggy left because there's some crisis at the tree farm again. But they're always going to have a crisis and I said he's never going to leave."

"Do you believe that?"

"I don't know. But then he more or less said that I wasn't ever going to make any type of commitment. Maybe he's right and I'm just using him to work through my grief. Maybe it's only a fling."

Paul sat and handed her a mug. "From my perspective, it looks like a relationship, not a fling."

"Maybe. I don't know. The whole thing is so stupid. We got into this big fight, both saying the same thing—that we want to be together. I don't even know what happened."

Paul folded his hands on the table and stared off into space. He looked back at her. "Perhaps you're simply both afraid."

"Afraid of what?"

"You tell me. What are you most afraid of right now?"

"I, um, well, I don't know. Life? Everything?"

Paul reached across the table to pat her hand. "You need to be honest with yourself. Is Dylan correct? Do you have reservations about all the time you've spent with him?"

"No. It's been amazing."

"Then what is holding you back? I think you know."

Erin took a deep breath. She did know. "What if something happens to him? I can't go through losing someone I love again, Dad. I *can't*."

"What I'm hearing is that you don't want to take the risk."

"No. Um, maybe. I'm not sure." Was she doing that? She took a sip of tea. "Well, what about him? I'm sorry, but how can I have a real relationship with someone who won't leave his parents?"

"He's been doing the same thing for a long time. Maybe that's what *he's* afraid of. Change is difficult. And having seen Melody and Greg lately, he may simply be worried about them."

"He is, but he has to live his own life someday. If not now, when?"

"I think that's something Dylan needs to work out."

Erin encircled the mug of tea with her hands, the warmth seeping into her palms. "Right now, he's extremely angry."

Jennifer walked into the kitchen and sat next to Erin. "Who's angry?"

"Ziggy. We had a stupid fight," Erin said. "Everything's so complicated, and I don't know what to do."

"Our consciousness fears the door of choices, but I'm sure you'll find consensus," Jennifer said. "He absolutely adores you."

"Not at the moment." Erin looked at her mother. "But you think so?"

Jennifer put her hands on Erin's shoulders and gave them a squeeze. "Oh honey, are you blind? Of course he does."

For the rest of the day, Erin read through some legalese about conservation easements and moped around the house, silently hoping that Ziggy might return. He didn't, and that night she tossed and turned, unable to sleep. She rolled onto her side, telling herself that she absolutely refused to resort to the little yellow ELF pills again. She looked at the clock. It was two thirteen in the morning, but it was time for the ELFs to go. Careful not to disturb Casey, she got up, went to the dresser, and pulled the pills out of the drawer.

She went downstairs to the kitchen, opened the pill bottle, and sprinkled the pills into the mortar bowl. Grinding them up with the pestle seemed symbolic somehow. When she was done, she sprinkled the remains into the garbage. Never again.

The next morning, Erin was sitting at the table spacing out and waiting for her coffee to kick in when the phone rang. Her mother called from down the hall that it was for her.

Without preamble Bea said, "Good morning. I'm sorry to call so early, but I need to talk to you. We have a problem."

Erin sat down heavily. She was way too tired and sad for problems. "What happened?"

"After talking to me, many of the owners called Spencer to see if they could find out what he's doing and to tell him how they feel about the land."

"I'm guessing that didn't go over well."

"No. I'm told that he won't budge. He wants money and tried to convince everyone that they'll make a mint if they sell out."

Erin scowled. What a greedy creep. "I'm not surprised."

"This morning Leah called me."

"Leah?"

"You probably know her better as Meadow."

"Okay, yes. I'm sorry. I think I need more coffee."

"Leah is a stockbroker now. When she talked to Spencer, she took a different approach. Rather than explaining her feelings and thoughts about conservation, she discussed money."

"I suppose she wants to sell out too?"

"No, she doesn't, but she didn't tell him that. Apparently, she talked to Spencer for quite some time. There's some bad news."

Erin braced herself. Bea was always Ms. Positivity, and if she said something was bad, it must be. "I hate to think what he said."

"Meadow said that it was still a secret, but he's enlisted a company to make a bid for the land. He tried to make a play for her to get in on the action."

"I assume she said no."

"She left it ambiguous and called me in a panic. Erin, you must resolve this lien problem as soon as possible. We need to get this conservation easement done sooner rather than later. I'm afraid the vultures are circling."

Erin wasn't sure what she could do. "Did you talk to the Bryants?"

"No, because the last time I saw him, Dylan said he'd ask his parents about the lien." Bea paused. "I know they've had some financial problems, but they're recent. Unless Spencer took a trip to Alpine Grove I don't know about, no one has seen him in twenty years."

"If this goes back years, it's going to be difficult to track down." Erin sighed. "I'm not sure what to do. Spencer won't tell me anything. It's like he's maliciously delighting in tying up the title."

"Did Dylan say anything to you?"

"No, I definitely would have told you if he'd mentioned anything. I think he's at home now."

"Oh dear, there's a customer outside the door. I need to open the store. Good heavens, the Christmas shoppers are busy this year. Could you call him? Thank you, bye."

Erin looked at the phone as if it could explain why the holiday season was so stressful. Being in retail during the Christmas shopping madness was harsh. No wonder Ziggy had been so grumpy about it.

~

Erin left what probably was a mildly incoherent message for Ziggy, but hopefully it got across the fact that she wanted him to call her.

She tried calling Spencer again, but his snippy secretary wouldn't let her through. Maybe the campaign of harassment from people involved in the commune was getting him down. If so, good.

At a loss for what to do with herself when no one would talk to her, Erin decided to take Casey for a walk. The dog was thrilled at the idea and ran around in circles. Erin felt a little bad that she hadn't taken him out over the last week, but she'd been gone all day, every day.

The weather was gray with heavy clouds, but not too cold, so it shouldn't be too hard on the elderly little dog. She grabbed her coat and clipped on his leash. "I know. I missed our walks too."

They started down the street, which was unusually quiet. Maybe everyone was off shopping. The clouds seemed to muffle sound like a heavy gray blanket had been thrown over the neighborhood. Almost all of the trees had lost their leaves, with only the occasional brown straggler hanging onto the otherwise bare branches.

Even the squirrels that had been chattering and frantically enjoying the last blast of late fall warmth at the end of November had given up and disappeared. The air felt like winter now, as if the snow were waiting on a precipice to dump a blizzard on them.

Erin wondered idly if her parents owned a snow shovel because they were going to need one soon. At this elevation, they'd largely missed out on the surprise early snow they'd had at Dancing Cedars, but it was only a matter of time before winter arrived for real in town.

She stood and waited for Casey to embark on a complex sniffing routine. Apparently, the boxwood he'd stopped at held the secrets of the canine universe, and he needed to catalog them. The house beyond was one of the historic ones, built at about the same time as the house her parents had restored. It was pretty, but it didn't have a cool tower room.

Casey suddenly ran back toward the sidewalk, wagging furiously, and Erin turned around. She was surprised to see Ziggy's beat-up old truck. Jeez, this was *such* a small town. The truck was still sporting the hideous camper shell, and he was reaching down to get something from the passenger side. He must have seen her. What was he doing?

He sat up, and when he spotted her, their gazes locked, and he smiled at her. She could tell that he had something he was absolutely bursting to tell her.

Something about the look of pure love and excitement on his face thawed Erin's miserable heart into syrupy lovesick goo. He jumped out of the truck and she launched herself into his embrace. He wrapped his arms around her and whispered, "I'm *so* sorry" in her ear.

She leaned back to look at him. "I am too."

"What I said was unfair. You lost someone you loved. If something happened to you, I don't know what I'd do."

"I shouldn't have said what I did either. It's stupid that we were arguing for the same thing."

"I know. All I want is to be with you."

"I do too. I don't know what's wrong with me. People spend their whole lives trying to find someone who loves them the way you love me. I'm an idiot."

"If you are, then I am too." He kissed her. "Let's not do that again, okay? Just so we're clear, I love you, and I want us to be together."

Erin laughed. "I love you too and I want the same thing. More than anything. So now that we've got that straightened out, what are you doing here?"

"I stopped by your parents' house, but no one was home. I'm taking a load of stuff out to the cabin." He gave her a half smile. "Joel's renting it to me. Wanna check it out?"

"Are you kidding? *Yes!*"

She picked up Casey and they loaded him into the truck. After a short detour back to her parents' house to drop off Casey for his afternoon nap, they rolled out of town, heading north.

Erin looked behind her through the back window at the truck bed, which was filled with boxes. "What are you going to do about furniture?"

"I've got an air mattress from when I went camping. It will work for now."

"What did your parents say?"

He glanced at her. "As you might imagine, they're not happy. Leaving home ain't easy."

"Queen. Unlike most Queen tunes, the vocals are by Brian May, not Freddy Mercury. The lyrics are certainly apropos."

"I memorized them years ago."

She leaned her head on his shoulder. "I hate to bring this up, but Bea told me that she talked to everyone, and no one remembers borrowing money from Spencer. Did you ask your parents?"

"I did. Given how terrible they are with finances, I figured it had to be them. But they both say they don't remember ever getting a loan from him."

"I'm not sure what we're going to do. I'd say that we should just leave things alone and forget about doing the conservation easement, but this morning Bea called me in a panic and said that Spencer has found a company that wants to buy the property."

Ziggy slowed to turn off the highway. "Uh-oh."

She sat up and put her hand over his on the gearshift. "If you have any ideas, speak now."

"Sorry counselor, but I've got nothing. I keep wondering why this is happening now. Why not twenty years ago? Or ten years ago?"

"Maybe the increase in land prices in the last few years?" Erin shook her head. "I have no idea."

When Ziggy pulled up the driveway to the little log cabin, Erin smiled. "This place is adorable."

"Wait until you see the inside." Ziggy held up the key. "First month's rent and deposits are all paid. I can't believe I finally have more than a single room to myself."

Erin got out and went to the back of the truck. Ziggy handed her a box and grabbed two. They went up the steps and stood under a small overhang while Ziggy unlocked the door.

The cabin was essentially a large open area with a small kitchen and a door to what was presumably the bathroom off to one side. A loft above was accessed using a ladder. The space held a faint scent of smoke mixed with wood.

Erin set the box on the scuffed wooden floor and walked over to the kitchen. She ran her palm across the smooth wood of a door. "These cabinets are so pretty."

"Joel built this place, and I think he made them. I guess he's redoing their kitchen now. He turned an outbuilding into a wood shop."

Erin looked up at the loft. "He built the whole cabin?"

"Except for the concrete work and some of the plumbing, yeah, he built it. I guess it took years because he did it on weekends and vacations." He gestured toward the door. "I'm going to grab more of my crap."

Erin followed him out. "It's so small, at least you don't have to find much furniture."

"I'm thinking after the reunion, I might bring the stuff back here. It was free, and I'm reneging on my donation."

"You're going to have to find some burly guys to move that couch again because it weighs a ton."

Once they had all the boxes inside, Ziggy started opening them. "The air mattress is in one of the bigger boxes. I suppose labeling them might have been a good idea."

Erin attacked a few boxes, pulling open flaps. She didn't find the mattress, but she did find notebooks. Hundreds of them. Ziggy certainly was prolific. "I think you need to get yourself a bookshelf. No wonder these boxes are so heavy."

Erin opened a box and saw that the spiral-bound notebook on top had the Rolling Stones logo and a photo of Mick Jagger on it. "Hey, check this out. Mick was such a youngster."

Ziggy looked over her shoulder. "That's an old one."

"How old?"

"I dunno. I should have thrown these away. Who cares what I thought when I was twelve?"

Erin grinned. "Hey, I was there. I *know* what you thought when you were twelve."

He kissed her ear. "Not everything. Probably most things though."

"Can I look at it?" She gazed into his eyes. "I'm dying of curiosity."

"I don't care. It probably has exciting information like what I had for dinner and whatever awful, terrible, things people had done that made me want to go climb a tree."

Erin sat cross-legged on the floor and flipped through a few pages. "1977. It sounds like you were living in an apartment in town. You're annoyed because your mother burned dinner."

"I told you. It's some riveting stuff." He leaned down to take the notebook from her and turned the page. "Ugh. This one is pretty depressing."

"That's after I moved away."

He gave the notebook back to her. "Yeah, I used to ride my bike past the house your parents had rented to see if your family had changed their mind and returned."

"Really? That's so sweet."

"More like pathetic, but I was pretty lonely then. Being fourteen stinks."

"That wasn't a great time in my life either." Erin returned the notebook to the box and reached for another one. "I'm guessing you didn't show this ABBA cover to anyone. Those are some serious sequins."

"Do you think I wanted to get beat up? These things have always been hidden in my room, far from prying eyes."

"How far back do these go?"

"Not sure. Probably as long as I could write. I'm kind of a pack rat."

"I noticed." She looked up at him. "I'm having a sort of odd thought."

He sat next to her on the floor. "I hate to ask, since you're busy dredging up the depths of my fourteen-year-old psyche, but what?"

"If Spencer loaned your parents or someone else money, do you think you might have written something about it?"

"Jeez, I don't know. Maybe."

"It's a huge long shot, but would it be okay to look? I mean, I might see something personal."

"What could you possibly find out about me that you don't already know?" He pulled the box closer and began digging through notebooks. "Apparently, I'm now, literally, an open book."

She laughed and grabbed another box. "I guess so."

∼

They sat quietly flipping through pages of notebooks, and Erin organized them into stacks by year.

Ziggy walked across the room to the pile of boxes and opened another one. "Hey, I finally found the air mattress."

Erin looked up from her reading. "Remember when we ran into each other on the street that time after the commune broke up?"

"We were standing near the old cafe. I had no idea what to say to you. I felt like such a loser."

Erin scanned the text. "I was so thrilled to see you again, but then you acted so different, I couldn't figure out what was wrong. I thought you hated me. If it makes you feel better, I went home and cried."

He sat next to her, put his arm around her shoulders, and leaned over to look at the text. "It doesn't make me feel better. Obviously back then, I didn't think about you in a romantic-love kind of way, but there was this huge hole in my heart. I missed you, but seeing you was confusing. I was a jerk, and then, as you can see, I beat myself up about it. So it wasn't a great day for me either."

"I guess not. I'm a little self-conscious reading about myself from your perspective."

He kissed her cheek. "Imagine how I feel having you read all this garbage."

"I know this has to be uncomfortable for you, but it's for a good cause."

"I sure hope so."

They sat next to each other reading quietly for a while, the flipping of pages the only sound breaking the silence in the remote cabin. She skimmed through countless poems and lyrics. There was everything from ballads about being alone to angry screeds about bad breakups. A profanity-laced diatribe about how someone named Robin hated him was particularly notable. The band names Black Sabbath and Judas Priest were scrawled next to it, so she was guessing the chords had a heavy-metal feel to them.

Erin opened a newer notebook with a plain blue cover. The first page included Ziggy's perspective of picking her up at the airport. The description was funny, sweet, and remarkably perceptive. He'd been able to tell something bad had happened to her, even though he didn't know what it was then. Somehow meeting him at the airport felt like a long time ago, yet also a violation of his privacy because in reality it *wasn't* a long time ago. The notebook was far too current to hold any long-forgotten clues about the debt, so she set it aside.

Ziggy reached to place his hand on hers. "Hey, I might have something here."

She looked over. "Wow, that's an old one."

"1973, right before Harry was born."

"That was a confusing time. So many people were there then. I don't remember much from when Bea had Rainbow, but I remember when your mom was pregnant."

"How could you forget? She barfed nonstop for months. It was a good thing she had multiple people taking care of her."

"She must have been miserable."

Ziggy pointed at the page. "If you read between the lines of ten-year-old me whining about having to haul buckets of water around the lodge all the time, it sounds like Mom had to go to the doctor."

"And your father borrowed money from Phoenix to pay for it." She looked into his face. "This could be it."

"Maybe, but my rambling means nothing. There has to be something written down somewhere. Maybe an IOU or something."

"They must have been notified about the lien too."

He stood up. "We need to go to the farm."

"Are your parents still angry at me? Maybe I shouldn't go with you."

"I don't care if they are." He grabbed her hand and pulled her upright. "Sorry, but you started this, so you have to go with me back to the Land of Christmas. I have to rescue Moose from his confinement anyway."

She gave him a hug. "For the record, I like your new home. Even without any furniture, this cabin has a good feel to it."

"Yeah, Joel refers to it as The Shack, but he said the last renters loved the place, and Kat doesn't want him to sell it. Now I understand why."

They put the notebooks back in the boxes, locked up, and got back into the truck for the journey south.

Ziggy said, "I feel like I'm driving a rut into the roads between Dancing Cedars and town."

"Although I love the cabin, I don't think you're going to have a big problem with people dropping by unannounced."

He turned to flash her a grin. "I know. Isn't that great?"

When they arrived at the tree farm, it was swarming with people. Erin got out, and a little boy about seven years old ran screaming past her holding a pine bough in one hand and a jingle bear in the other. She grimaced at Ziggy. "I think someone has had a little too much sugar."

"If you ever wanted to know what introvert hell is like, December at the Bryant Tree Farm is it." Ziggy grabbed her hand and led her to a young man who was climbing up onto a tractor attached to a wagon full of trees. "Erin, this is Barry."

"Nice to meet you." His gaze shifted toward the forest and he jumped off the tractor. "Uh-oh, we have a runner. Gotta go."

Erin smiled at Ziggy. "I thought he quit."

"I increased his hourly rate and told him he didn't have to wear the bear suit. It's still worth it to me."

They went inside the house and Erin followed Ziggy to the kitchen. No one had done the dishes in a long time, and dirty cookie trays and mixing bowls were stacked everywhere.

Ziggy moved a ten-pound bag of flour and pulled a couple of cookbooks out from behind it. He handed her a decrepit copy of *The Joy of Cooking*. The cover was held to the book with rubber bands, and it was stuffed with slips of paper, pages from magazines, and newspaper clippings.

Erin looked down at the disintegrating book in her hands. "What am I supposed to do with this?"

"Mom puts anything she thinks might be important into her cookbooks for safekeeping. Don't tell, but the deed to the farm is located in the *Better Homes and Gardens* cookbook, next to the brownie recipe."

Most of the cookbooks were falling apart, and it was difficult to avoid scattering papers all over the messy kitchen. When the pages of Julia Child's *Mastering the Art of French Cooking* exploded all over the floor, Erin said, "There aren't enough rubber bands in the world to save this one."

"Keep looking." He pulled another cookbook from the stack. "If anything was written down, it's here somewhere."

They dug through stacks of decomposing, stained cookbooks for a while, and Erin was getting discouraged. What Melody deemed important ranged wildly. The property deed was exactly where Ziggy said it was, but other cookbooks were filled with recipes clipped from magazines and coupons from 1983.

Erin picked up a copy of the *Moosewood Cookbook*. "I should get my parents a copy of this one, so we don't get award-winning gelatinous green food next Thanksgiving."

"I'll chip in."

Erin held up a sheet of paper and set the cookbook aside. "This has to be it. Look, it's an IOU."

Ziggy bent to examine the paper. "Holy chick peas, that's it."

"Thank you Gypsy Soup!"

"Do you find it odd that Spencer is going through all this for a fifty-buck loan?"

"I know. But look at this. It may be handwritten, but it's alarmingly complete, with payment terms, interest, costs, and recourse with terms that include taking ownership of collateral. I wonder if back in the day, Spencer was pre-law."

"It figures. The next step is to go to the office and look through the mail. Mom and Dad wouldn't have opened a letter from someone they didn't know."

"I hate to ask, but how much mail?"

"A lot. My parents don't throw things away."

"Uh-oh."

Lawyer Clothes

She followed him out of the kitchen and down the hall to a door, but stopped in the entryway when he opened the door. "Oh my God."

The room was filled with paper stacked on every available surface. A desk on the far wall was piled high with books, magazines, newspapers, and other detritus. Next to it, a filing cabinet was so full that the drawers couldn't close because of all the papers bursting from within.

Ziggy pointed to a heap of papers. "It's a disaster, but the mail tends to be in separate stacks, so start digging until you find a group."

An old sofa sat on one side of the room, and Erin started with those piles so she could dig out a place to sit down. Ziggy dragged an old portable CD player out from behind a mountain of magazines and pressed the Play button.

The Rolling Stones blasted "Get Off of My Cloud" and Ziggy turned it down. "Sorry."

"It's a miracle you're not stone deaf."

"What?"

She threw a stack of mail at him. "Very funny. Start looking."

He laughed and flipped through the letters. "Bet you're not wondering why I demoted myself to hourly laborer anymore, are you? Would *you* want to manage this business?"

"I think your pack rat tendencies must be genetic. This is a nightmare. How do they stay afloat?" Erin threw more envelopes into a stack of paper she'd reviewed. "Some of these are collection notices. You can't *not* open your mail. It's nuts."

"They open the mail they recognize, like bills from the electric company. But if they don't know who it's from, they throw the mail in here to deal with later. But later never happens."

"There's a lot of junk mail, but some of this could be important." She pulled a letter out of a stack. "This one looks like a loan foreclosure."

"It probably is. When a company sells a mortgage, Mom and Dad don't recognize the name anymore. But when the calls from collection agencies start coming in, the mortgage gets paid again."

Erin held up two envelopes. "I don't know how you could stand to watch this go on for so long."

"Any time I tried to intervene, we got into huge fights. *So* many seriously horrible fights. They said I was interfering and didn't understand anything. After I dropped out of college and came back here, I decided that continuing to have a relationship with my parents was more important, so I backed off. Harry was still a kid, and I was able to avert some of the worst crises, so he didn't end up homeless. What would you do if it were your parents?"

Erin used a letter opener to zip open an envelope. "I don't know. I can see how you've been stuck. But now that you're leaving, what happens when there's another crisis? Because clearly, there's going to be one."

"I don't know. That's why I went back the other day. It's always something." He flipped an envelope onto a stack. "That's why it's been so hard to leave for so long. I'm focusing on one problem at a time. First, we have to deal with Dancing Cedars. But if you have any ideas, let me know."

Erin shook her head. Her mind was as jumbled as the room. What a mess.

After several hours of sorting, Ziggy suddenly stood up, holding out a letter. "I've got it."

Erin jumped up, pulled his hand toward her, and gripped the edge of the paper so she could read it. "After twenty-four years, the interest and fees sure rack up. Your father should never have signed that IOU."

"He may not remember it, but he did." Ziggy sat down heavily on the sofa. "I think this guy has a legitimate claim, Stardust. What are we going to do?"

"The law is a funny thing. It's incredibly nitpicky. Every little detail matters." Erin sat, took the sheet of paper from him, and smoothed it out on her leg. "At first glance, something looks cut and dried, but then you look closer and find the holes. And if there's a hole here, we're going to find it."

They both stared at the paper in silence.

Erin put her hand on Ziggy's. "I've read over those property documents about a hundred times, and this is wrong."

"I know. It makes me sick. Morally, who would do this to a bunch of peace-loving hippies who opened their home to you and let you stay for free? This guy must be a real piece of work. If my mom was sick, my dad would have been freaking out and signed anything."

"Spencer is loathsome, but that's not what I meant." She pointed at the paper. "Look there. That's not how you spell your father's name. On the tax notices Greggory is spelled with two g's. Here it's spelled with one."

"You're right." He looked into her eyes. "That's a family thing. The story goes that my great-grandfather spelled his name that way."

"This mistake could invalidate the lien. At a minimum, it turns the case into one person's word against the other. Spencer hasn't created a secret company for no reason. If we can convince him that this misspelling is going to lead to a long, publicly revealing lawsuit, he might sign a lien revocation. Then all of this goes away."

Ziggy said, "How's that going to happen?"

"I'm not sure. It's a pretty thin argument."

He grinned and widened his eyes. "Hey, I have an idea."

"Wait. I know that face. That's the look you had when you suggested we go on that stupid adventure that almost led us to freezing to death."

Ignoring the comment, he tugged on the sleeve of her sweatshirt. "Did you bring any of your lawyer clothes?"

"Lawyer clothes?" She laughed. "You mean like a dress?"

"Whatever lawyers wear when they go to court."

"You know I can't practice law here. Even if we sue Spencer, someone else will have to do it. I could do a lot of pro bono paralegal work to help, which would save money, but…"

"You don't have to *be* a lawyer. You just have to look and sound like one. Do you need to shop for some lawyer clothes? I can give you wardrobe money if you need it."

"No, I can probably borrow something from my mom. She has some gorgeous outfits she wears at their seminars. I covet her shoe collection. But what are you getting at?"

"We go to LA and give Spencer this revocation thing. Tell him we know this is a legal fight he can't win. Except you say it in lawyer-speak."

"Although I might relish the opportunity to throw some Latin jargon at that turd, I don't know where his office actually is." She held up the envelope and pointed at the return address. "It's an anonymous Delaware corporation that uses a post office box for an address."

Ziggy looked thoughtful. "But we have a phone number, right?"

"Yes, and I can tell you that his secretary is quite an unpleasant woman."

"I have an idea."

"Another one?"

"Let's go back to your parents' house. I need that phone number."

They went to let out Moose for a short romp around the yard. When Ziggy corralled him to return him to the barn he said, "I promise I'll be back soon. Then you get to go out to your new home, which is not filled with screaming yard apes riding a sugar high." The dog seemed pleased at the news, but resigned to his current confinement.

Back in town, they gave Casey an outing, and then Erin went through her Dancing Cedars files. She handed Ziggy a piece of paper with the phone number for Spencer's office. "Be prepared. He's a real jerk."

"I don't plan to talk to him." He picked up the phone and dialed. He raised his eyebrows at Erin and said, "Hey, I'm from Federal DH Parcel. I got a package for you, but I can't deliver to a PO Box."

He smiled and did a melodramatic eye roll. "So you want that I throw it away? I'm not supposed to do that, and I'll get in trouble with the boss, ya know." He made a gimme gesture and mimed 'pencil.' Erin dug through her mother's desk and handed him a pad and pencil.

He waved the pencil in the air and pointed at the window. "Hey lady, I'm just sayin' it looks important. But not my problem, ya know. We can send it back." He paused. "Okay, that's off the 101, right? Got it. Thanks."

He hung up and grinned at Erin. "I even got directions. Pack up your lawyer clothes. We're going to the big city."

~

The next morning when Erin woke up, Ziggy wasn't lying next to her. He certainly was up and out bright and early. Maybe he wanted to make sure Moose was okay at the farm. It looked like the dog would have to spend a couple more days cooped up before he got to enjoy his new home.

She staggered down to get coffee and found her parents in the kitchen eating breakfast. Her mother got up, went to the coffeemaker, and poured her a cup. "Dylan said you're going to Los Angeles today."

Erin nodded and gratefully accepted the coffee. The revelations and running around the day before had left her mentally and physically exhausted. "Do you know where he went?"

"He said he had to run an errand, and that you need to make sure you're packed and ready to go by nine."

Paul asked, "Why are you going to LA?"

"It's a long story. If this works, it will be a miracle. If it doesn't, well, I don't know." Erin glanced at the clock on the stove. She didn't have time to explain. "I need to take a shower. Mom, can I borrow your blue suit?"

"Of course. My closet is a shared domain."

"Thanks Mom." Erin gave her mother and father hugs before running up the stairs to gather her things.

Erin had her suitcase packed with Mom's suit, heels, makeup, and the relevant paperwork related to Dancing Cedars. The previous day, after determining that they were going to LA, Erin and Ziggy had gone to the law offices of Larry Lowell, the only lawyer in Alpine Grove. He'd kindly lent her a couple of books from his law library, which she promised to return the next day. Then she and Ziggy had holed up in her mother's office while she used her mother's computer to type up the lien revocation document.

Erin brought everything downstairs, and at a knock at the door, she detoured through the living room to answer it. Ziggy leaned against the doorjamb and held out a lollipop. "For luck. As I recall, grape is your favorite."

Instead of his typical attire of baggy flannel shirt and faded jeans, he was wearing a tailored dark suit that fit him well. Extremely well. He had shaved and gotten a haircut, which made his eyes even more striking than they usually were and his facial features more chiseled. Clean-shaven,

Ziggy's face was more like the way she remembered it from her childhood, except slimmer and more handsome.

Erin took the lollipop, too stunned to speak. Finally, she mustered, "What did you do?"

"Went to Joe's. I think I made his day. He was so happy he gave me a couple of lollipops. I ate the green one."

Joe was the barber in town who was known for his talent for taming even the most unruly hair. Long hair was his nemesis and he made no secret about his disdain for men who didn't visit the barber regularly.

Erin ran her palm across Ziggy's smooth cheek. "I haven't seen your upper lip in so long. You'll think I'm shallow, but this look is incredibly hot. Where did you get the suit?"

"Dad made me buy it for my grandmother's funeral. I dug it out of my parent's bedroom closet. You don't want to know what *that* was like. I'm relieved it still fits." He leaned to kiss her. "Are you ready? I need to get my stuff from your room and change my clothes. The dirt in my truck is trying to glom onto this spendy fabric."

After loading their stuff into the truck, they took off down the hill for what Ziggy was referring to as their magical mystery tour to the big city. To celebrate the road trip, he put a CD into the player and they blasted the Beatles at high volume, singing along.

In LA, they found a motel near the business district where Spencer's office was located and changed their clothes. Erin emerged from the bathroom in her mother's blue suit and spread her arms wide. "Ta-da! Lawyer clothes."

Ziggy gave her a wolf whistle, grabbed her hand, and twirled her under his arm. "You look incredible. I feel like we're going to the prom."

"Except talking to a slime ball like Spencer is going to be a lot less fun."

He leaned to give her a hug. "At the big reunion on Sunday, at least we can tell everyone we tried."

"True, and if this doesn't work, maybe someone else will have another idea."

Ziggy called the office number, asked for Spencer, and hung up when the receptionist said she'd put him through. "He's there. Let's do this thing."

They took one of the blankets from the motel and threw it over the truck seat to cover up some of the filth and Moose drool. Ziggy smiled, "I hope Spencer doesn't look out the window and see the hunk of junk we're driving up in."

"Park next to a BMW, then sneer, and look horrified like you own the pretty car and don't want to touch the truck."

"How are we going to get in to see this troll?"

"I have a plan," Erin said with a smile. "Leave that to me."

The Ignite Enterprises office was not in one of the impressive glass high-rises, but was located in a nondescript blocky beige building that had a grubby, tired appearance, as if it had survived hard times.

They went in and took the elevator to the second floor. Erin straightened her shoulders, hoisted the strap of her mother's leather briefcase onto her shoulder, and took a deep breath before opening the door to Spencer's office.

She marched up to the receptionist's desk. The woman looked startled, hurriedly stuffing her nail file into her desk drawer and straightening her large purple-framed glasses. "May I help you?"

Erin said, "My name is Erin Quinn, and I need to discuss an important legal matter with Spencer Widman."

"Do you have an appointment?"

"I do not. But he will want to talk to me. I am the de facto representative for an individual concerned with an incident that transpired circa 1973."

"What *incident*?"

"I'm not at liberty to say. It's a private matter." Erin leaned closer and added, "However, have you ever heard Mr. Widman say that you can remember his name because he's a wild man? That was true twenty-four years ago as well."

Erin watched the wheels turning as the woman's expression became increasingly uncomfortable under Erin's fixed glare. Finally, the receptionist stood up and said, "I, well, fine. Let me tell him you're here."

Erin inclined her head to indicate that Ziggy should follow her, and he winked in acknowledgment. The woman opened the door to Spencer's office and Erin and Ziggy crowded around her before she could say a word.

Ziggy shoved the door closed on the sputtering woman and flipped the lock. Erin sat down in a chair across from Spencer. "Good afternoon. I talked to you ten days ago about a situation in Alpine Grove."

Spencer stood up. "You can't barge into my office like this."

"Actually, I think we can," Ziggy said. He hadn't moved from the doorway, effectively acting as a well-dressed seven-foot bodyguard.

Erin said, "Please sit down Mr. Widman. We need to discuss the lien you placed on the Dancing Cedars property in Alpine Grove."

Spencer looked smug, sat down, and leaned back in his chair, resting his folded hands on his stomach. "Why? Problem solved when the land sells. They get money for the land, and I get repaid. Everybody wins."

Erin pulled a file out of her briefcase. "I'm afraid the owners don't see it that way. When we talked before, you weren't amenable to discussing a mutually beneficial solution to satisfy the obligation."

"Why would I do that? Like I said, selling the land solves the problem."

Erin glanced over her shoulder. "My associate, Mr. Bryant, has discovered some inconsistencies in the paperwork."

Spencer sat up. "What's that supposed to mean?"

"As it happens, he wrote down what actually transpired in 1973."

"What do you mean wrote down?" Spencer scowled. "How old are you? You must have been a little kid."

"Apparently the loan was to pay for a doctor's appointment for his mother." Erin gestured toward Ziggy, who was standing with his arms crossed, looking unusually surly and imposing. "Melody had been terribly sick because of her pregnancy. In that desperate time, his father, Zappa, reached out to his friend Phoenix for a loan of fifty dollars so he could take his wife to the doctor."

Spencer slapped his hand on the desk. "Why are you telling me this? I know what happened, girlie. I was there."

"But were you? Legally, it appears we have a situation that may be difficult to resolve." She slapped the lien notification on the desk. "It seems that you've placed a lien because you loaned someone named Gregory Bryant fifty dollars in 1973, and the obligation has not been repaid."

"Well, duh, girlie. That's what you just told me."

"Perhaps. But perhaps not." Erin smiled and folded her hands on the desk. "Unfortunately, the name on the lien is not Mr. Bryant's father's name. His father spells Greggory with two g's."

Ziggy said, "It's a family name."

Erin pointed at the paper sitting on the desk. "As you can see on this document, Gregory is spelled with one g. In the United States alone, potentially thousands of people are named Gregory Bryant with one g," Erin explained.

"Who cares? It's a typo. Zappa owes me money—including a bunch of interest and fees—and you know it."

Erin leaned forward. "No one with the name Gregory—with one g—Bryant is listed as an owner of the Dancing Cedars property. And you referred to someone named Zappa. Some doubt exists as far as the identity of the parties involved."

Spencer scowled. "For God's sake, you *know* who I'm talking about. You just told me."

Undeterred, Erin continued, "Additionally, none of the twelve people who do have legal interest in the property want anything to do with you. Ergo, I have been tasked to make the sales process as legally problematic and publicly humiliating for you, your organization, and your associates as humanly possible."

"What's that supposed to mean? Are you threatening me?"

Erin leaned back in the chair and raised her eyebrows. "I am most certainly not threatening anything at all. I'm simply contemplating my future goals. You should be aware that I intend to put my law degree to its highest and best use, fighting this matter in court until the day you leave this mortal coil."

Spencer looked down at his feet and frowned. "You can't do that. This sale has to go through quickly."

Ziggy said, "You can't always get what you want."

Erin flashed on a mental image of Ziggy saying that at Dancing Cedars when they'd worked so hard cleaning that he'd fallen asleep. It reminded her why they were here. She looked over her shoulder and mouthed, "Rolling Stones" to Ziggy, and turned back to Spencer, more determined than ever.

She pulled a piece of paper from her briefcase and held it in her hands. "Perhaps we can reach an agreement that will keep your questionable business dealings and financial issues from reaching the media."

Spencer narrowed his eyes. "How do you know I have financial problems?"

Erin hadn't known, but she'd guessed by his comment about the quick sale and by his body language that something was off with the housing project that Ignite Enterprises was working on. "I did some research on your current business activities. And I suspect an eager young reporter would love to know what I've learned."

"Hey, it's not as bad as they made it out." Spencer spread his arms wide. "Everyone's out to get me. They're making things up. It's all fake stories. They don't know what they're talking about."

"Don't they?" Ziggy asked. "That deal's looking pretty dicey to me."

Erin slid the lien revocation document across the desk. "It would be in your best interest to explore other avenues for expeditious revenue. Signing this document could prevent quite a bit of expense and anguish on everyone's part."

"What's in it for me?"

Ziggy walked up to the desk and threw fifty dollars in cash onto the desk. "You never hear from us again."

Erin smiled. "In other words, the status quo continues unabated. We forget this unfortunate event ever happened, and we all return to our lives. The owners set up the conservation easement they desire, and the land remains as it has been for millennia."

"And the newspapers never find out how you heartlessly repaid a sick pregnant woman who compassionately fed and sheltered you by extorting money from her family years later," Ziggy added. "It's quite a human-interest story."

Spencer grabbed the sheet of paper, scrawled his name on it, and thrust it at Erin. "Get out of my office."

~

The short drive back to the motel passed in a blur because Erin was still reeling from the fact that she'd managed to completely bluff her way through the meeting with Spencer.

They walked into the motel room and Ziggy closed the door behind them. He reached for her hand and pulled her to him. "You were absolutely brilliant."

"So were you. I can't believe we pulled this off."

He grinned. "I think it was all the Latin. You intimidated him with all the brainy words."

"A lot of that was for your benefit because I know how much you like it."

He pushed the blue jacket off her shoulders and it fell to the floor. "I do. Who knew a dead language could be so sexy?"

Erin smiled and reached to tug at his tie. "I think we're overdressed. It's time for the post-prom party."

They ever-so-carefully stripped their clothes off each other, gently folding them and laying them on a chair, and then they leaped onto the king-sized bed. Later, they ordered pizza and had it delivered to their room, so they could eat dinner in bed.

Ziggy grabbed another slice of pizza from the box. "I like food that shows up at your doorstep."

"Don't get used to it. No one is delivering anything to your new cabin, ever."

"Still worth every penny of the rent I pay to be there."

Erin sat up, tugging the blanket around her. "Have you figured out what you're going to do about your parents? In the office, I saw threats of foreclosure. They don't owe Spencer anymore, but they owe everyone else."

"I know. It's been getting worse again." He put the slice of pizza aside. "The last time they ended up in the hole was about eight years ago. The only option was to do a home equity loan. Basically, a second mortgage on the farm."

"Is that one of the foreclosure notices?"

"Probably. They're running out of options. They need to consolidate the loans, but now their credit is so bad, they can't refinance."

Erin scrunched down next to him and laid her head on his shoulder. "I can't believe they're going to lose the farm. That's heartbreaking."

"I don't know what to do. I've been tossing around ideas, but I haven't come to any conclusions yet. I don't want to live there anymore, and like I said, when I try to fix anything related to the business, it usually ends in a huge fight."

"That's hard. I wish I could help."

He ran his fingertips along her temple, smoothing her hair back from her face. "You already have. Being able to talk to you about this has helped me more than you can imagine. I've felt completely alone and stuck for a long time."

The next morning on the drive back to Alpine Grove, Erin gazed out the window watching the changing topography and reflecting on what Ziggy had said about feeling stuck. She'd been stuck too, trapped by grief. Ziggy had called it a prison and thought she might be breaking free. And maybe she was. Although mentally she felt like she might be ready to think about being a lawyer again, the decision to stay in Alpine Grove made that idea difficult.

Alpine Grove had only a one lawyer. Even if he asked her, which he wouldn't, she didn't want to join Larry Lowell's law practice. A general law practice looked pretty tedious—a fact that was apparent when she'd dropped by Larry's office to borrow the books. She didn't want that life. And having talked to Larry, she wasn't sure he did either. In her experience, countless lawyers secretly yearned to do something else.

Andy used to call Erin a tree hugger. Perhaps he was more right than she thought. Preserving the Dancing Cedars land for future generations was the first thing that had captured her attention since she'd worked at Natural Justice, the environmental firm where she'd been a paralegal.

She'd hoped to work there after she got her law degree, but once she finally made it through law school and passed the bar, they didn't have any openings. Her boss, Carson, had said that she could use him as a reference and had given her a list of places where she might apply. Then Andy died, and she couldn't face it. Now she couldn't even bear the thought of living in DC. Times had changed. She'd changed. After Andy died, she wasn't the same person anymore. But who was she now?

She glanced at Ziggy, who was focused on driving and lost in his own thoughts. In the short term, she could continue to freeload off her parents. Maybe that had to be good enough for right now. Rather than making herself miserable fretting about her lack of direction, she should simply let go and enjoy the big reunion and holiday festivities. No matter how much you tried to plan, life was going to happen anyway.

When they got back to her parents' house, several cars were parked out front. After she got out of the truck, Erin yanked her suitcase from behind the seat. "So are my parents throwing a party while the kids are away?"

Ziggy chuckled. "You never know what Saffron and Arrow might have gotten up to while we weren't looking."

Inside, a group of people were sitting in the living room playing with the kittens. Jennifer waved at Erin, "Welcome back! We're having an adoption party. The kittens are going to their new homes. Everybody, this is my daughter, Erin, and our friend, Dylan. They are the ones who rescued these furry rascals."

Paul pointed at a red-haired woman in the circle who was cuddling the black-and-white kitten. "This is Brigid. She runs the rescue group in town. And Tony over here is adopting the kitten she's holding."

Jennifer held out the kitten in her arms. "Anna is adopting this one."

The woman next her said, "I'm Doreen, and this little love is going home with me. My kids are going to be beside themselves. This will be the best Christmas ever. I can't wait to see their faces."

Ziggy and Erin chatted for a few minutes about the kittens' feral heritage and their feline relatives who lived at Dancing Cedars, before they went upstairs to unpack.

In Erin's room, they collapsed onto the bed. They hadn't gotten much sleep the night before, and after the long drive, Erin was glad to lie down.

Ziggy was sprawled out on his back staring up at the ceiling, his long legs hanging off the end of the bed. "Well, if we did nothing else, we saved some innocent kittens from the perils of winter."

Erin rolled over onto her stomach, propped herself up on her elbows, and grinned at him. "Yeah, isn't it great? We did a good thing. Those kittens are going to be spoiled rotten."

~

Erin and Ziggy spent the next couple of days preparing for the big solstice party on Sunday. Erin and her parents went to Gleasonville so they could go Christmas shopping and she could meet with Joanna at the land trust offices. Erin enjoyed spending time with Joanna and learning more about the nonprofit organization. The woman certainly seemed to be overwhelmed with work. Dancing Cedars was one of many conservation projects the group was working on.

Meanwhile, Ziggy spent a lot of time out at Dancing Cedars with his brother, Harry, who was on holiday leave from the Navy. They helped get the lodge set up for the party. According to Ziggy, his mother had foisted approximately ten-thousand decorations on them, and because of the need to power both the Christmas lights and the music, they'd cleaned out the battery display at Lowell's Hardware.

At night, Ziggy returned to her parents' house and told her funny stories about Harry, who hadn't been home in a while. Because Harry's old bedroom had been turned into the Kris Kringle barf zone, he'd had to sleep in Ziggy's old room, which was already so full of Christmas clutter that Harry claimed he had more space on the aircraft carrier.

While they were moving stuff around out at the commune, Erin got a look at Harry for the first time since he was two years old. Like Ziggy, he was obviously taller than he had been the last time she'd seen him. He could walk and talk a lot better too.

Interestingly, he also looked a little like her father, but even more like his brother, her Uncle Arthur. The person Harry didn't look like was Ziggy. Although the two men both had the same brunette hair color, Harry was about a foot shorter and had brown eyes and a completely different build. Ziggy had long arms and long legs, which he often said made him resemble a goofy, klutzy giraffe. Harry, on the other hand, was all muscles with huge shoulders, a lot like Uncle Art and her grandfather. Genetics was an interesting thing.

On Sunday, Erin went with her parents to Dancing Cedars for the big reunion. Everyone had been assigned a type of food to bring, and Mom and Dad were given bread, so no scary green gelatin was involved.

Erin entered the lodge carrying her basket of bread and was greeted by extensive constellations of twinkling

Christmas lights strewn throughout the building. Ziggy hadn't been kidding about the need for battery power.

Every kerosene lantern was lit, and the staircase and many surfaces were strewn with evergreen boughs and ribbon. A huge Christmas tree sat in the middle of the room, decked out with more lights and countless ornaments. When the Bryants did Christmas, they did it in a large way. The Kris Kringle room was probably naked at this point.

A woman screeched, "Stardust!" and Kristen and Lila ran toward her. Before she could put her bread down, it was snatched from her hands, and she was wrapped in a hug by two of her "aunts."

More hugging ensued when another commune member, Emily, and her daughter, Maureen aka Harmony, came over to say hello. Dean and Leah were in a corner talking. Erin was amused to note that Mom had been right. Dean did look like Santa, complete with beard and jolly old gut.

She scanned the room, searching for Ziggy. He was talking to Harry over by the Christmas tree. She smiled when their eyes met and he mouthed silently, "Right back where we started from." She grinned and silently replied, "Maxine Nightingale."

After saying hello to Ziggy's parents and Kevin, she scoped out the food situation and continued over to the Christmas tree to see how Ziggy was faring.

He leaned down to give her a kiss. "No green goo, right?"

"Nope. You're safe from Quinn family recipes. How are you doing?"

"I'm okay, although I don't want to see another string of Christmas lights for a while."

Harry said, "*So* many fornicating lights!"

Erin burst out laughing. "I didn't look too closely, but did you hang up a bunch of porn lights or something?"

Ziggy shoved Harry's shoulder. "He got in trouble with Mom for swearing like a sailor, so now he says 'fornicate' a lot. I'm not sure it's an improvement."

"I don't know what her problem is," Harry grumbled. "I *am* a fornicating sailor. Why can't I cuss like one?"

Erin and Ziggy stared at him for a moment, and Erin said, "You don't seem to be fornicating right now."

Ziggy chuckled. "Sometimes Stardust can be a bit literal."

She looked up at Ziggy. "Are we still going back to the cabin later?"

"You bet," he said. "I need some serious alone time with you to recover from this. The bad news is that you're going to be stuck helping me and Harry clean up and move furniture tomorrow."

Erin returned to her mingling, leaving Ziggy to savor his brother's peculiar profanities on his own. While she was chatting with Bea's daughter, Tracy, and her boyfriend, Rob, Erin noticed that Ziggy's parents and hers were sitting together at the long table and laughing about something. They were actually *laughing*. Maybe after all this time, they'd finally accepted what had happened and decided to move on.

Bea walked to the head of the table and waved a stack of papers to get everyone's attention. "Before we have dinner, I'd like to say a few words. Today, in addition to celebrating the solstice and the thirtieth anniversary of Dancing Cedars, as you know, I need you to sign the paperwork for the conservation easement."

Kristen and Lila clapped their hands and cheered. Bea smiled, and continued, "Some of you know that making this happen has been a long, complicated, and often frustrating process." She pointed at Ziggy and Erin, who were sitting next to each other at the table. "When everything was looking impossible, I told these two that we needed a miracle. And because of their love for this place and each other, they made that miracle happen, against all odds. So I want to publicly say thank you to them for all their hard work cleaning, repairing, sleuthing, vetting cats, wrangling legal complexities, and finally finding a way to make that horrid developer go away."

Everyone in the room cheered and Erin smiled, although Ziggy was squeezing her hand so hard under the table, it was getting uncomfortable. She wriggled her fingers and said through gritted teeth, "Ouch." He let go and widened his eyes in silent apology. Erin gave his hand a squeeze, understanding how much Ziggy absolutely hated being the center of attention.

Hours later, after lots of eating and chatting, Ziggy had retired to a corner with a piece of cake, and Erin went to retrieve him. "You look like a guy who is ready to go home."

"So ready."

Both sets of parents were sitting at the long table again, and Erin walked up to her mother and put her hands on her shoulders, "We're taking off. I'll see you Christmas morning."

"Happy solstice, sweetheart." She put her hand on Erin's. "We left the back of the SUV unlocked. Don't forget."

"I won't."

She and Ziggy went outside into the crisp, bright, starry night. He looked back at the lodge. "I'm even more glad we cleaned the place up. I don't think any of them are leaving tonight."

"Well, it is a long drive back to town."

Erin walked to her parents' car and opened the back hatch. She pulled out a suitcase and a large black guitar case, which she handed to Ziggy. "Happy solstice. There wasn't a way to wrap it, and it would be obvious what it is anyway."

He took it from her and looked down. "Hey, you can't afford this. It's way too expensive."

She shut the hatch and started toward his truck. "Mom and Dad wanted it to be a joint gift from them and me. I told them you're too cheap to ever buy a guitar for yourself."

He laughed as he stowed the guitar behind the seat of the truck. "I am cheap, but I also told you, I stink at playing."

"I don't care. You promised you'd play some of your songs for me, and now I'm collecting on my Christmas present."

Back at the cabin, Moose greeted them happily, leaping around with great joy at the presence of his favorite human. After letting the dog out to run around in his fenced area behind the cabin, Ziggy returned and sat on the floor next to the guitar case. He opened it and ran his palm across the wood. "This is a nice one."

"If you don't like it, we can go to Gleasonville and exchange it. I don't know anything about guitars, but Dad got into a big conversation with the sales guy and they came up with this one."

Ziggy put the guitar in his lap and strummed a few chords.

Erin said, "Hey, I recognize that. It's 'Smoke on the Water' by Deep Purple."

"It only has four chords. I told you I suck."

She went over to the boxes and started rummaging around through the notebooks.

He played a creepy, spooky chord progression. "You seem to be on a mission."

"I'm looking for a notebook. There's a song I want you to play."

"Is it the one about how I think goats are insane? Even after all these years, I *still* don't miss Vince."

"I know Vincent van Goat was off his nut, but none of the goats were psycho like that hen Dad called Crazy Mother Clucker."

"You're still pissed about that time she chased you across the pasture. That was one speedy chicken."

Erin handed him a notebook opened to a page with chord notations on it. "Found it."

"Oh…wow…okay." He plucked at the strings and turned the tuning pegs. "I haven't tried to play this in a while."

The song was about memories of blue skies, green fields, childhood dreams, and losing your best friend. Wondering if she still remembered those times. Gazing at the dusting of stars across the pitch-black night, and hoping she was loved and happy wherever she might be.

He started singing, haltingly at first, but seemed to remember the feelings that had inspired the song.

By the time the song was over, Erin had tears streaming down her cheeks. Struggling to express how moved she was, she simply wrapped her arms around him. "That was beautiful. I didn't forget either. I might have tried, but I couldn't. Thank you."

"I love the guitar, but I love you more. Having you here with me is the best present I could ever have."

Chapter 16

Take a Chance

They spent some time over the next few days at Dancing Cedars cleaning up after the big solstice party. As predicted, everyone stayed over and people started filtering out late Monday afternoon. After everyone was gone, Harry helped Ziggy move the furniture back to the cabin. There had been some speculation that some of it had lived at Dancing Cedars "back in the day," so it was hard to say where the ancestral home of the furniture actually was. Everyone did agree that the ugly couch had never lived at the commune though. Sure it was hideous, but Erin was still glad to see the return of the couch. Sitting on the floor or the air mattress when she was at the cabin wasn't particularly comfortable.

Even though the cabin was empty and echoey, she loved all the time she'd spent alone with Ziggy not worrying about much of anything. They spent a lot of time cooking and reading. He played more songs while Moose slept on an old rug that had been restored to the cabin. After all their running around, it was nice to simply relax and be.

On Christmas Eve, they took down the last of the Christmas lights at Dancing Cedars and loaded them into the farm truck Harry had borrowed from his parents. Ziggy and Erin gave him a hug, and Ziggy said, "Tell Mom and Dad we'll be there tomorrow afternoon. We're spending

Christmas morning with Stardust's parents, then we'll head over to the farm afterward."

"Okay. Man, I wish you were still living there. It was fornicating easier to be there when you were around, dude. Mom gets on my case about *everything*."

Ziggy patted his back. "Good luck. We'll see you tomorrow."

After Harry left, they walked back to the Hodgepodge Lodge to take one last look around for anything that might entice a critter to eat its way into the building over the winter.

Erin swept some dirt into a dustpan and threw it outside. She hung the old broom back up on its hook and proclaimed, "It's done."

Ziggy picked up his toolbox and walked toward the door. "Until next time. All that talk about a summer reunion sounded pretty serious."

"We'll see. How are your parents doing?"

"The same. Harry pulled me aside and yelled at me for abandoning them, as he called it."

She put her hand on his arm. "I'm sorry."

"It's okay. He's going to think what he's going to think."

"It doesn't help that he's so much younger. He probably has no idea why things are the way they are."

"I know. He'll go back to his aircraft carrier and forget all about it." He opened the door for her and locked it behind them. "I have been thinking about the situation though."

"Uh-oh. Do we need to go to the thinking spot?"

"You know, I think we do." He put the toolbox in the truck and slammed the door. "Let's go."

They walked across the meadow and into the forest, following the trail down the incline to the creek and the gigantic rock. Ziggy hoisted her up and clambered up after her.

He settled in and pulled his knees up, wrapping his arms around them. "So I've been thinking about the whole mess with the farm, and I had an idea."

She looked up at his face. "Am I going to like this idea?"

"Maybe. Maybe not. But it does concern you."

"Okay. What are you thinking?"

He stretched his legs out, pulled her into his embrace, and began stroking her hair slowly. "So here's the thing. My parents got the second mortgage when interest rates were at almost record highs. And second mortgages have higher rates than standard mortgages. They're paying almost thirteen percent on that, and the rate for a thirty-year mortgage is at seven point two now."

Erin closed her eyes. The way his fingertips felt grazing her temple was utter bliss. Why was he talking about interest rates? Attempting to focus, she opened her eyes again. "So what? You told me before that they can't qualify for a refinance because their credit is so bad. Having seen the office, I certainly believe that."

"They can't qualify, but I can. I have enough for a down payment. If I buy the property, everything gets refinanced and consolidated."

Erin moved her head to look at him. "You can't be serious. You finally moved out. What about the adorable little cabin? Staying there has been wonderful. Have you changed your mind?"

"Not in the slightest." He pulled her close again. "Don't look so horrified. I'm not done explaining."

"Okay, but how would this work? You have no job and you have to pay rent now."

"Joel asked me the same thing when we talked about me renting the place. I told him I had enough money for a year of rent and offered to pay it up front."

"Did you really pay for a whole year?"

"No, he said not to worry about it. But I also asked if anyone happens to be hiring."

"Are you going to get a job?"

"I don't know, but I have a lead. The guy we met who used to live in the cabin, Jack, is a forester."

"Yes, he did the forestry management plan for Dancing Cedars."

"Jack has been complaining to Joel about having too much work. He's worried that if he keeps working long hours, his girlfriend will give in to her workaholic tendencies now that they're living closer to town."

"And I gather he doesn't want that?"

"Apparently not. I don't know the details, but Joel encouraged me to ask Jack about a job."

"You do know a whole lot about trees." She poked his stomach. "Probably from spending so much time climbing them."

"I doubt it will work out because I don't have a degree in forestry. Or a degree in anything at all. But it doesn't hurt to ask."

"Okay, suppose you get a job, still, why do you want to buy the tree farm? Then you're on the hook for the next financial catastrophe."

"I know, which is why there will be stipulations for my parents to continue to live there."

Erin raised her eyebrows. "You have certainly put some thought into this."

"I decided to turn around what I was doing. Instead of me working for them, they technically work for me. They live there, but an outside manager runs the business. That way they're employees, not owners, and someone who isn't me calls the shots. It would work like it did in the beginning when Dad got the job at the tree farm."

"Do you think they'd go for it?"

"They might. I have some other ideas too. Initially, we need to harvest some trees that have gotten too large because they over-planted." He waved a hand. "Don't ask."

Erin pulled her legs up and wrapped her arms around her knees. "So you'd have it logged?"

"There are five acres that have a bunch of trees that aren't marketable as Christmas trees anymore. The money from thinning that section pays for the business manager's salary to start with. Then to manage the endless cash-flow issues, the manager helps turn it into a year-round business with you-pick blueberries, pumpkins, and a farm stand."

Erin placed her hand on his arm. "You've done some homework, haven't you?"

"I've written the outline for a business plan. I think it can work." He sat up and looked into her eyes. "My parents get to do what they love, which is sharing the joy of Christmas with the community. And I get to do what I love, which is being with you."

Erin smiled and gave him a kiss. "Ooh, nice business pitch. I'm all for it."

"Good, because like I said, this affects you."

Erin gave him a hug and rested her head on his chest. "Well, obviously."

Gently, he moved her away so he could look into her face. He took both of her hands in his. "It's more than that. If I do this, it could affect you financially because I want to ask you to marry me."

"What? You can't do that."

"Why not? I love you. You love me. You're the only person who has ever understood me, and going forward, I can't imagine my life without you."

"You know I love you too, but I have no job and absolutely no idea what I'm doing next. My life is a mess. I have to move and find a place to live. A job might be nice too. As we both know, finding work in Alpine Grove is next to impossible."

"I know you'll figure it out, and I'll help any way I can."

"But we haven't spent enough time together."

"How much time do you need? You said sometimes you wished you hadn't had a long engagement before."

"That was different."

"How?" He raised his eyebrows. "What were you waiting for?"

Erin frowned. "Well, first we were figuring out our relationship, then we were waiting for Andy's job to settle down. Then he was hoping for a promotion, and I was working to graduate from law school and pass the bar. Then I wanted to get married in June, so we put it off again."

"But then he died." He squeezed her hands. "What if we don't do that? What if you take a chance on me?"

"ABBA. Way too easy." She gave him a kiss for emphasis. They still wanted the same thing, but this time she wasn't going to fight it. "I suppose this is us doing everything out of order again." With a laugh, she pulled her hands out of his, placed her palms on his cheeks, and stared into his amazing blue eyes. "So you'd better ask me. Or I'll ask you first."

"Stardust, will you marry me? Preferably as soon as possible."

"Yes I will. Whenever you want. Carpe diem."

He grinned. "Oooh, more Latin. That's totally sexy."

"Yeah, the things we do for love."

Before kissing her, he whispered, "Nice one. That's by 10cc."

Chapter 17

Epilogue

A couple of days after Christmas, Ziggy loaded Moose into the truck for a trip out to the boarding kennel. Erin got in and shoved Moose's ample butt out of the way. "This isn't your good side. Sit down."

Moose turned around a few times and settled himself in the middle with his gigantic muzzle on her lap. She stroked the fur on his head between his ears. "Hey, don't look so sad. You get to play with your buddy Gizmo again."

"Driving to the airport feels different when you actually get to get on the plane for a change," Ziggy said. "Let's hope this storm holds off until we get down off the hill."

When they arrived at the kennel, Kat and Joel were outside with Linus, the giant brown dog, and Lady, the collie mix. Moose stood up and wagged his tail, whapping Erin in the face. She shoved his prodigious rear aside again.

They got out and unloaded Moose, who was thrilled to see all his canine pals. Lady leaped happily around the big dog. Linus was more circumspect, perhaps because he was used to being the largest dog in any room.

"Thanks for letting us drop him off early. I'm a little worried about the storm moving in," Ziggy said.

"Getting out shouldn't be a problem," Joel replied. "Getting back to the Shack might be trickier."

335

"We can always stay at Erin's parents' house if it's nasty up here. They're getting ready for a trip, and Erin is going to be house sitting and studying for the California bar exam."

Kat said, "You're a lawyer?"

"I have a law degree, but I haven't practiced," Erin said.

Ziggy added, "The Cedars Land Trust could use her help with more conservation work once she passes the bar."

Erin grabbed Ziggy's arm. "And he needs to talk to Jack about the first timber cruise they're doing next week."

Joel said, "Well, you have a plow, which will help getting home."

"If it's bad and we end up stuck in LA, it wouldn't be the worst thing, assuming you have room for Moose here," Erin said. "Then we could celebrate by going to a fancy hotel or something."

Kat took Moose's leash. "The Christmas rush is mostly over, so give us a call if you run into weather problems. What are you celebrating?"

Erin grinned. "Well, I told you that we're going to DC to clean out my apartment. But DC is a no-waiting, no-blood-test, no-residency-requirements location. So we're also planning on getting married."

Ziggy added, "Don't tell. We'll let our families in on it when we get back."

Kat threw her arms around Erin. "We'll then, I'm the first to congratulate you. That's wonderful."

After more hugging and congratulations, Erin and Ziggy climbed back into the truck for the trip to the airport.

Erin said, "I can't believe we're doing this. It's like a dream. Well, a good dream, that is. One without jingle bears, stoned cows, or dancing chickens."

"I'm glad to hear it. I can't believe I'm finally going to get on an airplane. I hope I don't freak out."

"I think you're gonna make it."

"We'll see. You need to hang on to yourself."

"Nice one." Erin moved closer and placed her hand on his. "That's by David Bowie performing as Ziggy Stardust."

Thanks for Reading

Thank you for dedicating some of your reading time to *Yowliday Inn*. I hope you enjoyed the adventures with Erin and Ziggy. I'll be writing more books that will feature Kat, Joel and various other residents of Alpine Grove who bring dogs to the boarding kennel, so keep your eye out for the next book in the series.

If you would like to be notified by e-mail when I release a new book, you can sign up for my New Releases e-mail list at SusanDaffron.com.

I know that not everyone likes to write book reviews, but if you are willing to write a sentence or two about what you thought of *Yowliday Inn*, I encourage you to post a review at your favorite book vendor site or share a message with your social networking friends.

If you would like to share your thoughts about the book with me privately, you can reach me through the contact page on the SusanDaffron.com web site.

I look forward to hearing from you!

~ Susan C. Daffron

Acknowledgements

Writing a novel is never easy and I'd like to thank my husband James Byrd for his support and encouragement throughout the publishing process.

I'd also like to thank my alpha and beta readers for their eagle-eyed reading and great feedback.

About the Author

Susan Daffron is the author of the Jennings & O'Shea mystery series and the Alpine Grove romantic comedies, a series of novels that feature residents of the small town of Alpine Grove and their various quirky dogs and cats. She is also an award-winning author of many nonfiction books, including several about pets and animal rescue. She lives in a small town in northern Idaho and shares her life with her husband and three really cute dogs.